Unforgotten

by

Cassie Laelyn

The Fallen Guardians, Book 2

This is a work of fiction. Names, characters, places, and incidents are either the product of the author's imagination or are used fictitiously, and any resemblance to actual persons living or dead, business establishments, events, or locales, is entirely coincidental.

Unforgotten

COPYRIGHT © 2020 by Cassie Laelyn

Cover Art by *Diana Carlile*

The Wild Rose Press, Inc.
PO Box 708
Adams Basin, NY 14410-0708
Visit us at www.thewildrosepress.com

Publishing History
First Black Rose Edition, 2020
Print ISBN 978-1-5092-2996-3
Digital ISBN 978-1-5092-2997-0

The Fallen Guardians, Book 2
Published in the United States of America

Pivoting around, he peered over the cliff. Flames consumed the mountainside like bright orange burning fingers reaching for him.

Fuck. The fire surrounded him. No way out.

"Help!" Willow shrieked, her voice screaming through the roaring flames.

He had to find her before it was too late. Shielding his face with his arm, he crept closer to the flames.

"Willow, where are you?" A blast of heat scorched his face, forcing him back. "Fuck!"

Any gulp of air he managed burned in his chest. The smoke swirled around his body making his head swim and legs wobble. His stomach rolled.

The moment his throat squeezed shut, his legs gave out, falling to his knees in the ash, gasping for breath. Fire licked his arm as he reached for Willow.

He couldn't find her. He couldn't save her.

Dedication

For you,
for giving me the strength to hold on

Acknowledgements

I can't believe I'm lucky enough to sit here again and write acknowledgments for another book. I'm still incredibly humbled by the encouragement I receive from my closest friends and family, and the romance community.

A huge thank you to every reader who has supported this series—read my books, wrote reviews, sent me messages about your favorite characters or pestered me for the next book! Every time I hear from you it feeds my soul and keeps me tapping away at the laptop.

Danni and Karina—thank you for the late nights and brainstorming sessions while I drafted Aric's story. I couldn't have done this without you.

To my tribe of writing buddies who lift me up, cheer the loudest and basically keep me sane. Linda, Dana, Sue-Ellen, Shelley, Jess, Shona and Ally—you guys are amazing.

Finally, for those readers who begged to hear more from Blaine…you're welcome!

Cassie x

P.S. Reader support is the lifeblood for any series. If you loved reading *Unforgotten*, please consider leaving a review, recommend it to your reader friends, or request your local library purchase a copy. Thank you.

~*~

A **Glossary of Terms** is on page 341
for your reference while reading.

Prologue
Blaine

Ten months earlier

Blaine swung his legs back and forth in the air as he sat on the wide, crispy branch of a singed tree that threatened to snap at any moment. Thick smoke hung low in the air while tiny pieces of ash fluttered around him, reminding him of his time in Hell. Now that place was a buzzkill, and somewhere he had no intention of returning to until the time was right to unleash war.

He scooted a little to the left for a better view of the burned valley. Lucky for him, only two catastrophic wildfires happened worldwide this week. He took a gamble appearing here rather than the other location, mainly because he had a thing for Britain—that tiny little café on the outskirts of London made one helluva trifle.

If the Ariel he waited for didn't appear today, he'd come back tomorrow. Then the day after that. Since his spectacular Fall from the Heavens, patience and time were two things he had in abundance.

Balancing the takeout container in his palm, he took a giant spoonful of the decadent dessert, moaning as the rich, creamy goodness slid down his throat.

"Love," he said, speaking to Fate as though she stood before him rather than hiding in the Heavens.

"This trifle is to Fall for. It's such a shame you'll never venture from your sanctuary long enough to taste it."

He swallowed another mouthful, licking the underneath of the plastic spoon. "It may even be better than that."

If the recruitment of the Ariel wasn't at stake, Blaine would lower the glamour concealing his presence for a moment. Long enough for Fate to hear him and see he wasn't spending eternity curled up in Hell pining for her. Nope. Pining wasn't half as much fun as revenge, and his revenge was now in full swing.

Recruiting angels and syphoning their heavenly powers was a necessary step in his plan, the whole reason he hung out in this burned forest. He'd recruited Azraels to harness the ability to collect souls and recruited Raziels to glamour his presence in the mortal realm so Fate, the Ice Queen, couldn't track him. Soon, thanks to the Ariel, he'd possess the ability to regenerate. Once he possessed the power of five angelic factions, he'd challenge Zath for the throne.

Between the bare, singed branches, Blaine peered through the veil of smoke at the muted colors filling the dusky sky. "And then, my love, you better hold onto your pretty crown."

He scraped the last remaining bits of trifle from the box before balancing the empty container on his open palm. Summoning a burst of hellfire, a deep crimson flame ignited in the center of his hand, reducing the container and plastic spoon to ash in seconds. After a moment, Blaine closed his fist, extinguishing the flame. He never tired of that party trick.

A shimmer of power over to the left caught his attention. He narrowed his gaze waiting to see which

Ariel materialized. He didn't want just any Ariel. Only one resulted in a two-for-one deal.

The moment fiery red locks appeared Blaine knew he'd scored the jackpot.

He leaped off the branch, landed on the sooty ground and strolled toward her. A few feet away, still concealed by his glamour, Blaine paused, watching the angel summon those Ariel powers he craved. Tucking the knee-length dress behind her knees, the Ariel crouched and brushed her fingers over the blackened earth. Warm orange power glowed from her fingertips, but it sparked and spluttered before extinguishing.

"Damn it," she muttered.

The Ariel closed her eyes and a second later, the glow reappeared, but far dimmer than Blaine remembered from his time in the Heavens. The instant her fingertips connected with the earth, a tiny shoot sprouted from the soil. Her brows knitted, hardening the look of concentration on her face as she placed both palms on the ground.

The earth beneath his feet hummed, bright green shoots rising from the dirt, while new leaves uncurled on the branches of burned trees. Blaine remained hidden within the glamour for an agonizing amount of time while the Ariel regenerated the forest surrounding them. Her Ariel magic had faded quicker than he anticipated, if he didn't recruit her soon, her powers would be useless to him.

A smile curved her lips as she stood, but it quickly disappeared, replaced with a tired and worn out expression.

The time for hiding was over. With a flick of his wrist, Blaine expanded the glamour to include the Ariel.

She staggered back the moment she discovered him standing there.

He extended his arm in a royal bow. "Hello there, Willow. Fancy seeing you here."

She sucked in a sharp breath. "Blaine?"

"Were you expecting someone else?" He peered around for potential visitors, even though he knew there weren't any.

"I…uh." Willow shook her head. "I haven't seen you since…well, you know. Since you Fell." She lowered her voice. "I thought you were in…Hell?"

Blaine waved his hand in the air, dismissing the subject. "Been there, done that. I burned the shirt."

A nearby shoot grew higher, and he watched it rise beside his leg, gradually forming a miniature tree. Tiny leaves sprouted on the delicate limbs.

He craved that power. Needed it.

"Actually." He turned back to Willow. "I thought I'd drop by and say hello. See how you were doing."

"See how I'm doing?" Her voice rose a notch. "Well, let's see…after your spectacular exit from the Heavens, my existence has been crap, to be honest. My soulmate abandoned me without saying goodbye, and now…" She waved a hand in the air. "My Ariel powers are suffering." Her eyes narrowed. "All because you became a Fallen. Thanks for that." She sneered.

"You're welcome, love."

She gaped. "Really? You don't feel an ounce of remorse for the damage you caused?"

Fine. Maybe she didn't thank him now, but she would. She'd thank him when he gave her the only thing she wanted more than her Ariel powers.

"I sense you're still a little disheartened about my

sudden departure." He reached to one side and curled a shoot around his index finger. "But that's all right, you'll forgive me once you hear my offer."

"Offer?" She retreated a step as though she now realized who stood before her. "You're a Fallen, Blaine. What could you possibly offer me?"

Releasing the plant, he glanced to her. "Freedom, love."

"What are you talking about? I have freedom."

He narrowed his gaze, zeroing in on every twitch of her features. He could probe her mind but toying with her was way more fun. A challenge of sorts. As an angel of the Heavens, Willow couldn't lie, but some angels had perfected the ability to scoot around the truth. Like his brother, Raven.

He sensed Willow wanted to play a little game of cat and mouse. No matter, he may not convince her today, but now that he had her attention, she'd agree soon enough. Blaine had Willow's soulmate to thank for planting the seed of resentment. All Blaine had to do now was nurture those seeds until they grew nasty little thorns.

"Really, love? That's not what I heard." He cocked his ear, catching the slight skip of her heart rate. "After I left, I heard Fate put you and all her other Ariels on lockdown." He paused, for effect. "I heard you can only mist to your designated assignments and then back to the Heavens. How frustrating it must be to possess the ability to mist but never be able to visit your soulmate."

Willow held his gaze for a moment before walking to a tree, its trunk split through the middle as though struck by a vicious bolt of lightning. When she brushed her fingers along the blackened bark, he hardly noticed the dull orange glow of her magic.

"What kind of freedom?" Her voice came out barely above a whisper.

Swaying her may not be as difficult as he expected. The fact she'd considered him family for a good chunk of her existence might be in his favor.

Foreign pain simmered behind his ribs, which was ludicrous. Willow was simply another angel he planned to recruit. The fact her soul would blacken shouldn't change his decision. With war came sacrifice.

"Freedom to leave the Heavens...for good."

She spun to face him. "And how could you possibly give me that?"

"I'll take care of that part, love. All you need to do is embrace your simmering rage and pop down to join me."

She drew back. "Join you by becoming...a Fallen?"

Blaine rolled his eyes. His potential recruits were always so dramatic.

"Falling isn't as bad as it's made out to be. Plus, what better way to give your soulmate a little payback for choosing that brotherhood of Boy Scouts over you?" Willow winced, and he stepped closer. "I can offer you a chance to free yourself from Fate's chains, free yourself from an existence of waiting around for a Guardian who will never return." He lowered his voice. "I can restore your power."

Interest sparked in her eyes. "How?"

Hook, line and sinker. "Fallen power is more powerful than you could ever imagine, love. With me, you could have it all."

Willow didn't answer. Instead, she peered at the

blackened forest for so long the sun slipped below the horizon, blanketing their surroundings in a thin veil of darkness.

Finally, she turned to him. "I have to go before Fate sees me with you."

Blaine's glamour took care of that tiny detail, but he kept that knowledge to himself for the time being. Now was not the time to reveal his plan to an angel whose every choice was visible to the Ice Queen. Fate would have her private viewing soon enough.

"Very well." He stepped back. "Think about what I said, Willow. I'll drop in and say hi again soon."

The air around Willow shimmered with glimmering Ariel power, surrounding her body in sparkling dust of vibrant colors, misting her back to the Heavens. Before she vanished, Willow locked her gaze on his and gave a curt nod.

A smile curled Blaine's lip. He always got what he wanted. He allowed Fate to win their last round, but only because it served his purpose. Tayla healing Raven's soul meant his brother remained in the mortal realm. Exactly where Blaine needed him.

This round belonged to Blaine, and he'd ensure it counted.

Now that he'd nudged Willow's seeds of doubt, he'd wait for them to fester. After a few more catchups, those seeds would grow into long wiry vines covered in sharp poisonous thorns. Making her transition that much more seamless.

Whistling to himself, Blaine sauntered into the night with a spring in his step. Soon, he'd have the power of regeneration and another angel on his crimson-winged army. If all went as planned—it would—a Guardian, the most powerful faction, would quickly follow. Because if Willow meant anything to her soulmate, that Guardian would move the Heavens and Hell to be with her.

Chapter One
Aric

Current day

Aric wiped the thick black ooze from the blade of his dagger on the thigh of his jeans. Before him, the crimson-winged Fallen exploded into mist, drifting away into the crisp night air. Aric one, Fallen zero.

River slapped his shoulder. "That bastard didn't even blink."

Until that point, the Fallen had taunted the two of them all night. Baited them. Then the next minute, the Fallen gave up, standing there with a bored expression on his face, accepting his fate like a complete dumbass.

Aric stilled for a moment, staring at the filthy pavement where the Fallen had stood, before turning to face River. He had his back against the brick wall, one leg bent up, dressed in their standard combat gear, with his wild mess of dark hair pulled into a semi-tamed state. There was no chance of missing his bright moss-green eyes though, beaming like beacons in the dimly lit alleyway.

"Maybe the mop on your head mesmerized him?"

River drew back. "It's called a 'man-bun,' bro. All the mortal guys are doing it these days."

Aric rolled his eyes. Just when he thought River's fashion sense couldn't get any worse, he labeled his hair style.

Faint tingling tickled Aric's nape and he ducked his head around the corner, narrowing his eyes at the entrance to SubZero—the club where he and River were enjoying a drink until that damn Fallen ruined his buzz. A second later, Aric's assigned Chosen stumbled out the door onto the sidewalk, thrown out by the bouncer for the second night in a row.

River scoffed. "You must've seriously pissed off Fate for her to assign him to you."

"You have no idea."

Not that he'd spoken to Fate in…oh, well over three centuries. That bitch sure held a grudge.

He glared at the pathetic excuse for a mortal. What extraordinary destiny could that dumbass achieve? As a Chosen created by Fate, the mortal's path, his destiny, contributed to Fate's greater plan, ensuring the scales tipped in her favor. The Heavens had lowered their standards since Aric's exile.

Nevertheless, Fate assigned Aric as the Guardian to protect the chauvinistic mortal. Again, he put on his big-boy boots and sucked it the hell up.

Preventing the Fallen from infecting the Chosen's soul became harder and harder. Not because of Aric's track record, but because, lately, he struggled with finding a reason to save the mortal's ass.

Maybe he should let the Fallen win, sending the Chosen's soul to Hell instead, and take the assignment off his hands. It wouldn't be the first time he'd failed a Chosen. No way could that scumbag be destined for the Heavens unless there had been one royal screw up.

At the curb, Leon, the Chosen, tripped over his own feet before falling into the backseat of a taxi. What kind of name was Leon, anyway? Probably the name printed on his fancy business card, giving him an excuse to parade around all king-of-the-jungle-like, when his name was probably Ratcliff. Emphasis on "Rat."

As the rear door to the taxi closed, Raine stalked from the club toward the alley that concealed him and River. Dressed in skin-tight black leather pants, she paired them with a figure hugging singlet and a shiny red pair of heels that could gouge an eye out. God, as siblings, she and River were chalk and cheese.

"That disgusting Chosen is a piece of work, Aric," Raine sneered, rounding the corner to join them.

Aric remained on watch until the taxi disappeared down the street. Rat better head home because Aric was ready for this train-wreck of a night to end. Protecting that mortal was a fucking full-time job, and not only from the Fallen. At the rate that mortal pissed him off, by the time Leon completed his destined path, Aric might consider handing him over to the Fallen, so he didn't murky the Heavens.

With all imminent threats eliminated, Aric sheathed his dagger and turned to face the brother/sister combo. Gabe had sent the siblings to join him, Raven and EJ a little over a year ago. In that time, Raine impressed them with her skill for forging a variety of new weapons out of Purah—heavenly water from the Eternal Fountain—including the bullets loaded into the 0.40 caliber Glock tucked in the back of his jeans. For emergencies…or for when he didn't give a shit.

"Somehow, I don't think that Chosen will be your soulmate." River snorted.

Aric glared back. Negative. The title of soulmate

belonged only to her. The angel he gave his eternity to until Fate screwed them over.

Maybe Fate had softened during the Guardians' exile. Maybe that's why after over three centuries of radio silence, she had assigned Raven a Chosen to protect. The assignment became more than a standard protection mission because Tayla turned out to be Raven's soulmate, and the key to restoring the light in his soul. Their connection restored Raven's faith, preventing his soul from plummeting to the fiery gates of Hell. The assignment from Fate came right when the Guardians needed it the most.

Just because Fate threw a single flotation device to a sinking ship in the middle of the ocean, it didn't mean she gave a shit or had changed her ways. Besides, Aric didn't need his faith restored. Faith was the key that fueled the light in his soul and maintained his connection to the Heavens. Faith was the key to return home, to her. He'd hold onto every goddamn thread.

Grabbing the phone from his jeans pocket, Aric created a group text to Raven and EJ. "I'm calling it a night," he said aloud to the other two.

The phone pinged a second later, and he read the reply from Raven, who finally had the hang of basic technology.

"Raven's good," Aric said to the siblings. "You two can carry on here, if you want. I have things to do."

River pushed off the wall. "Nah, I'm callin' it a night, too. You want a ride somewhere?"

Aric shook his head. "I'm gonna stretch these wings while it's cloudy."

"Righty-o, take it easy, bro." River gave him a brotherly handshake before heading down the alley with Raine to the parked car.

The clicking of Raine's heels echoed louder than the thumping bass coming from inside the club. How the hell did she sneak up on an enemy wearing those?

Aric took off in the opposite direction onto the street, following the pavement to the end of the road before slipping into the forest. Removing his jacket, he held it in one hand and unfurled his black wings, rolling his shoulders and neck to loosen the muscles. He peered into the stormy night a second before taking flight. His favorite time to fly.

Soaring high above the river, flanked on either side by towering trees, he followed a path up the mountain. Had it been darker with less chance of a mortal spotting him, he would've glided inches above the surface of the water, closing his eyes as the icy spray misted his face. Just so he could inhale a scent like hers.

The town lights of Summit Creek faded in the distance, replaced by the dark ominous treetops of the Snowy Mountains. Banking left, he soared over a nearby ski resort. Through the uncovered windows, he spied mortals milling around inside the lodge while smoke puffed from various chimneys. Flood lights lit the main ski run, hazy fog swirling around the bulbs, and toward the top of the run gurgling machines pumped artificial snow onto the slopes. That was one thing he missed from his time in Europe—there was never a shortage of snow.

The neighboring town of Pine Valley came into view and he flew over the town center, all but deserted in favor of a restful night. Larger than Summit Creek in size and population, the town wrapped around a manmade lake. Again, the residents had lit the front of the buildings along the shoreline, this time reflecting vibrant pink. It happened more often over the past couple of years, different colors representing different causes. If only they realized that lighting a building didn't cure the problem.

He flew over a small hill at the far side of the lake—the fancy-ass hotel sitting proudly on the top, its flag drooped down the length of the pole. On the other side, he spotted his destination. Ancient leafless trees surrounded an early twentieth century neo-gothic church, with a pointed steeple stretching high into the night as though reaching for the Heavens.

Don't bother. They don't answer.

He eased to the ground, landing in the center of the landscaped grounds. He trudged up the stone steps to the side entrance, wiped his feet on the mat and slipped inside. After a moment to steady himself, he gravitated to his usual spot in the last row and planted his ass in the pew.

Subtle hints of burning candles and incense, mixed with furniture polish calmed his mind. The tension in his shoulders flowed along his arms and out through his fingertips, like a lazy wave rolling over the shore. Leaning forward, he crossed his arms on the pew in front of him and rested his head on top, allowing his mind to drift back to the history of the church.

The townsfolk erected the church back in the early 1900s, when he, Raven and EJ had arrived in the region following EJ's first semi-useful vision from Fate. Since the day of its completion, he came every goddamn Wednesday night to sit in this pew. Though he never revealed his true self to the church's caretakers over the years, he was damn sure they sensed who, or rather what, he was. Because each Wednesday night without fail, the side door remained unlocked, heater turned on during the winter months and candles lit along the altar, as though the church awaited his visit. Like tonight.

Awareness danced along his spine a second before the wooden doors to the church creaked open. Without lifting his head, Aric slid a steady hand inside his jacket to grip the hilt of a dagger. A nippy draft drifted under the pews, whispering against the calves of his jeans. He inhaled through his nose, sifting through the scents in the air. Recognizing the intruder, he released his hold on the dagger, returning his arm to the pew in front.

Sneakers squeaked along the wood floor before the pew creaked and bowed as another Guardian sank down beside him. Aric sat upright, stretching his spine to release the pressure in his lower back—man, how long had he been there?

Raven relaxed, extending his legs under the next row of pews. "I thought I'd find you here."

Aric glanced at his brother—by choice rather than blood—staring at the ceiling. "I thought you'd be tangled in the sheets with that beautiful woman of yours."

The corner of Raven's mouth twitched. "The night's still young, my man."

Aric shook his head. Those two were still like fucking mortal newlyweds. Almost a year had passed since Tayla bargained with Fate, scoring herself immortality by Raven's side. Aric was happy for his brother, an eternity away from a soulmate was downright hell. He of all angels knew that.

Comfortable silence stretched between them and Aric closed his eyes again, drifting away in the peaceful stillness. Until Raven ruined the moment.

"I'm worried about you, Aric. We all are."

Great. Raven's drop-in just turned into a mini intervention. Ellen probably sent him. "I'm fine. I have a reason to hold on, remember?"

Raven turned his way. "I know. Just remember we all made the same choice that day when we agreed to Fate's twisted deal. I'm not saying had we known the consequences, each of us would have chosen differently, but maybe…just maybe this was our path all along." Raven gazed toward the altar. "I mean, if I didn't take Fate's deal, I never would've crossed paths with Tayla. I doubt Fate would've created her in the first place." Raven exhaled a long, drawn out breath. "You can't keep punishing yourself, Aric. Trust me, it doesn't help."

Aric's chest tightened, and he looked away. Anything to avoid this conversation. Instead of replying, he focused on the floor to ceiling stained glass window behind the altar, counting the individual pieces of vibrant blue, red, and yellow glass in each pane. A helluva lot better than coughing up some bullshit response.

One, two, three…And easier. *Four, five*…What was he supposed to say anyway? *Six, seven…I'll punish myself for as long as it takes? Until I figure out how to return to the Heavens? Eight, nine…Until I get her back?* Nope. Not answering hurt a lot less. Goddamn it, he lost count.

"You'll see her again, Aric. We'll complete our mission to save Blaine, and you'll have her back in your arms."

Aric clenched his jaw. For once, he didn't agree. "I

wish I was that sure."

Why did his chest ache so much every time he came here? Why did he keep coming here?

The pew creaked as Raven stood. "Let's go home. I don't know about you, but I could use a drink. Plus, when I left, EJ had challenged Raine to another game of pool and it'll be fucking hilarious to see him get his ass kicked."

About time someone knocked EJ's ego down a notch. He considered Raven's offer. Coming together as a family pulled him out of his slump every single time. For a little while at least. Plus, he could use a whiskey…or seven.

After a moment, Aric nodded. "Give me a sec."

Raven squeezed his shoulder before stepping out of the pew to exit the church through the side door. Aric stood and shuffled out of the pew to face the altar. With his head lowered, he trudged toward the stained-glass window he failed to count, stopping at a side table. He tugged open the top drawer, grabbed a fresh tea-light candle and held the miniature wick against an already burning one to ignite the flame. With a shaky arm, as though moving too fast extinguished not only the tiny flame but also life as he knew it, he eased the candle onto a stepped platform.

He despised himself for lighting one each week. The action changed nothing. Past or future. The pain in the center of his chest sharpened, and he gritted his teeth at the constant agony. No, anguish. But he didn't want it to disappear. The suffering served as a constant reminder of the choice he'd made and the fact he lived with that guilt for the rest of his fucking existence.

Not that I'm truly living.

He was pathetic, just like those mortals lighting the outside of their buildings. Lighting a tiny-ass candle didn't magically let her know he thought of her. Lighting a candle didn't tell her he was sorry.

Chapter Two
Willow

Willow screwed up her nose. "What is that putrid smell?"

Beside her, Blaine threw his head back and laughed. "It's the scent of alcohol and sweat, love, all mixed with a touch of desire."

She wiped her clammy palms down her dress, the fabric glowing under the colorful lights. "Personally, I don't see why mortals congregate in places like this, night after night."

Although she was an Ariel, who spent most of the time outdoors, she knew enough about mortal establishments to know they sat in a nightclub. From their position in the far corner, she scanned the club. Colored lights hung from the low ceiling, flickering on and off at such a rapid pace it caused a dull ache behind her eyes. To her left, mortals congregated in a sunken section, grinding their bodies in time with the thumping music. While farther over, they squished together like cattle in front of a long bench, lining up for their next drink. To the right, on the same level as her and Blaine, stood tables and chairs surrounded with non-dancing mortals. Bar staff wandered back and forth delivering orders and collecting empty glasses.

She and Blaine had sat at a small circular table, surrounded by that filthy smell seeping into her pores for the past hour, waiting for something. What? She didn't know because Blaine refused to say.

Was he waiting until she became intoxicated like the surrounding mortals making fools of themselves on the crowded dance floor? Was he preparing her for life as a Fallen?

She turned to Blaine. "I still don't understand why you brought me here. Why couldn't we speak in the forest like all the other times?"

Blaine took a long sip of alcohol and a smirk formed on his face. "You'll see, love. Be patient."

She'd known Blaine for over a millennium, though he'd changed in so many ways since she last saw him in the Heavens, back when she considered him family. He and the other Guardians were once like brothers, fighting side by side since the beginning of time. With a bond so strong, she recalled them vowing to lay down their lives for one another.

Willow scoffed. *Guess they meant it.*

She looked closer at him. As a Fallen, shouldn't he focus on corrupting mortals and blackening their souls? She wasn't naïve. Every angel knew the dangers of getting too close to a Fallen, especially one who possessed the ability to manipulate a soul. Until Blaine, though, she'd never interacted with a Fallen. She definitely hadn't conversed with one. How times had changed. Because right now she sat engaged in a confusing half-conversation with Blaine, whose choice to become a Fallen had shattered the Heavens. The resulting shockwave had ripped apart her own existence.

Instead of appearing how she imagined a Fallen would, Blaine slouched beside her in a worn leather jacket, his midnight black hair longer than she remembered but still perfectly styled in a bad boy kind of way, sipping a drink without a care in the universe. That carefree attitude lured her to meet with him a second time, then a third and a fourth. She'd pay any price not to care, not to feel.

She sipped her soda, the cool bubbles fizzling down her parched throat. Blaine had compelled the mind of a mortal waitress to deliver drinks to their table but somehow the rest of the club goers were oblivious to their presence. As though they sat enclosed in an invisible bubble. Blaine must've obtained the ability to glamour since his Fall.

The compelled waitress leaned between her and Blaine to collect his empty glass, brushing her over-sized breasts against Blaine's shoulder. "You want another, handsome?"

Blaine winked. "You betcha, sweetheart."

Giggling, the waitress trotted off in the bar's direction. Willow rolled her eyes. Did anyone wonder where the waitress delivered the drinks? Perhaps the mortals were so intoxicated they didn't notice?

What the heck were they doing here? As the thought formed, a tingle danced along the nape of her neck. She narrowed her gaze at the lower level, searching for the source, roaming over the faces of the mortals on the dance floor. Nothing. Casting a wider net, she scanned the packed never-ending line at the bar...passed the single-file line in front of the restrooms...up the metal staircase leading to the entrance—

Her breath jammed in her throat. The world seemed to skid to a halt. He stood on the bottom step.

The Guardian she wanted to avoid at all costs.

Her stupid heart skipped a beat while her gaze roamed over him, all the way from his chocolate-brown leather lace-up boots, up the form-fitting black jeans, over the dark Henley that did absolutely nothing to conceal the rigid muscles she knew hid underneath. What caused her blood to heat was that chiseled jaw, recalling how the groomed line of facial hair had grazed her neck as he kissed her.

She gripped the hard edge of the table, sharp pain piercing her fingers as her nails sank deep into the fake wood. Anything to hold her still. Otherwise, she'd break free of Blaine's glamour, walk right up to that Guardian and wipe the sexy grin off his damn face, using her lips.

Damn it!

Willow sank lower in the chair. Why had she agreed to meet Blaine?

The Guardian stalked through the parting sea of mortals as though they instinctively sensed the power radiating from him. She tried hard not to track his every move. Her chest tightened the closer he came.

The sharpness of Blaine's stare scratched her skin. Was this the reason he brought her here? Surely, he wasn't that cruel? Curling up under the table seemed like a fine idea right now.

Just as the Guardian arrived at a sectioned off area toward the opposite end of the club, he paused, one hand on the rope. As though in slow motion, he glanced her way.

She sucked in a sharp breath. Their gazes locked. The same whiskey eyes she remembered so vividly now stared back at her. The same eyes that forever haunted her dreams.

"Aric," she murmured.

A thousand questions instantly flooded her mind. *Are you okay? What are you doing here? When are you coming home?* Her chest heaved in and out...*Why did you leave me?*

Her eyes stung. She had to leave. She wasn't ready to face him, let alone speak to him. She shot up, shoving her chair back.

Blaine touched her forearm. "He can't see you, love. There's no need to rush."

With her heart lodged in her throat, she braved another look at Aric. The Guardian who'd held her heart in the palm of his hand, before he ripped it into a thousand pieces. His smoldering gaze narrowed in her direction.

Blaine better be right.

A conversation with Aric was not wise, especially now. He'd only convince her she'd made a mistake, use that sculpted body of his to soothe her worries. Then, she'd be right back in the Heavens crying herself to sleep. Nope, not happening.

After what felt like an eternity, Aric's shoulders slumped. He turned, released the clasp on the rope and walked away from her. Again.

A shudder ran through her body as she exhaled a long, ragged breath. As much as it hurt to see Aric, she couldn't turn away, like when mortals gawked at tragic accidents to fulfill their morbid curiosity. Aric stalked to a table, turned the chair backward and sat with his arms resting on the back, facing another Guardian. A female Guardian. Hang on. Weren't only Aric, EJ and Raven banished? *He lied about that, too.*

Blaine shifted his chair closer to her. "That's Raine, aka Killer Blonde. She and her brother, River, arrived just over a year ago…in mortal time."

Breaking her death stare at Ugly Blonde, Willow glared at Blaine. "I suppose she's on the same mission to save you?"

Blaine shrugged one shoulder. "Dunno, love. I haven't figured her out yet."

Willow sighed. Aric didn't see her, but that didn't ease the churning in her gut. "Tell me why we're here, Blaine. Was it to gloat over Aric meeting a female Guardian in a mortal nightclub?" Of all the times she met with Blaine in the mortal realm to discuss her current…dilemma, he never once pulled a stunt like this.

Blaine's eyes narrowed. "You're sitting on the fence, love, which must be a tad uncomfortable." He motioned to the club full of mortals. "I brought you here to aid your decision, help nudge you over to the other side."

She bit the inside of her lip and looked away. Blaine was right. She'd hovered on that fence for a while now, but each time she prepared to jump over it, an image of Aric rose in her mind. The adoration in his gaze as he made love to her, the sweet words he whispered in her ear. With a broken heart, she climbed off the fence again.

Though, over time, doubt returned. She couldn't forget the fact Aric left her in the Heavens and chose his brothers over her.

I thought he loved me…

She clutched the table as the compelled waitress approached Aric, performing the same maneuver with her breasts. That bitch. Didn't she know he was spoken for? With a schoolgirl giggle heard a mile away, the waitress pivoted, heading toward Blaine. The waitress delivered his drink, without bothering to ask if Willow wanted one. She didn't, but that wasn't the point. The waitress ignored her. The entire club ignored her. Aric ignored her.

Glass in hand, Blaine motioned to Aric's table. "He seems right a home here, don't you think?"

"Who? Aric?"

Blaine exhaled an exaggerated sigh. "Who else, love? Jeez, keep up."

Ugly Blonde and Aric chatted away at the table. He didn't look miserable, nor did he appear heartbroken. In fact, he looked happier than the last time she saw him in the Heavens.

A massive cavity opened inside her heart. To avoid remembering Aric's sword roughened hands on her waist, she focused on the events leading to this moment. Focused on when she saw Aric last, on the day he abandoned her in the Heavens. The day he threw everything away.

She glared at Blaine. "What's your point?"

"I'm only showing you how it is. While you sit up there in the cloudy paradise waiting for him to return, he's down here enjoying all the pleasures this realm offers." Blaine swirled the ice in his tumbler. "I would've thought he'd be desperate to return to you."

She mulled over Blaine's words while shooting death-stares at Ugly Blonde. Did her clothing have to be that tight? Did the Guardian's stunning platinum hair have to be so straight and perfectly under control while Willow could barely contain her unruly curls?

"Your bond mustn't mean much if Aric willingly abandoned you, all for a battle he knew bloody well he wouldn't win." Blaine sniggered. "Do I look like I'm about to waltz through the Heavenly gates?"

Blaine's words left a bitter taste in her mouth. He was right. Aric didn't love her, he abandoned her. *After I begged him to stay.*

"Seems a shame holding your breath waiting for a Guardian who will never return," Blaine added.

Oh, that hurt. Because Blaine spoke the truth. She did hold her breath in the Heavens for Aric's return and by the looks of it, he wasn't in any hurry. His mission, or so she thought, was to return Blaine to the Heavens. If that was true, why was Aric drinking at a mortal nightclub with a female Guardian she didn't know?

Her hands curled into tight fists. Why did she bother waiting for Aric? Why did she waste her time thinking of him? In fact, why did she bother to still love him?

"There it is, love." Blaine circled her face in the air with his finger. "There's the key that'll break you free. All you need to do is hold on to it and I'll catch you on the other side. The fun side." He winked.

She snuck another peek at Aric. He turned her way as though he somehow felt her inner turmoil or sensed the invisible bubble hiding her. His whiskey eyes drew her in, as they had thousands of times before, expanding the gaping hole in her chest until it threatened to swallow her whole. Even though Blaine portrayed Aric as an unfaithful liar, she couldn't help but search for a hint of sorrow in his gaze, a sign he missed her. Something that showed Aric remained the same honorable, protective, passionate Guardian she

26

gave her heart to more than a thousand years ago.

When Aric's eyes softened, she leaned forward. She caught a sense of…longing. Before she confirmed it, he diverted his gaze and curled his finger, motioning for the chesty waitress. The waitress hurried to his table, wasting no time performing her maneuver. Aric whispered in her ear.

Willow pushed away from the table. That was it. The tipping point that forced her to take control. No longer would she allow Fate to hold the reins, imprisoning Willow in the Heavens because of a choice Aric made. Fate created a destiny of incredible happiness for them only to rip it away, crushing her future into a million pieces. No. She was done with the Heavens and with Fate. She was done with Aric.

She faced Blaine. "Do you guarantee Fate won't intercept my Fall?" If Fate caught her trying to escape, the punishment would be horrific. After Blaine's shocking Fall, Fate held all her angels on a tight leash, especially Willow.

"She can't see your choices, love, not when you're with me."

She raised her chin. Now was the time to leap. Her powers and her soul wasted away each day she remained in the Heavens waiting for Aric's return. They wasted away each day she remained connected to him. Obviously, he had no intention of returning to the Heavens. He had no intention of returning to her. If by some twist of Fate he did, she wouldn't be there waiting.

"I'm ready."

Blaine turned in his chair and smirked. "Very well." He downed his drink and stood facing her. "It's better this way Willow, you'll see. He doesn't deserve you."

Yes. Becoming a Fallen would be better than failing as an Ariel. It had to be. Now she prayed she had the strength to survive her Fall.

Steadying her shaky voice, she asked Blaine, "You'll be at the gates to meet me?"

He bowed in a low regal way. "I give you my word."

Could she trust the word of a Fallen? She had to because she either trusted Blaine to meet her at the gates of Hell or she climbed off the fence again and drowned in the agony of Aric's abandonment. *All over again.*

She gave another long, lingering stare in Aric's direction. At her movement, he turned her way. A tiny spark lit inside her blood, like a match striking against the box repeatedly but failing to light. Did he sense her presence through their dormant soulmate bond? He scanned the club before his gaze settled directly on her. He knew she was there even though he couldn't see her.

His hands flattened on the tabletop, his shoulders tense. She was out of time. She needed to Fall before Aric discovered her.

For the final time, she took a mental snapshot of his features. The love of her existence, who she thought was her soulmate forever. Hurt, resentment and anger rose from within. For once, she embraced it all, welcomed the emotions, filled her soul with them until nothing but darkness consumed her.

Chapter Three

Beneath Aric's skin, under the thumping beats of music, a foreign sensation stirred to life. A slight prickle along the back of his neck told him someone watched from a distance. Slowly, he turned, discreetly scanning the crowd, searching for the cause of the humming in his blood. The swell of power so faint, if he had downed another whiskey, he wouldn't have noticed.

The sensation compelled him to look toward the seating area, filled with tables and chairs, mortals shouting conversations above the music, and bar staff scooting back and forth with drinks. All seemed normal. Except, a vacant table in the far right corner drew his attention. Why? No clue. No one sat at the table and given the clear, clean surface, no one had sat there all night. Positive the pull came from that direction, he narrowed his gaze. Nope, still no one there.

This damn club screwed with his head. Why couldn't that Chosen drink at the intimate whiskey bar on the outskirts of town, instead of SubZero? At least then, Aric's eardrums wouldn't have to endure the constant thump of shit music. Thank fuck for the VIP section where he sat, the only place in the club where his glass remained full without lining up. Priority number one. Watching that moron would drive any sane immortal to drink, let alone a semi-unhinged Guardian already exiled from the Heavens.

Four weeks, two days and close to seventeen hours, he had protected that scumbag, and not only from Fallen. There were plenty of mortal males lined up to beat him to a pulp for groping their women. That sleaze bag couldn't keep his hands, or mouth to himself.

Shrugging off the weird sensation humming through his veins, Aric turned back to the table. "What the hell is that?" He nodded to the fancy cocktail glass pinched between Raine's fingers.

She shrugged. "Jimmy said I'd like it."

Jimmy, the bartender on a Saturday night, had a serious hard-on for Raine. Poor guy.

Aric cocked an eyebrow. "And do you?"

Raine peered in the glass, swirling a piece of lime skin in the clear liquid. "Yup."

A neat glass of whiskey arrived on the table, courtesy of their usual waitress. Aric lifted it in the air and thanked Jimmy from afar, who returned a thumbs-up.

"Any issues?" he asked Raine.

She downed the rest of her cocktail. "Nope. Your Chosen's still a dick, but that's nothing new. EJ arrived about twenty minutes ago but quickly disappeared with some mortal female."

Aric clenched his jaw, not because of EJ getting all hot and heavy with some random mortal, but because of his fucking Chosen. Raine had kept an eye on the Chosen until Aric arrived in case Leon got himself into some shit with a Fallen or mortal male. Each time the stupid Chosen stepped in public, he was drunk or high on something, making it near impossible to rely on the spiritual connection linking a Guardian to their assigned Chosen.

He should accidently—on purpose—forget to watch Leon. The idea appealed to him, but he vowed never to fail another Chosen and Aric didn't break his word.

Scanning the club again, he found Leon stumbling to the bar. Sweat beaded across his forehead, his brown scruffy hair styled to one side with so much gel it wouldn't move for a week. His skin-tight jeans hung low on wiry hips and tonight, Leon wore a fluorescent colored short-sleeve button-up that glowed under the light. River wasn't the only one with zero fashion sense.

A waitress, with a tray full of empties balanced on her palm, weaved past the Chosen and that damn piece of shit slapped her square on the ass. Aric clenched the tumbler in his hand. Cocking his ear toward the action, he tuned out the music to hear the conversation unfold.

Man, did that waitress give Leon an earful. Aric smirked. When it came to females defending their honor, he'd let that scumbag get what was comin'. Nothing was sexier than a woman who fought her own battles. However, Chosen or not, if Leon touched her one more time, Aric would fucking deal with him. The waitress told Leon to stop once and once was more than enough.

The prickling sensation at his nape intensified. While he scanned the club again for the source, he caught the attention of a waitress and waved her over, at the same time dreading the thought of having her rub those breasts against his shoulder. If only she got the hint, he wasn't interested and never would be.

"See that scumbag in the three sizes too small fluorescent shirt."

The waitress flicked her hair to the side, glancing in the direction Aric pointed. "Yeah?"

"Do me a favor and get Jimmy to cut him off. He's groping the staff."

The waitress shook her head. "We should ban him."

"Best idea yet." EJ chuckled, pulling up a chair to join them at the table.

The waitress hurried to the bar and spoke in Jimmy's ear. A second later, Jimmy gave Aric another thumbs-up. Good. Now that idiot Leon no longer had access to alcohol, he could stumble his drunk ass home. The advantage of VIP status and being on good terms with the head bartender who happened to own the club.

"Now that EJ's back from his make-out session, I'm heading home." Raine pushed her empty glass to the center of the table and stood. "Babysitting that asshole is on you two." She left via the rear emergency exit, leading to the parking lot out back.

EJ gaped at Aric. "Make-out session? What does she think I am? Twelve?"

Aric raised a brow. "Then maybe you should wipe that lipstick off your neck."

"Nah…" EJ grinned. "I'm gonna wear that a little longer."

This club had always been EJ's scene. Since it opened, the Guardians enjoyed access to the VIP area positioned a few steps higher than the dance floor, where the air resembled oxygen rather than fake smoke. EJ, on the other hand, took full advantage of the private rooms hidden in the back.

A jolt shot through his body. What the hell was going on? A split second later, a familiar thread stirred to life in his soul, like the skin of a wound stitching back together. A thread MIA for over three centuries. A thread which tied his soul to…

He sucked in a breath. Aric jumped off the chair so fast it tipped backward. He scanned the crowd, this time with more focus and determination. Willow was here. His soulmate. He'd recognize that pull anywhere.

EJ stood beside him. "What's up, Ric?"

Aric shook his head. He couldn't breathe, let alone speak with the massive lump forming in his throat.

He searched for Willow's fiery red hair amongst the crowd. Mortals laughed, drank and danced but she wasn't there. He was going mad. His subconscious played tricks on him because he missed his first ever Wednesday visit to the church. *Because of that scumbag.* He lit a candle just after midnight, but then it was Thursday and felt all-kinds of wrong. While the tiny flame burned, he had pleaded for forgiveness. A stupid move, given she couldn't see or hear him. Even knowing the odds weren't in his favor, his heart still ached for the chance to see her. For the chance to hold her in his arms.

Aric's body stiffened, a knot tightening low in his gut. His gaze halted on the vacant table. The table that remained vacant the entire night, even with mortals standing a few feet away.

"Do you see her?"

EJ leaned forward to follow Aric's line of sight. "See who, Ric?"

Without another thought, Aric took off. One minute he stood in the VIP section, the next he bolted toward the vacant table, drawn to it for an unknown reason. He shoved mortals aside.

Urgency screamed to life in his blood. Willow needed him. Something was wrong. He had to find her.

Why the fuck can't I see her?

A few steps from the vacant table, the feeling vanished. The faint thread binding his soul to Willow's once again faded, just as it had the moment Fate exiled him from the Heavens.

He sucked in gulps of air, pressing his palm against the crippling pain behind his ribs. It felt so real. For a second, he convinced himself Willow had escaped from the Heavens. But no, his mind played tricks on him. His chest squeezed tighter at the thought of never reuniting with his soulmate.

EJ squeezed Aric's shoulder. "You look like you've seen a ghost. You good?"

Aric exhaled a shuddering breath. "Was nothin', man. S'all good."

EJ's ice-blue eyes narrowed, but he didn't push the topic. Instead, EJ nodded toward the dance floor. "Your Chosen's at it again."

Aric glared at Leon, thankful for the distraction. "Yeah, but I reckon that blond waitress is gonna swing around and kick him in the balls."

"Awesome." EJ laughed. "I got back just in time."

Aric's gaze drifted back to the vacant table where, moments ago, he sensed Willow. God, he was pathetic. As if she snuck past Fate. Fate wasn't stupid.

A tiny sliver of hope secured its claws deep inside him, renewing his determination to hold on for Willow. One day, he'd figure out a way to return to her.

When they reunited, he'd replace his last memory

of her, the image that haunted his dreams every single night.

Chapter Four

High-pitched screams of terror pierced Willow's ears the instant her body materialized. Fire tore through her blood, consuming her insides with white-hot flame, causing her to scratch and tear gashes in her flesh. Bending at the waist, she coughed and gagged, struggling to suck in oxygen. Only, there wasn't any. Gulps of foul, thick smoke coated her throat, blackening her lungs with each sharp inhale.

She stumbled forward. Heat singed the soles of her feet, her once pretty ballet flats shredded and burned, the fabric barely holding together. Bubbles of fire popped from the ground beside her, spurting tiny fireballs into the air. If she stood there much longer, it wouldn't be just her shoes that caught fire.

Up ahead, a monstrous set of black wrought iron gates appeared, flanked by a never-ending brick wall. Flames licked the surface of the iron making it glow in the darkness. The gates of Hell.

She peered around for Blaine but didn't spot him. Her stomach churned. Where was he? Maybe he meant to meet her inside the gates? If so, she needed to enter on her own. She could do this. She wouldn't be there long. Once inside, Blaine would mist her back to the mortal realm as they agreed.

Pushing forward, she forced one foot in front of the other. The heavenly light remaining in her soul roared to life, burning as bright and hot as the sun, screaming for her to stop. But she wouldn't listen. This was her choice. Aric abandoned her, lied to her, and because of him, her Ariel powers faded. If she wanted control back, her powers back, she had to walk through those terrifying gates.

Sinister laughter echoed around her, sending a wash of cold terror down her spine. Her pulse kicked into overdrive as she spun in circles searching for the source. The voice wasn't Blaine's.

The gates. She had to make it through the gates. Fast. Picking up her pace, she rushed forward, willing the gates to open—

Less than a few feet away, a figure appeared out of nowhere. She sucked in a sharp breath, skidding to a halt. No. It couldn't be. Her gut churned, she staggered back.

Concealed under a thick layer of ominous shadows and smoke, stood a powerful Fallen. She couldn't see his face clearly, but she didn't need to. Everyone knew him.

"Zath," she gasped.

His sickening laugh sent a chill over her flesh, her heart racing so fast it made her dizzy.

Zath didn't move, instead he straightened, as though tormenting her in a sick, horrible way. His soulless red eyes glowed in the darkness like the heated metal of the gates behind him.

To go through, she had to face Zath. She swallowed the bile rising in her throat. No way in…well, *Hell*, that would happen. She'd never win. Zath would strip her remaining light and keep her as his own personal pet for the rest of eternity. She'd heard horror stories about what that involved.

If Blaine was inside the gates, would he hear her? Would he know she'd arrived? It didn't matter, her only option now was fight Zath or mist herself to the mortal realm. In Hell, Fate couldn't control where she misted. But with her light fading by the second, she had to trust she'd been in Hell long enough to transition. If she misted to the mortal realm before she became a Fallen, Fate could immediately return her to the Heavens.

Zath spread open his blood-red wings. The next minute, he leaped in the air toward her. Fierce strength came to her from nowhere. She summoned her remaining sparks of light and misted away.

A split second later, she landed on all fours, retching soot from her lungs. Her heart sank as the choking scent of ash registered. She didn't mist out of Hell. Panicked, and without the time or mental ability to clearly visualize a destination, she ended up in the middle of god-knows where. At least she escaped Zath.

She took a moment to lower her heart rate before standing. Her legs wobbled, so weak and unstable she braced her arms out in front of her for a minute while they steadied. As the landscape registered, she sucked in another breath and gagged. Blinking hard, she tried focusing on the…wasteland.

What have I done?

Coarse crimson dirt topped with a heavy layer of soot, covered the sparse flat landscape far into the distance. Ripples of heat hovered above the surface as though she stood in the middle of a bare, rocky desert on a scorching summer day. She shielded her eyes from a blaring red sun consuming the sky, so large she could almost reach out and singe her fingers on the surface.

In the far distance, twin black volcanoes spurted glowing red lava. The thick, bubbling liquid spewed down the sides, creeping into a lava river at the base. Dirty gray ash floated through the air, landing on her trembling palm—a sickening contrast to the delicate, white snowflakes she experienced in the mortal realm.

She slapped a hand over her mouth, holding back a cry when she scanned left and right, finding nothing but the same bare, sterile landscape, void of living things.

No rolling green hills, no blooming wildflowers, no lush grass. No life.

Ice shot through her blood when the memories flooded back. The choice she'd made. How could she have thought this…nothingness…was better than her restrictions in the Heavens?

God, I've made a mistake.

No. This was the result of her quest to escape the pain. But this—she surveyed the desolate landscape once more—was not what she imagined. The thought of navigating through the endless realms of Hell terrified her. She'd heard the horror stories of angels like herself. Falling and tortured for countless centuries before, best case scenario, they were released into the mortal realm as a Fallen. She wanted no part of that. Emotional strength would only get her so far.

Ignoring her epic failure for a moment, she brushed off the ash and soot from her hands and knees. Cleaning her dress proved pointless, it no longer resembled the white summery fabric she wore when she…Fell.

She accepted the risk of Zath intercepting her Fall. Blaine didn't withhold that information from her, but during their meetings, he had assured her the risk was slim. Next to nothing he said. To put her mind at ease, he agreed to meet her at the gates and immediately mist them to the mortal realm. That way she severed her connection with the Heavens without remaining in Hell.

If only Blaine had kept his word. Why did she trust him? Deep down she knew she shouldn't. After all, he was a Fallen. The one who instigated the biggest shake-up the Heavens had ever seen.

She couldn't dwell on past mistakes. Finding a way out of Hell became priority number one while she still possessed a sliver of light to mist. Once in the mortal realm, the only realm as familiar to her as the Heavens, she could work out her next step.

Different locations floated around in her mind before she settled on one: her last assignment in the mortal realm. Blaine could find her there as he had each time they met. He promised to return her powers, and she'd make sure he kept his end of the bargain. Once she was up and running in the mortal world as a Fallen, she'd leave Blaine and set out on her own.

The mortal realm was large. If Willow remained on the opposite side of the world, she could exist without Aric knowing. Without ever seeing him again. He'd betrayed her, abandoned her and no way she'd let him ruin this, too.

Closing her eyes, she imagined a vivid picture of the location, pouring all her strength and concentration into creating the scene. Lush green grass, towering trees, a slow trickle of water in the distance as it slid over smooth rocks, landing in a small pool.

The tips of her fingers illuminated with Ariel power, sparking to life, a weightlessness lifting inside her chest. What remained of her heavenly light tingled beneath the surface of her skin, flesh and bones preparing to mist. Warmth spread through her chest, expanding as her limbs hummed with power—

A violent jolt jerked her head back. The image instantly erased.

"Argh!" she screamed, flinging her hands behind her head.

Digging her heels into the dirt, she fought to regain her balance. Someone yanked her backward by her hair. Thick red curls flung across her face. She screamed louder, twisted and turned to get free. Whatever held her was too powerful. She flipped to the side and ended falling flat on her face in the red dirt.

A familiar wicked growl rumbled in her ears, sending chills down her spine. Attempting to flee, she scurried along the dirt, but Zath tightened his grip on her hair.

"Well, well, well…what do we have here?" he snarled.

Her eyes stung, vision blurred.

Zath yanked her head back again so forcefully he might snap her neck. He hovered against her ear. "He shouldn't've left you unprotected. He knows better than that."

No time to process the meaning behind Zath's words. She had to escape. Now.

Standing tall, Zath dragged her along the ground by the hair, like a dead animal he intended to feature on his wall.

She kicked harder. Dug her heels in the dirt. Reached behind and scratched at his fist clenching her hair.

Her attempts were pointless. Zath overpowered her in every way that counted including sheer strength, while hers depleted by the second.

"Aric!" she screamed for help, the first name that came to her. Which was stupid. As if he would save her.

Zath's chilling laugh froze the blood in her veins. "This is gonna be soooo much fun."

Oh, please no…

Chapter Five

The engine of Aric's custom-built motorcycle rumbled between his thighs as he accelerated, pure raw power screaming for release. Knocking it back a gear, he hugged the bike between his legs and leaned to the left, curving around a sweeping bend inclining up the mountain, pulling back on the throttle when he entered and kicking it in the guts on the exit. The wind whizzed around him. Golden afternoon rays streamed through the towering pine trees flanking the road, lacking enough warmth to melt the light dusting of snow.

The highway across the top of the mountains was his favorite place to ride. A windy road where he focused solely on the motion of leaning in and out of corners, easing off the throttle to kick it down a gear, and letting it rip on the straightaways.

The Snowy Mountains were breathtaking this time of the year. Fresh forest pines and rich earth, mixed with the stormy scent of bulging dark gray clouds, reminded him of Willow.

Calmness washed through his body as he inhaled, and he slowed down to a Sunday cruise. An image of Willow's fiery red hair appeared in his mind, thick curls cascading past her shoulders like the sun rested upon her head, afternoon rays beaming over her body. His chest warmed at the memory. Her bright hazel eyes and the way a delicate smile curved her lips each time she caught him staring at her, something he did all the time.

Though the memories caused an intense ache in his chest, he never wished them away. They were all he had left to keep him holding on until he saw her again. Which, given his screw up, could be a long fucking time.

He leaned the bike around another sweeping bend and accelerated onto a straightaway. Up ahead, a pullover came into view and he eased off the road, parking the bike. After unzipping his leather jacket, he wandered to a nearby boulder, perching himself on top to take in the view.

From here, three-quarters up the slope, he spied the road he traveled far in the distance, curving around the edge of the mountain. The road led to smaller, less popular ski resorts, so he could avoid mortal traffic. Directly below, shadows bathed the mountainside, preparing for the evening ahead.

He took a deep, full breath. Relaxing back on one outstretched arm, he closed his eyes and replayed memories of him and Willow.

Smoke caught in the back of his throat. His eyes snapped open. Jolting upright, he sucked in another breath, but coughed and choked as though he'd misted right into the middle of a wildfire.

He leaped off the boulder, searching for the source of the smoke, breathing through the neck of his shirt to ease the coughing. Wildfires were common in this part of the country, but they rarely occurred during the winter months when snow and dampness covered the vegetation.

He scanned the area. No sign of fire, yet, smoke continued filling his lungs. Spinning around, he searched higher up the mountain. Nothing. Where the hell did the smoke come from?

The air thickened. He peered along the road heading up the mountain. His heart sank. Gloomy gray fog drifted around the corner toward him. Wait, that wasn't fog. The thickening cloud was smoke.

Inching closer, holding the neck of his shirt over his mouth, he zeroed in on the orange glow in the center of the smoke, resembling a fire without flames.

The smoke continued rolling toward him. He shot a glance at his bike. If he got on now, he could out-run it for sure. As the thought formed in his mind, the bike's corporal form flickered and faded into thin air.

"What the fuck?" he muttered.

He staggered back, stumbling on a burned tree stump appearing out of nowhere. He gaped as the landscape transformed into something more sinister and no longer resembled the mountain lookout.

He kicked the charred branch at his feet, recoiling when it disintegrated before his eyes. Holy shit. With a sinking feeling consuming his gut, he turned around. He must've misted into the aftermath of a wildfire with the entire forest destroyed. But how? Fate revoked his ability to mist, so how the hell did he manage it after so long? He had no clue, but he needed to flee, stat.

Along the road, smoke rolled toward him, building high into the air, consuming the forest in an eerie orange glow. Waves of heat rolled over him but still without visible flames.

"Aric!" a female voiced screamed.

His heart stopped. Willow. Spinning in tight circles, he searched for her.

The rational part of his brain knew she wasn't here,

knew this was another trick of his subconscious, but he couldn't take the chance. If Willow misted here, then she needed his help. He had to save her.

"Willow?" he shouted back.

Thickening smoke curled around his body, surrounding him. His eyes stung. Coughing and wheezing, he gasped short sharp breaths through the fabric of his shirt.

Flames licked his boots a moment before fire roared to life, searing heat forced him backward. His feet faltered, a rock tumbled over the edge and fell a thousand feet to its death. Pivoting around, he peered over the cliff. Flames consumed the mountainside like bright orange burning fingers reaching for him.

Fuck. The fire surrounded him. No way out.

"Help!" Willow shrieked, her voice screaming through the roaring flames.

He had to find her before it was too late. Shielding his face with his arm, he crept closer to the flames.

"Willow, where are you?" A blast of heat scorched his face, forcing him back. "Fuck!"

Any gulp of air he managed burned in his chest. The smoke swirled around his body making his head swim and legs wobble. His stomach rolled.

The moment his throat squeezed shut, his legs gave out, falling to his knees in the ash, gasping for breath. Fire licked his arm as he reached for Willow.

He couldn't find her. He couldn't save her.

I failed her again.

"I'm sorry, baby."

He collapsed on his side as the flames engulfed his jacket.

****

Aric shot upright and slapped at the flames on his sleeve. Only…there were none. He sucked in a lung full of air. Clean, fresh air.

What the fuck?

His heart thumped inside his chest, racing so fast it broke records. Taking a minute to catch his breath, he glanced around, re-orientating himself. He sat on the ground, nestled at the base of a boulder, his bike parked a few feet away. Darkness blanketed the mountains.

Damn it. He must've fallen asleep.

The motorcycle ride worked off the unease stirring in his gut, but obviously, he needed more rest than he thought. He hadn't focused clearly since the incident at the club three nights ago where he swore he sensed Willow. The thought messed with his fucking head.

Willow wasn't in the mortal realm. She remained in the Heavens, safely tucked away where he'd left her. Why now did he possess an overwhelming urge to see her? The past few weeks his yearning to reunite with her shot to a whole new level.

The unease returned. What if she had moved on? What if she gave up hope? Although he always wished for her happiness, a selfish part of him longed for her to wait. They were soulmates, destined to be together until the end of time. She was the only one for him.

That dream was so vivid, so lifelike, he still felt the flames singeing his face. The burn in his throat evident each time he swallowed.

Bracing himself on one side, he stood, dusting off the pine needles and dirt covering his black jeans. Fuck. He needed to get his shit together.

After zipping up his jacket, he swung his leg over the bike and settled into the seat. A shower, Ellen's steamy beef casserole and a body packed full of weapons were what he needed. Not the imaginary screams of his soulmate. He slid on his helmet and cranked the engine, giving it a little rev for the hell of it before pulling onto the road, leaving that horrid nightmare behind him.

Chapter Six

"Show me your wings, little pet."

The sinister voice grated against her ear, making Willow's stomach churn.

Where was she? For what seemed like hours, her mind drifted in and out of a heavy fog. One minute her eyes shot open to the vast deserted landscape, the next darkness swallowed her. This time, with the chilling voice wrenching her subconscious from the depths of nothingness, something felt different. Something *sounded* different.

Oh, God, where has he taken me?

How could Blaine find her if he had no clue where she'd gone? Fate had imprisoned Zath in Hell. Did that mean she'd remain there, too? Though, without any idea which of the countless realms in Hell Zath dragged her to, she had no hope of escape.

A sob caught in her throat. How could she have messed up her Fall so spectacularly? The only angel in the history of angels to fail Falling to Hell. First, she failed to hold onto her soulmate, and now she also failed to sever her connection with him.

Argh! She'd planned this for too damn long, given up too much, for it to crumble apart. She refused to end her existence like this.

Falling was her only choice. The only path that restored her Ariel magic, which had fizzled away over the past three centuries. Falling to Hell should've broken her connection with the Heavens. Instead, it led to her capture. Her muscles tightened. If she didn't escape, she kissed goodbye her plans of freedom in the mortal realm.

Inhaling stale air, she attempted to figure out where Zath held her captive before opening her eyes and alerting him to her conscious state. Smoke caught at the back of her throat, a familiar smell from her assignments in the mortal realm. The scent likening charcoal and burned wood, that lingered in the air after a catastrophic wildfire. The same smell she remembered from the gates of Hell. Whew. At least he hadn't taken her to an unknown realm.

She focused on the sounds, picking up faint screams in the distance, followed by liquid gushing over a stone floor but on a much grander scale. The cold, jagged surface she lay on pressed firmly against her right side.

Heavy footsteps made her tense. Her heart rate sky-rocketed through the roof. The heavy steps circled behind her. Bile rose in her throat when foul breath skated along her nape.

"Show me your wings," Zath's sickening voice demanded.

Nope. She wouldn't show him a damn thing, but the thought piqued her curiosity. Had her wings changed to crimson?

Stop! Exploring her new appearance had to wait; she needed to escape.

Get the hell out of Hell. Great. Now she was looney, too.

When the footsteps trailed away from her, she

peeked at her surroundings. She blinked a few times, trying to clear her vision, but only one eye functioned. The other refused to open. As soon as the injury registered in her brain, her eye socket throbbed.

It took a moment to realize she lay on a dark stone floor with her hands bound in front by thick metal chains. Not an ideal situation. Without thinking, she sat up, totally forgetting her ploy to remain unconscious.

"Well, well…the pretty one awakes."

Damn it. Mistake number one. Two, if she included Zath capturing her. Three, if she included her failed Fall.

Bracing her hands on the floor, she curled her legs beside her. A quick glance confirmed she still wore her filthy summer dress.

Her gaze lifted, and she sucked in a sharp breath. Zath crouched before her, his long leather clad legs in front of her face, his naked torso glistening with sweat. Thick jagged black scars marred his chest. A lump grew in her throat as she peered at the deep crimson wings extended behind him. Rather, what remained of them. Gross infected wounds covered the inside of his wings where feathers had once been. Black blood splattered across the gossamer tissue, gaping holes at each tip instead of poisonous talons. Her gaze settled on Zath's fiery red eyes.

"Now that you're awake, the fun can begin." He snickered.

Fun wasn't the word she would use but thought better of correcting him. Stalling him became her mission. She didn't know how much strength she had left and needed every ounce to escape this place.

"There's no point trying to escape, my pretty Ariel.

The iron forged in Hellfire prevents misting."

Mistake number four. God, her failures increased by the minute.

Up went her mental wall so Zath no longer heard her thoughts, otherwise escaping was pointless.

"What…" She swallowed to clear the burn in her throat. "What do you want from me?"

The monster chuckled. "It doesn't matter what I want. What you should be worried about is who I am."

You can do this, Willow. Summon that strength.

"I know who you are," she snapped, lifting her chin.

His lip curled, revealing sharp, pointy incisors. "And here I thought that bitch and her fragile little angels had forgotten me." He stood and moved behind her.

Her breath quickened. *Distract him, Willow, distract him.* "You're just another Fallen. Like I am now."

Her muscles tensed and because they refused to budge, she lost sight of Zath.

"You see…when an Ariel Falls, there's always a spark of light left inside." He dragged a finger through her hair, making her gag. "I've waited a long time for another Ariel."

Do not vomit…do not vomit…

"You're mistaken." She steadied her voice. "I severed my connection with the Heavens. There's no light remaining in my soul. You're wasting your time."

She prayed Zath bought her lie. Willow sucked in a breath. The ability to lie. *I guess I truly am a Fallen now.* Though, she knew a sliver of light remained, stirring deep inside her soul. No way she'd let Zath get his filthy hands on it. That light was her ticket out of there…once the chains came off.

Zath inched closer. "I know you're lying."

Her pulse pounded in her ears. "Why me?" *Distract.* "Surely, there are more powerful Ariel who Fall." How could she get the damn chains off?

"Yes, but they are so rare I take whoever Falls." He caressed her hair. *Gag.* "But your power is not the only reason I chose you."

Her heart sank. What other reason could Zath have? Did she even want to know? "Why then?"

"Revenge is my favorite pastime, my little pet."

Her mind raced with thousands of questions. *Revenge for what? Revenge for who? What did I do to him?*

Zath's foul, hot breath exhaled at her ear. "Now, be a good girl and show me your wings."

This time he layered his words with a powerful compulsion she couldn't disobey. Her wings exploded from her back with incredible speed, leaving her powerless to stop them. She choked back a sob as his rough hand gripped the top of her left wing, stretching it further. No matter how hard she tried, her wings refused to return inside her back.

"Hmm, just as I thought." His sweaty palm roamed along the top of her wing.

Out of the corner of her eye, she braved a peek. Tiny specs of bronze shined bright against the abundance of crimson feathers, a clear sign her Fallen transition wasn't complete.

I'm so doomed…

Zath sniggered. "Maybe next time that Guardian of yours will think twice about leaving you unprotected."

She recoiled and spun to face him. "Guardian?"

A wicked grin curved on his blood-red lips. "He made it clear to my legion of Fallen that you belonged to him. Though, I'm curious why he let you Fall."

Surely, he wasn't referring to Aric.

Zath turned his back to her. "It's taken me a long time to gather the strength to regenerate my power after Fate had him strip it from me. Once I remove your wings, pretty Ariel, I'll be one step closer to harnessing enough light to break free of this prison."

What? Remove my wings? Her heart plummeted through the stone floor.

Metal scraping against stone made her shudder. She inhaled slowly, trying to steady her heart rate. "You're making a mistake. Aric wants nothing to do with me. I'm dead to him." Saying it aloud reopened the wound she'd mentally stitched closed.

Zath pivoted to face her and the glint of metal in his hand caught her eye. "I wouldn't be so sure of that. But only time will tell." He shrugged with a dangerous smirk. "Perhaps I'll ask him when I return to the mortal realm. I can only imagine his outrage when I relay all the gory details."

As though in slow motion, Zath grazed his thumb along the sharp blade of the curved dagger, cutting his flesh. Black blood pooled at the wound before dripping to the floor. Sickening satisfaction washed over his features.

Willow thrashed against the chains. She whipped her arms back and forth to break free, but to no avail. She tried to stand but stumbled back to her knees, the iron chains secured to the floor.

She froze the moment Zath stood directly behind

her. "Take my light. I want to be a Fallen." Her voice cracked. "Please don't take my wings." Her wings harnessed her powers, without wings she had no hope of restoring them.

Zath yanked her hair, leaning close to her ear. "I'll enjoy hearing you scream, my little Ariel."

Searing hot pain sliced through her wing. She screamed at the top of her lungs, adding to the millions of other screams echoing around her. Jerking the chains, she reached behind her, to twist away from Zath, to break free. But her muscles seized with shock as the pain consumed her.

A second later, a heavy thud sounded on the floor. She gagged, catching sight of her hacked-off wing laying on the cold stone. Bright red blood gushed from the flesh.

Zath's sickening laugh boomed in her ears as fire ripped through her other wing. She screamed louder until her voice cracked and violent convulsions racked her body. She fought against the blackness, to remain conscious, but the pain took over.

One last thought burned before the darkness swallowed her whole.

I hate you, Aric.

****

Distant grunting roused Willow from the deep depths of her subconscious. She fought to open her eyes, but her lids were too heavy. The cold, hard surface pressing against her cheek did nothing to temper the blaze roaring across her back.

Vivid memories assaulted her mind, just as Zath had assaulted her with that dagger. Her throat tightened, choking back a sob. The last thing she remembered was excruciating pain when Zath sliced off her second wing.

Loud thuds followed by rocks tumbling to the ground made her jolt, and she found the strength to open her eyes. Several blinks failed to clear the vision as the grunting and snarls continued. She rolled her heavy head to the other side and caught a blurry image of two shadows engaged in a vicious brawl.

Had Aric saved her? No, he didn't care. Aric was the reason Zath hacked off her wings. At that thought, her flesh burned hotter over her shoulder blades and her eyes slid closed again, as she drifted off away from the agony.

****

"Willow, love, wake up." A familiar voice stirred in her mind.

Something cool patted her cheek. She forced open her eyes a notch and found a dark-haired male crouched on the floor before her. Through her hazy vision she recognized Blaine.

"Chop-chop, we have to get a move on." Blaine lifted her body to a sitting position.

Pain sliced along her shoulders. The world spun. Her stomach lurched. "Let me be." She tried pushing Blaine away, only she lacked the strength to raise her arm.

"No can do, love. It's now or never."

The fight in her vanished the moment that monster hacked off her wings, leaving her powerless. Without her wings she was nothing; not an Ariel, not an angel, not a Fallen. Nothing.

Turning her head away from Blaine, she closed her eyes. "I choose never."

How could she have been so stupid, thinking she

could sneak past Zath? Blaine had told her it would be easy, a quick step through the gates. He'd told her he would mist her back to the mortal realm. Blaine abandoned her like Aric had when he left her in the Heavens.

A stupid error in judgement diminished her powers. And now, another stupid choice, supposed to fix the first one, left her in some sickening realm of Hell without wings and powers. Without an identity. Without a home.

All she wanted was to drift away in the blackness and cease to exist. No pain compared to what she endured, and she had no reason to exist without her powers.

Weightlessness rushed through her body like she floated off the ground, a familiar tingle traveled along her flesh. A sudden drop in temperature washed over her skin, chilling the beads of sweat on her forehead. A moment later, her body lowered onto a soft, plush pallet.

"You're safe now, love. Time to rest."

Pain reared in her back, bringing fresh tears to her eyes but she gritted through it to roll onto her side away from Blaine.

Who cares where I am?

Everywhere was Hell without her wings.

Chapter Seven

"It's been three weeks and it still feels real. I swear I smell smoke every time I wake." Aric took a long sip of his favorite whiskey.

The dream of him standing in the middle of a wildfire hadn't returned, but each time he closed his eyes, Willow's screams echoed around him and choking smoke caught in his lungs.

Raven pursed his lips. "I hate to say it, but maybe Fate's at work again?"

That was all Aric needed. Fate and her OCD to meddle in everyone's goddamn existence.

"She's already assigned me a Chosen. Though I have no clue why she wasted her time creating that loser."

Raven scoffed. "Yeah, I got a helluva better deal than you, my man."

Aric tilted his glass to Raven. "Speaking of which, why aren't you back at home with Tayla?"

"She has some girls' night planned with Raine." Raven frowned. "What does Raine do on girls' night anyway?"

"Hang dead-beat males from the ceiling by their balls?"

Raven chuckled and clinked his glass with Aric. "Exactly."

Warmth expanded in Aric's chest, filling his soul

and lifting the weight from his shoulders a fraction as he settled back in the chair. It had been too long since he and Raven chilled. Raven called an end to their shift about an hour ago due to the lack of Fallen. They ended up at a small bar halfway between Summit Creek and the closest ski field, stocked with every flavor combination of schnapps and a few top-shelf spirits. His new favorite location. Besides the handful of mortals mingling around a tasting table at the other end of the bar, he and Raven were the only patrons.

Comfortable silence stretched between them and he relaxed back in the leather armchair, facing the lit double-sided hearth positioned in the center of the establishment. The flames roused his dream of Willow until his chest squeezed so tight, he looked away.

Sitting in the armchair to Aric's left, Raven turned slightly to face him. "Tell me again about the dream. We must be missing something."

Aric inhaled a long, deep breath before rattling off every detail, from the time he arrived at the lookout to the moment the flames closed in around him. The smoke burning his lungs freaked him the fuck out. It felt so real as though he'd misted to the location, even though he knew misting was impossible.

Willow's screams playing on loop in his head caused the most pain, and the fact he had no clue whether they were real or not. Real meant acknowledging Fate was at play. If they weren't real, it meant he'd lost his goddamn mind. Both possibilities scared the shit out of him.

Chilly wind blew under the coffee table and circled Aric's ankles. His gaze shot to the door as a Fallen strolled in like he owned the place. Aric's entire body tensed, preparing for action, his hand twitching to grab the dagger concealed in his boot. The Fallen turned their way.

"Fucking great," Aric groaned realizing the Fallen's identity. What a way to ruin a perfectly good night.

Blaine strutted to their spot before taking a seat to Aric's right. "Evening, gentlemen."

"What do you want, Blaine?" Raven snapped.

Blaine shrugged off his worn leather jacket and peered around the bar. "This place is cute. A tad quiet but cute."

A waitress appeared and addressed Blaine. "Can I get you something, sir?"

Blaine glanced at the empty glasses in front of Raven and Aric. "Refill theirs and I'll have one of those fancy schnapps thingies. Why don't you surprise me?"

He winked at the waitress making Aric shudder. When did Blaine become such a creep? The waitress, oblivious to Blaine's creepiness, giggled and trotted back to the bar.

Aric leaned forward resting his forearms on his thighs, unable to sit still with the amount of tension crackling in the air between the three of them. Centuries ago, he would've welcomed catching up with Blaine, but now, he dreaded every second.

How could he not? If Blaine didn't Fall, then he wouldn't be on this screwed up mission. He'd be back in the Heavens with Willow.

He lowered his voice to avoid drawing the attention of the few mortals hanging around. "Why the fuck are you here, Blaine?"

"No need for hostility, friend. I couldn't help but

hear you talking about you-know-where and I'm intrigued to hear more."

Raven popped his knuckles. "And where exactly is you-know-where?"

Blaine frowned as though Raven had asked the world's stupidest question. "Hell, of course."

The pit of Aric's stomach plummeted to his boots. "Did you just say—"

Before Blaine could answer, the waitress returned with their drinks, placing them on the coffee table.

The waitress batted her thick brown lashes at Blaine. "I thought a man like you would enjoy schnapps with a little kick." She handed the glass to Blaine. "This one is called Devil's Sin."

Raven spat out his drink causing sprays of bourbon to dot the table. The waitress glared at him with an "I hope you're cleaning that up" look, before returning her attention to Blaine.

Blaine cackled. "Sounds perfect, sweetheart." He crooked his finger at the waitress, and she leaned closer, locking gazes with him. A moment passed before she straightened, beamed at him and trotted back to the bar, swaying her hips so wide she could've knocked out anyone who walked in her vicinity.

Just fucking great. Not only did Blaine ruin Aric's buzz, but he also compelled a helpless mortal to probably continue a steady flow of drinks without charge.

"Devil's Sin," Raven grumbled, using a napkin to wipe the bourbon from the table. "How appropriate."

Blaine's throaty laugh echoed around the bar. "Uncanny, isn't it?" He motioned between them. "This is nice. Like the good ol' days."

With a sparkling clean table, Raven relaxed back and crossed his ankle over his knee. "Before you screwed it all up."

Blaine shrugged. "Semantics."

Aric grabbed his glass off the table. "Yeah, it's been a great chat, Blaine. Can we get back to the part where you said we were talking about Hell?"

Blaine shot down the schnapps and shuddered. "That does have a kick."

"I think you're meant to sip it, asshole." Aric clenched his teeth to control the rage bubbling inside, so he didn't punch Blaine in the middle of a mortal bar. "Fuck, man, tell me what you meant."

Blaine narrowed his eyes. "Why don't you tell me how you misted to Hell?"

Aric drew back. "I didn't…" He hadn't misted to Hell, he'd dreamt it. Sure, the dream felt real but…*fuck.* Had he misted?

He couldn't have. Fate revoked their ability to mist when she exiled the Guardians to the moral realm. The dream felt real, but the flames on his jacket hadn't burned the leather. Besides, Willow was in the Heavens, not in Hell. Still, finding out any info Blaine had was a good strategy.

Aric shot a quick sideways glance at Raven, trying for an "exactly how much should I reveal to Blaine?" look and hoped Raven caught his drift. With Blaine around, they locked the padlock on their mental walls nice and tight. They could never be too careful.

Raven's lips thinned. Right, not much then.

Aric turned to Blaine. "I didn't mist there. I was telling Raven about a dream." The statement wasn't a lie if he believed it. Besides, he still wasn't sure he misted in the first place.

Blaine smirked, not convinced. "I could've sworn you described the fiery gates." Waving his hand in the air, he dismissed the conversation. "My mistake."

Aric described the fiery gates of Hell? Describing Hell was one thing, but to describe the gates? Now he was invested in the conversation. "Why would I dream of the entrance to Hell? I haven't been there. I wouldn't even know what it looks like."

Raven took a slow swig of bourbon, acting all calm-like. "Don't worry 'bout it, Aric. We'll figure it out. Fate's probably twisting things up a little, that's all."

The waitress appeared and placed another round of drinks on the table between them, no doubt thanks to Blaine's little compulsion trick earlier. Blaine winked, and she trotted off again.

Blaine reached for his glass and smirked at Raven. "Brother, I'm pretty sure it's not Fate's turn."

"What's that supposed to mean?"

Blaine dismissed the question with a shrug. He tapped his forefinger on his chin and peered at the ceiling. "I wonder who else you would dream of, Aric, who might pass through the gates…"

Aric's blood felt like the tiled roof had flung off and a blizzard landed in his fucking lap. Blaine didn't mean…no, that scenario was impossible…but the dream felt so real. Nothing else explained it.

"Willow," Aric muttered.

A devilish grin curled on Blaine's lips.

Raven leaned in. "It's not possible. She's in the Heavens."

Aric couldn't speak. Words formed in his head, but

his brain had short-circuited, no longer communicating with this mouth. Blaine baited him. He knew that. *But what if...*

His brain kick started again. He glared at Blaine. "Why would Willow pass through the gates?" he snapped through gritted teeth.

Blaine sipped his stupid, appropriately named schnapps as though he enjoyed a Sunday afternoon tea party, making Aric's rage increase by the second. "I dunno. Maybe she got sick of waiting for you to return?"

Aric lowered his voice to a menacing growl. "You're the reason I can't return. You're the fucking reason I left."

"True. But I wasn't the one who abandoned her."

Aric clenched his jaw, his grinding molars crunched in his ears. "The fuck you weren't. She loved you like family. It would've broken her heart when you tossed us all aside."

"Oh..." Blaine waved his hand in the air. "She's forgiven me for that little indiscretion." He slapped a hand over his mouth. "Oops...did I say that aloud?"

Red spots invaded Aric's vision. He tightened his fists and fought with every ounce of self-control not to beat the shit out of Blaine right fucking now. "What do you mean she's forgiven you?"

"Never mind." Blaine shot back the rest of his drink and slid the glass to the center of the table. "Anyhoo, I have to get a move on. Places to see...people to be. Or is it the other way around?" He stood, sliding on his jacket. "It's always a pleasure."

Aric sat frozen as Blaine strolled out of the bar as though he hadn't just hurled a grenade at them and laughed while it fucking exploded. The armrest creaked underneath his grip.

"Don't do it, Aric. Don't take the bait. You know this is his thing."

Raven's voice trailed off, lost in thousands of unanswered questions appearing in Aric's mind. *What if Blaine knew something? What if Willow is in Hell? What if she needs me…?*

Aric slammed his glass on the table. "I have to know."

He didn't wait for Raven's reply. In an instant, he shot across the bar, shoved open the door and stormed outside.

"Took you longer than I expected," Blaine called from Aric's left.

Aric stalked toward Blaine. Blood boiled in his veins. If this was another one of Blaine's tricks, he'd kill the bastard. Screw the deal with Fate.

"Tell me what you know," he growled.

Blaine relaxed against a tree trunk, one leg bent up, his arms crossed in front of his chest. "Now, that's no way to talk to an old friend."

"I'm in no mood to play, Blaine. Tell me."

Blaine's brows furrowed. "Everything has a price."

A fucking price. He should've realized Blaine no longer felt any loyalty to the brotherhood he'd once fought alongside. *Until he Fell…*

The bar door swung open and Raven strolled out. "I thought you'd have him hanging from a tree by now. You need me to call Raine to give you a hand?"

Blaine grinned. "Now there's an idea."

Raven halted a few steps behind Aric, leaving him to control the situation. The fight was Aric's and Raven wouldn't deny him that.

Aric inched closer to Blaine. "What's your price for information on Willow?"

"Depends what type of information you desire."

"This is not a fucking game," he roared. "If she's in Hell, I need to save her. Tell me if she's there."

Tiny flames lit in Blaine's irises. "That's a big request." He tapped his chin again.

One more time and Aric would break his fingers.

"A request that large requires an equally large payment."

Whatever. He didn't give a shit about payment. "What's your price?"

Blaine peered to the Heavens and grinned before returning his gaze to Aric. "I want your Chosen's soul."

What the fuck? Did Blaine say that aloud? Surely, he wasn't serious.

Aric sensed Raven inch closer. *I've got this,* he mentally snapped to Raven. He didn't give a shit anymore about upholding mental walls.

"You've gotta be kidding me." Getting right in Blaine's face, he growled, "I want no part of your fucked-up revenge on Fate. This is Willow's life. Her soul. If you have any shred of humanity left, now's the time to use it."

Blaine held his composure. "I'll let you think it over. But if Willow is in Hell…" He shook his head, a grim expression on his face. "We both know, as an Ariel, she won't make it out of there." Blaine stepped to the side, out of Aric's reach, and unfurled his crimson wings. "Be sure to let me know when you choose her over your brotherhood." Blaine chuckled before he shot into the night sky.

"Fuck!" Aric roared.

Raven stepped beside him. "You gotta know it's a trick, Aric. He's setting you up."

Aric squeezed his forehead, the pressure inside his skull building like the inside of a cooker about to explode. "But what if she is there? What if she Fell?"

Authority boomed in Raven's voice when he said, "Don't even consider it, Aric. Leon's a Chosen, for God's sake. We don't know his destined path. This could be why Fate assigned him to you."

Aric glared at Raven. "We both know that scumbag doesn't deserve to be a Chosen. He doesn't deserve entry to the Heavens. He should go to Hell."

"I can't even comprehend what Fate would do if you willingly failed your Chosen. Think about what it would do to your soul, Aric. Think about what happened last time."

Aric shoved his fingers through his hair. He didn't give a shit about his soul. He'd give up everything for Willow. "Have you considered that, maybe for once, Blaine's telling the truth? He's our only connection to Hell, unless you feel like torturing a Fallen for the info."

"I don't like where you're going with this."

He turned to Raven. "I have to know. I have to know she's safe."

"You will." Raven squeezed his shoulder. "But sacrificing your Chosen's soul to a Fallen isn't the way."

Peering off in the direction Blaine had flown, Aric mentally sifted through his options, searching for the right answer. Not an easy task with Raven staring him down as though at any moment Aric would turn rogue and do something stupid.

Going rogue was one thing. Sacrificing his assigned Chosen? That move would score him punishment beyond his comprehension. He got off lightly last time. He doubted Fate would be so lenient again. What if Fate paved these two paths for him? What if she was more twisted than he gave her credit?

After a few moments of pacing in a tight circle, Aric decided. Would he risk punishment from Fate to know Willow wasn't in Hell? Would he betray his oath as a Guardian to know she was safe in the Heavens? Would he risk destroying his soul to save her?

Yes. Yes. And Yes. For Willow, of course, he fucking would.

Chapter Eight

Willow opened her eyes and peeked at her surroundings.

Yep, still here.

She'd opened them to the same extravagant room each day for the past seven days, each time hoping the memories were a horrific nightmare. Hoping her subconscious had created them. No such luck. Because once again, she lay on the same cushiony bed, in the same room, bathed in the same warm light filtering through the same uncovered windows. The fact she lay cocooned in glorious linen made no difference to her current mood.

Rolling onto her back, she stared at the patch marks in the ceiling. Her back no longer blazed with heat when it touched her clothing. Smoke no longer lingered in her hair, and her eyes no longer refused to open. What remained, though, were the nightmares that occurred each time she fell asleep.

Over to her right, she spotted a tray of uneaten food and an unopened bottle of water on the nightstand. How long would her body function without nourishment? Another week? Another month? Was she still immortal?

Returning her gaze to the ceiling gave no answers. Snippets of memories teased the back of her mind. Blaine's voice, full of urgency, while she drifted in and out of consciousness, then him assuring her safety.

Yeah, right.

She wasn't naïve. Zath severed her wings and she knew one day he'd come for her. A hint of blood hit her tongue when she bit her bottom lip. She had to toughen the hell up and take it one day at a time. She would survive.

A long, deep breath of fresh air filled her lungs and for the first time since her…ordeal, she realized she was in the mortal realm. Through the walls in her room, she sensed the forest outside. It called to her, roused her from her nightmares and stirred what was left of her soul.

Every day she fought a battle to give up or carry on, but today was different. For the first time, she woke without pain.

"It's time to get up, Willow," she muttered.

Her plan to arrive in mortal realm wasn't a complete failure. She just took one massive detour. Nevertheless, she made it. She had to trust her wings would regrow, eventually. She was immortal, her body should regenerate. If she lost a limb, it would regrow so why wouldn't her wings? If all went to plan, her powers would return when her wings did. Then she'd never think of, or see, Aric again. Their bond would no longer diminish her powers. Once her wings grew back, she'd no longer be a failure.

She rolled to the side of the bed and planted her feet firmly on the cool floorboards, wiggling her toes to revive the circulation.

"Here goes…"

Standing, she braced a palm on the nightstand to steady herself. After a moment, she took a sip of water and explored the room. Behind internal door number one, she found a closet full clothes and shoes. She grabbed some garments and padded to door number two. Inside, she discovered a luxurious bathroom, fitted with all the modern facilities.

She stripped off the horrific dress she'd worn for what felt like an eternity, all torn and singed, and tossed it in the bathroom corner. When the smell of smoke didn't send her into a panic, she'd burn the dress. After fiddling with the taps to find a suitable temperature, she submersed her body under the spray. Wow, it felt good. Taking her time, she emptied every bottle of fragranced goodness, scrubbed and scrubbed until her skin returned to its usual ivory tone. She gave her long, wavy bright copper hair the VIP treatment, several washes and a whole bottle of something labeled "treatment." Feeling like new again—on the outside—she shut off the taps and stepped out of the shower, coming face to face with her reflection in a foggy mirror.

Do not look.

No good came from peering at the gaping holes in her back where her wings once were. The thought of seeing if crimson wings had grown made her stomach churn. She turned from the mirror, took a step and paused.

One little peek wouldn't hurt…

Peering over her shoulder, she looked at the mirror. Her shoulders sagged. Twin jagged, gray scars ran parallel down her shoulder blades. She willed open the slits in her flesh, unfurling her new wings. They didn't emerge. The skin refused to part. Her new wings still hadn't formed.

Her eyes stung. The scars hadn't healed either.

Perhaps her whole body hadn't healed. She sucked in a sharp breath. What if she wasn't in Hell long enough to transition? That meant she needed to mist back to Hell to regenerate her wings. *Gag.* If that was the case, no way. Returning to Hell required a level of strength she didn't have.

Heaviness weighed on her chest, making her turn from her reflection. She was a Fallen who was once a powerful Ariel. She refused to sob like a little mortal baby. Surviving a little longer in the mortal realm without her powers wasn't a big deal, she didn't need them straight away. Hopefully, her wings just took a little longer to heal.

At least she was out of the Heavens. She wasn't a powerless puppet dangling on a piece of string while Fate, the almighty puppeteer, controlled her next move. She was no longer the laughingstock of her faction for being the only Ariel in history who tied her powers to her soulmate. At the time, she didn't know he'd abandon her. She didn't know he'd drain her magic to refill the light in his soul after he tortured those Fallen.

Tying her Ariel powers to him gave their souls a continuous stream of light. They'd never be susceptible to Falling. She'd never lose him.

Huh. Another failure. Stupid, stupid move.

Folding the wet towel neatly over a rack, she dressed, slipped on the pair of heels, and headed out of her room with her chin held high.

****

Willow wandered along the corridors on each floor, opening several doors to find rooms decorated with rich timber furnishings that oozed old money and generations of wealth. Thick dust layered the surfaces in the kitchen and meal area as though unused since the turn of the century. Perhaps Blaine used this place as a recovery location, and the inhabitants didn't require formal meals? That thought brought her back to the question of how long she could survive without sustenance.

At the end of a long corridor, she stopped in front of a set of double doors with brass handles. On the other side, Blaine's deep throaty voice spoke with another male voice she didn't recognize. She rapped her knuckles on the door.

"Come on in, love," Blaine replied.

She stepped inside to find Blaine perched on the edge of a large mahogany desk, at the rear of the room, facing two leather chairs. The other male sat in one, peering over his shoulder at her. His dark chocolate eyes rimmed with crimson told her he was a Fallen.

With a lift of her chin, she straightened and entered the room, crossing to the empty chair. Instead of sitting, she stood tall behind the backrest, while she glanced at the stranger. He had smooth dark brown skin, a bald head with a trimmed goatee around his mouth and chin. Thick metal bands wound around his forearms and cords of strength bulged from his biceps, on display courtesy of the cut-off sleeves. She appreciated well defined biceps, but that much muscle was way over the top. She preferred a naturally strong physique proportioned equally over the entire body, exactly the way…*Do not think of him.*

The Fallen smirked. "So…this is Aric's girl?"

The chair creaked under her grip. "No," she snapped. "I most definitely am not Aric's girl." *Anymore.*

The Fallen raised an eyebrow challenging her.

Blaine snickered and slid off the desk to stand. "This is Willow. Willow, this is Slater, my second in command, who may or may not have his head by the end of the day."

Jeez. Out of her room for less than an hour and she had already made an enemy, one who easily baited her. *Way to go, Willow.*

"I see you two will get along just nicely," Blaine chuckled. *Yeah, right.* "All healed up now I presume?"

Her stomach dropped. Should she tell Blaine her wings hadn't healed? Should they have healed by now? Her gaze shot to Slater as he stared at her. Nope, she'd keep that information to herself for the time being. At least until she didn't have to announce her latest failure in front of an audience.

"Yes, I'm fine." Her stomach churned as she spoke the words…another lie.

Blaine smiled, but it didn't reach his eyes, like he knew she didn't tell the truth.

"Excellent. Did you find everything you need? I trust the garments were to your liking?"

She recoiled. "Really?"

Blaine left her fending for herself at the gates of Hell, which led to Zath capturing her and slicing off her wings. How dare he stand there asking if she liked the clothes? Her hands curled into fists. Just because he rescued her, didn't mean she wasn't pissed at him.

She moved around the chair. "You want to know if I like the clothes?"

Blaine narrowed his pitch-black eyes and turned to address Slater. "Why don't you hurry along? Let me know when it's all set."

Even with her death-stare fixed firmly on Blaine, she didn't miss Slater stand. Thank goodness he sat that whole time because she couldn't support her current level of confidence with him towering over her.

"I'll be in touch," Slater said before he left the room.

When the door shut behind Slater, Blaine turned his attention back to her. "I thought we might celebrate tonight."

Bubbling anger rose in her belly. "Are you for real?"

Blaine tilted his head to the side. "Why not?"

Seriously? Could Blaine be that heartless? He acted as though he was oblivious to her anger, like he couldn't care less that she had her wings hacked off and required rescuing from Zath's torture pit. "What could we possibly celebrate?" Her voice rose with each word. "The fact Zath captured me? That I severed my connection with the Heavens? Or perhaps the fact that psycho cut off my wings?"

Tiny flames ignited in Blaine's onyx eyes, reminding her of the fire surrounding the gates of Hell. Triggering the memory of the rim around Zath's pupils. Despite Blaine's relaxed body language, she felt the power rolling off him in waves. The same power he promised her when she Fell.

Exhaustion slammed into her body. She rounded the chair and collapsed on the seat, her limbs achy, shoulders heavy, feet feeling as though they'd walked a thousand miles even though she'd barely strolled around the house. Her recovery would take longer than expected. Without power, she couldn't speed up her healing. After severing her connection to the Heavens, she couldn't use the sun's healing power either.

Blaine pulled a chair closer and sat facing her, his expression a little less frightening. More of the old Blaine seeped through his dark eyes.

Relaxing in the chair, he crossed his ankle at the knee. "We're celebrating the new you, love." He circled her body in the air with his finger.

She exhaled a long, heavy breath, releasing a good chunk of anger along with it. Maybe Blaine felt bad for ditching her at the gates and this was his way of making it up to her. Though she wasn't in the mood for celebrating. "It's too early to celebrate the new me. I've only just gotten out of bed."

"Every achievement deserves a little hurrah, regardless of how small. Plus, I have a surprise for you."

She groaned. "I'm not really a fan of surprises." Since Aric gave her the biggest surprise in history.

His lips curled in a mischievous grin. "Oh, I think you'll enjoy this one. It'll help with your recovery."

She took his word on that, given she knew nothing about how to speed up her recovery. Regenerating her wings needed to come first. Without them, she had no chance of regaining her powers. If the surprise Blaine had planned helped with her transition, then she'd take the chance.

****

After leaving the house, Blaine took her into town to shop, free of charge, courtesy of a compelled shop assistant. At first, compelling a mortal felt wrong, causing a churn in the pit of her stomach. Relieving a mortal's trauma was the only time she considered using compulsion, not personal gain, like many Fallen did.

They followed a different set of rules, if they followed rules at all. That mentality took time to sink in.

To get the ordeal over sooner rather than later, she threw on a dress, tied her crazy hair in a messy bun and exited the store. At least on the outside, she looked like she had herself together.

Back in the car, her mood lifted a little. She no longer felt the urge to tear Blaine to shreds, but that didn't mean she had forgiven him.

The car slowed to a stop and she peered through the tinted window. "Why are we stopping here?" she said to Blaine, sitting beside her in the back.

"I have to take care of a little business, love," he replied, exiting the car.

She waited a moment staring at the open door while thumping music filled the street.

Blaine poked his head back in. "C'mon, chop-chop."

"Please tell me this isn't another one of those mortal nightclubs," she groaned.

"Consider it a pre-entertainment drink."

She knew Blaine well enough to know she fought a losing battle by arguing with him. Plus, hiding in the car got her nowhere and wasted a good outfit.

Sliding across the seat, she exited the car. The moment she hopped out, Blaine shut the door and slapped his palm twice on the roof for the driver to leave, driving away with her getaway car. Learning to drive became a necessity until her wings regenerated.

She looked Blaine up and down. He wore his usual black faded jeans and worn leather jacket. "If we're having pre-entertainment drinks, you could've made an effort to dress nicely."

Blaine recoiled as though she'd slapped him across the face. "What do you mean, love? I made an effort. I even wore my favorite jacket."

Without waiting for a reply, he sauntered across the road toward the thumping music. She waited a moment. If she made it to the other side of the street, she could sit at a table and rest her achy feet. Her body felt fatigued from the transition and the thought of a cool, bubbly drink and a little mortal-watching sounded like a good idea.

She took a step to follow Blaine but froze when she caught sight of the illuminated sign hanging above the entrance to the club. SubZero. They weren't at any mortal nightclub. She'd been here before. Only last time, she severed the final thread of connection to the Heavens, while staring into the eyes of the Guardian who'd destroyed her.

Chapter Nine

Aric's phone chimed with an incoming text and he snatched it from his jeans pocket, groaning as he read it.

EJ: *Dummy's on the move.*

Aric needed to head into town earlier than he thought. That Chosen never left the club before midnight. He thought he had at least another hour.

Aric: *On my way.*

He grabbed the two newly forged short daggers off the workbench in the armory. "Thanks, Raine. They're exactly what I'm after."

"You say that like you're surprised," Raine responded without turning to face him, her attention focused on the cooling chamber in front of her.

He bounced a dagger in his palm, testing the weight. "Nope, not anymore."

Sure, it surprised him in the beginning. Not only could Raine forge weapons, but she created ones at the exact weight and size ratio he wanted. Their little game of good versus evil had tipped in the Guardians' favor ever since Raine arrived.

Raine returned to the workbench and filed a dagger. "I wonder what Fate would do if you accidently missed a Fallen and took out that Chosen of yours instead? The way he harasses mortal woman, like it's a sick game, pisses me off."

Aric stilled. He'd thought about that exact

scenario—too many times to count—but it sounded fucked up coming from another Guardian. It made the whole idea seem foolish. Raine despised his Chosen more than he did, which was saying something.

"I agree he's a piece of shit, but if I fail, Raven will have my wings before Fate even knew what happened." He nodded at Raine and exited the armory, sliding the daggers into their new homes strapped to his chest.

Once outside the mansion, he unfurled his black wings and took to the sky, off to protect his stupid-ass Chosen. Halfway into town, prickles danced along his nape, originating from his Guardian connection with Leon. A warning alerted him the Chosen was in danger. Flapping his wings harder, he increased altitude and speed.

What's going on? he mentally said to EJ.

When EJ didn't reply, Aric tucked his wings in a tight V and descended rapidly. The clouds hung low, giving him the cover to soar closer to the ground than usual. The sensation across the back of his neck intensified, like someone increasing the pressure of a sharp blade on his flesh. The lights of Summit Creek appeared in the distance.

Ric! He's got Leon. EJ's voice roared in his head.

Who? Aric replied.

Blaine. River and I are chasing a Fallen.

Adrenaline shot through Aric's veins, pumping blood faster through his body. He wasted no time. If Blaine had Leon, that meant he also had the upper hand in gaining information on Willow. He'd mulled over Blaine's deal for six whole days and still couldn't decide. He wasn't ready to accept the deal, but he wasn't ready to decline it either.

If Blaine took the Chosen's soul, he lost his bargaining chip. Fate would have his head and once again punish him for failing a Chosen. But this time, more was at stake. His priority remained with Willow and her safety, which meant he needed to save the scumbag. For now.

I'll find Leon, he mentally said to EJ.

He hovered in the sky, closing his eyes, concentrating on the spiritual tether connecting him with Leon. The beacon instantly lit, firing in the distance like a bright orange flare shot into the dark sky. He dove toward the light.

The rear parking lot of SubZero came into view and he touched down, hoping like hell he landed in a safe location away from prying eyes. Mortals freaking out about a guy with wings would only add to the list of shit he had to deal with tonight. Standing there for a second, he scanned the parking lot searching for Leon. The connection led him here, but he didn't see the Chosen.

A Fallen materialized at the opposite end of the lot, one he instantly recognized. Slater.

Aric glared at the dark angel, once an Azrael until Blaine recruited him. Like so many others Aric had fought beside.

Slater stood in the light of a nearby streetlamp, wearing an ancient-looking sleeveless robe over the top of leather pants. More than a century had passed since he saw the Fallen, and clearly Slater hadn't updated his wardrobe.

"What?" Aric spat. "Blaine summoned you from Hell so he didn't get his hands dirty?"

Slater shrugged. "He's a little preoccupied at the

moment."

"I heard that." He inched toward Slater, assessing his tactical options. His weapon of choice, the speed of the breeze blowing across the parking lot, the angle of trajectory for his dagger. Halfway to Slater, he lowered his voice to a menacing growl. "Where's my Chosen?"

"Maybe you should keep a closer eye on him. Isn't that your job?"

Aric slid a dagger out of his jacket, gripping it in his hand as he continued inching closer.

Lightning fast, Slater whipped out a handgun and aimed it at Aric. "I'm not really in the mood for a knife fight."

Aric snorted. "I don't give a shit what you're in the mood for. A mortal bullet won't stop me from kicking your ass." Another step.

Slater tilted his head slightly to one side. "What makes you think these are mortal bullets?"

Aric froze mid-step. A tiny seed of doubt scratched the surface. Without a link to the Heavens, Blaine couldn't syphon water from the Eternal Fountain to create Purah bullets. Unless…Blaine had someone on the inside.

Was he willing to call Slater's bluff?

Under the right circumstances, Purah bullets killed any immortal, including him. The concentration of light in Purah was too powerful for any soul outside the Heavens. With his faith high, it wouldn't kill him instantly, but it would sure as hell injure him, leaving him vulnerable to decapitation. Now that did a helluva lot more damage than a mortal bullet.

He had to be smart. No doubt Blaine captured his Chosen to bait him, force him to decide, but if Aric screwed this up, his Chosen was toast. A mistake he didn't want repeated. He had one chance to throw his dagger at Slater's chest.

He raised his palms in fake surrender while assessing the direction and intensity of the breeze, rapidly calculating the right trajectory to hit Slater in the center of his heart. No room for sentimental shit for his former ally. Slater was a Fallen and long ago, Aric vowed to destroy every one of them.

Slater smirked, his handgun still aimed at Aric. "You surrender so easily. All for an insignificant mortal soul."

The breeze softened and Aric adjusted the angle of his dagger to compensate. "Some of us abide by a code of honor."

"What a boring existence you lead. No wonder she left."

Aric drew back, lowering his arms and his voice. "What did you say?"

Slater lifted his chin. "You heard me."

Aric flipped the dagger to grip the thin blade between his thumb and forefinger. Narrowing his eyes, he stepped closer to Slater. "Who left?" he growled.

Slater's eyes widened. "You haven't heard?"

Aric tightened his grip. The time for talking was over, he needed to find his fucking Chosen. *Three...two—*

The air to the right of Slater shimmered and rippled, diverting Aric's attention. A moment later, Blaine materialized, his arm curled around Leon's neck. That damn Chosen stared blankly into the night as though he were in a trance.

Aric relaxed his arm, racing to think of Plan B. He

couldn't risk wounding his Chosen. The last time he did that, Fate dished out a mission disguised as the biggest fucking consequence he'd ever received.

"You've had long enough, friend." Blaine's light tone sounded so out of place in the middle of the stand-off. "What's your decision?"

Fuck. He wasn't ready to answer. The choice had eaten away at him since he saw Blaine at the bar, torn between knowing Willow was safe and his oath as a Guardian. For his heart, the decision was a no-brainer, but sacrificing his Chosen? His head just couldn't agree. His loyalty lay with the Guardians, his brothers, and he wouldn't risk further punishment from Fate.

Stage left... The words whispered in his mind a second before EJ landed in the left-hand corner of the parking lot, a 0.40 caliber Glock aimed at Slater. At least now, the numbers balanced.

Blaine peered at EJ. "There's no need to get all hostile. I simply came for Aric's decision." He shoved Leon forward a step, snagging Aric's attention. "I completed my end of the bargain, obtained the answer you so desperately craved. Now...will you sacrifice your Chosen's soul to know if your precious Willow is safe?"

Blaine knew? Shit, what the hell should he do? Not knowing whether Blaine would double cross him was a major factor in refusing the deal. But if Blaine knew...the desperation to know Willow was safe doubled.

"Tell me," he snapped, lowering the dagger to his side.

Blaine *tsked* and shook his head. "No can do, friend. Payment before information."

Don't do it, Ric. We'll find Willow. Raven's right, this isn't the way, EJ mentally shouted at him.

Aric focused his attention on the blade clenched between his fingers. Once again, he assessed moves to control the situation. If he took out Slater, that left Blaine to mist away with the Chosen. Given neither he nor EJ could mist, they couldn't follow. Killing Blaine wasn't an option—saving Blaine was the whole damn reason Fate exiled their asses. Fate would unleash all her fury if either of them took out Blaine, then he and his brothers would be stuck in the mortal realm for the rest of eternity. No thanks.

Only one option kept his Chosen safe. It'd get him in the shit again with Fate, but the move was better than Blaine stealing Leon's soul. Slightly better. He was screwed either way.

In one swift movement, he raised his arm and threw the dagger. "Sorry, man," he muttered under his breath.

The dagger sliced through the air with the precision of a bullet and the grace of a perfectly folded paper airplane. Straight toward his Chosen.

He wouldn't relinquish his oath as a Guardian. At least this way, the scumbag's soul ended up in the Heavens—not that he was worthy. A second before impact, crimson flames roared to life in front of Blaine, engulfing his Chosen.

"No!" Aric roared, leaping forward.

The dagger disintegrated in the heat. The connection between him and Leon severed like a rubber band stretched so far it snapped. As quickly as it appeared, the fire vanished.

Blaine stood with a small pile of ash at his feet and

a smug fucking grin on his face. "I'd say that was a no-deal, wouldn't you?"

Through clenched teeth, Aric growled, "I'll fucking kill you."

"Then you'll be locked out of the cloudy paradise for your entire existence. How can you save me if I'm dead?" Blaine chuckled.

"I'm pretty sure my deal with Fate is void if you're dead." Aric curled his hands.

"Ric. Look at me." EJ stepped into his vision, pushing hard against his chest. "We'll figure this out. Let it go."

Red specks appeared before his eyes. He couldn't let go. Blaine pushed him too fucking far this time. His one chance to remove Blaine's leverage failed. Now his Chosen's soul was in Hell and he didn't know where the fuck his soulmate was.

Something inside him snapped. He shoved EJ, who fell on his ass. He bolted toward Blaine, fist extended, prepared for contact—

"Stop!"

He skidded to a halt at the familiar voice. The world around him froze. Time stood still.

He pivoted. A female stood at the end of the alleyway, concealed in shadows between the buildings. He couldn't make out her features but there was no need. Her fiery red hair illuminated in the darkness like those damn flames.

She stepped into the light of a streetlamp and his heart clenched. His gaze locked with hers.

"Stop it, both of you," she screeched.

Memories flooded his mind, ones he'd locked away deep inside, memories too painful. His gaze roamed over her features. The memories hadn't done her justice. They'd diluted the brightness of her hazel eyes, the curls of her long, red hair, the glow of her beautiful skin. The giant, gaping hole widened inside his chest. She was more beautiful than he remembered.

"Willow," he whispered.

He moved to step forward, but his feet refused. His heart thudded against his ribs. Where did the oxygen go? *How is she here?*

Willow glared at him, narrowing her eyes. "Yet again, Aric, you chose your duty over me."

Bile rose in his throat at her seething words. Fuck.

Chapter Ten

Willow suppressed the sob rising in her chest. Centuries ago, Aric chose his oath to Fate over his vow to her. He just repeated it.

At the far end of the parking lot, Blaine slapped his palms together in a slow clap. "Ta-Dah!"

Her stomach knotted. Great. Blaine set up this whole situation like some sick joke. Her earlier rage returned. "Oh, shut it, Blaine. Was this your big surprise? Because it's pretty low even for you."

"On the contrary, love. You were meant to be inside enjoying a drink."

She threw her hands in the air. "I should've known you'd pull a stunt like this."

"Wait a minute." Aric's wild eyes widened. He pointed at Blaine "You're here with him?"

God, she didn't have the emotional capacity to deal with Aric tonight or any other night. She should be on the other side of the planet, enjoying her freedom and the return of her powers. Instead, she stood in a dingy parking lot, facing a soulmate she couldn't relinquish. She just wanted to return to Blaine's house and fall into a deep sleep rivaling a princess. Transitioning to a Fallen played havoc with her energy level.

"Don't speak to me, Aric. I've stood here long enough. I heard everything. I guess some things never change."

A muscle popped in the side of his jaw, and she knew that meant he barely had control of his anger. *Join the club*.

"Tell me you're not with Blaine," he growled in a deep possessive voice causing goosebumps to sprout over her arms.

She straightened her shoulders. She wasn't with Blaine, but he had no right to question her. He no longer had any claim to her. "That's none of your business," she snapped. "You gave up on us when you abandoned me in the Heavens."

The words were way below the belt, but he deserved it. She refused to stand there feeling ashamed or embarrassed for severing her connection with the Heavens. That place was full of nothing but painful memories of his choice to throw away their future. In fact, she placed this whole situation firmly on his shoulders. Based on his actions a moment ago, she doubted he regretted anything. He hadn't changed one bit.

Still locked in a stare with Aric, she addressed Blaine, "Call your driver, Blaine. I'm ready to go home."

"We could just fly, love? It's such a lovely night."

Damn it. How the heck could she hide the fact she didn't have wings? No way would she reveal that little mishap, especially in front of Aric. Plus, earlier she lied and told Blaine she'd healed. If lying became a habit, she needed to keep track of them.

She motioned to her dress. "Fly in this? You can't be serious?"

Blaine pursed his lips. "Of course. That may be a tad awkward. I'm not used to having a female Fallen around."

A shudder ran through her body at Blaine's words. Fallen. The first time anyone had called her that. She wasn't ready to hear it, let alone publicly announce it in front of her ex-soulmate and his fellow Guardian.

Blaine strutted toward her. The second he was within range, Aric's arm shot out and clenched Blaine by the front of his leather jacket. "Touch her and I'll fucking kill you." Aric's voice raised the hairs on the back of her neck.

EJ inched closer. So did Slater.

"I'd like to see you try." Blaine shrugged off Aric's fist as though it were an annoying fly and continued walking. When he reached her, he offered the crook of his arm. "Let's go home, love."

She took one final glance at Aric. His whiskey eyes changed to pitch-black, confirming his level of rage. He stepped toward her.

She inhaled a long, drawn out breath before turning away. She wouldn't let Aric lure her in, even if the sight of him after so long still made her belly stir. No, he only caused her pain and would send her plan rocketing in the wrong direction. In a twisted way, Blaine was right. This interaction aided her recovery. She looped her arm through Blaine's.

"Lo-Lo…don't do this," Aric said, his voice laced with hurt.

Her step faulted. Her heart twisted. Damn Aric and the pet name he always whispered in her ear as they made love.

No, Willow. Focus.

She'd come this far. Her only choice remained moving forward, forcing one foot in front of the other.

"Don't ever call me that again," she said with a sneer. Without bothering to turn her head, she walked away.

****

Aric collapsed to his knees, the loose gravel digging into the fabric of his jeans. EJ's firm hand gripped his shoulder, holding him in place. Not that he'd move anyway. One minute his feet felt cemented to the ground refusing to walk, the next minute they were unable to hold his weight.

EJ's voice grumbled into a phone held against his ear, but Aric couldn't comprehend the conversation through the buzzing in his head. What the hell just happened? Did he see Willow in the mortal realm? Had she left with Blaine?

Sharp pain stabbed the inside of his skull from the questions, the pressure became so intense that any second now, his brain would explode all over the fucking parking lot.

Willow was…a Fallen. God, the realization made his stomach churn. How did he fight those bastards when his soulmate was one of them? How the hell had she become a Fallen in the first place?

EJ's palm squeezed his shoulder. "Rave wants us back at HQ, now. You all right to fly or you want River to bring a car?"

Was he all right to fly? What a stupid fucking question. He didn't even know if he could exist after that bombshell.

*Now I know how…*God. He couldn't even finish that sentence.

Aric pinned EJ with a glare. "Why didn't Fate send you a vision of her? Why didn't she stop Willow?"

EJ's lips thinned. "Dunno, Ric. I've never had a vision involving a Fal—ah…you know, one of them."

On Aric's right, the air rippled with power a second before Cole materialized, dressed in a black robe and black knee-high lace-up boots. Standard dress for an Azrael about to collect a soul. Only this time, there weren't any souls to collect.

Cole tucked his silvery-gray wings behind his back, taking long heavy strides in Aric's direction. "Do you mind telling me what's going on, Aric? Where the hell is your Chosen?"

Aric turned away. He'd wallow in that failure for a little while longer before admitting it aloud.

EJ cleared his throat. "Ah, Hell is kinda accurate."

"How in this world did you fail another Chosen? This was the easiest assignment ever, he only ventured to a handful of places and half the time he was drunk."

In a micro-second, Aric stood, getting right in Cole's face. He shoved Cole hard in the chest. "Maybe someone should explain how Willow severed her connection with the Heavens. And no one thought to fucking tell me," he roared.

Cole drew back. Arms up in surrender. His gray eyes narrowed. "Hang on. Did you just say Willow…Fell?"

Aric pulled at his hair until it almost tore from his scalp. "How did no one know?"

Cole's face tightened. "Did she…Aric, did Willow take your Chosen's soul?"

Aric's throat tightened, preventing speech. What if it had been her? What the hell would he have done? He turned away, unable to face Cole as the realization sank deep in his gut. Willow didn't take his Chosen's soul this time, but would she in the future? Could he stop her if it meant killing her?

EJ saved him answering. "Nope. That was all Blaine."

Cole shook his head. "Fate will lose her shit, brother."

Aric stared at the scattering of ash on the gravel that was once his Chosen. "Tell me something I don't know."

EJ steered Cole toward the other side of the parking lot. Pity it wasn't out of earshot.

"Listen, Reaper, this is the second Chosen assignment since Fate exiled us here. What are the odds she'll forgive this one-time screw up? Well…second time in Ric's case."

Why did everyone keep bringing up the last time he failed a Chosen? He didn't need the reminder. In some screwed up way, that failure led to joining Raven and EJ on their stupid-ass quest to save Blaine. A mission Fate manipulated to get what she wanted. A mission he wrongly assumed would be done and dusted the same day, not resulting in him banished to the mortal realm for centuries with no hope of returning to Willow. Failing a Chosen nearly four hundred years ago became the catalyst for the biggest mistake of his entire existence.

"I can't say," Cole murmured. "Fate hardly ventures from her sanctuary anymore. Not since Blaine's little stunt. Who knows what she's plotting amongst her cherry blossoms?"

EJ exhaled a heavy breath. "Maybe we should hunker down in one of those mortal doomsday shelters."

"Even that wouldn't keep her out, brother," he scoffed. "In all seriousness, Willow's here, in the mortal realm?"

Cole lowered his voice, but Aric still fucking heard it.

"She's a Fallen?"

"Afraid so, and I didn't see it coming. Which leads me to believe, neither did Fate."

Aric kicked the ash with his boot sending it fluttering into the wind. "There's no point standing here talking about it. I have to figure out what the hell's going on and I can't do that while staring at a pile of ash that was once my fucking Chosen." He turned to EJ and Cole.

EJ nodded. "Righty-o, Ric. Let's hit the sky."

Cole expanded his wings. "I'll go back and see if I can find out anything. I'll drop by later." The air rippled a second before Cole misted away.

Aric ripped off his jacket and held it in his hand as he unfurled his wings. He snuck a glance underneath his arm to check if the feathers had turned crimson—he wouldn't be surprised given this epic failure. When he spotted only black, his shoulders sagged, and relief burst inside his chest. At least he remained on the right side of the war.

Which wasn't the case for his soulmate.

Chapter Eleven

Willow threw open the door to Blaine's mansion. "How could you do that to me?" she yelled, stomping inside with Blaine following behind.

Holding in her rage during the car ride out of respect for the driver was nearly impossible, but now that she and Blaine were alone, civility went out the window. She spun on her heels, hoping the ferocity in her glare communicated the full force of her anger. Blaine deserved every ounce.

Blaine kicked the door shut with his foot. "Willow, love, you need to control the rage. I know it's all new, but you can't let it overcome you."

"Don't tell me what to do," she snapped.

Flames lit in his pupils before disappearing a second later, reminding her of Blaine's boundless powers. "The first few days are hard. A bit of an adjustment, that's all."

She ripped out her hairband. "Why would you do that? Why would you have me face him?"

Leaving her alone at the gates of Hell or forcing her to see Aric? She didn't know which one caused more anger. One left her without wings, the other smashed her heart into a thousand pieces all over again. The emotional scars of both were equally as painful.

Blaine curved an arm around her shoulders and steered her to the sitting room. She shrugged off his touch and crossed to the burgundy leather sofa on her own, collapsing in the seat. She'd never experienced exhaustion in the Heavens. Since arriving here, every cell ached with weariness that consumed her entire body, her shoulders so heavy she struggled to hold them back.

Accepting a glass from Blaine, she took a sip of the golden liquid. The alcohol stole her breath, and she exploded in a coughing fit. Blaine sat on the edge of the couch across from her, smirking.

"You could've warned me about Aric."

Would she have listened? Blaine cautioned her about Zath, and she took the chance anyway. But Aric…she could've prepared herself.

Blaine remained silent the whole time she sat, and each second made her feel worse. God, when did she become such a bitch? What the heck was wrong with her? One minute bubbling rage threatened to explode and the next, she felt utterly worn out.

Gripping the glass tighter, she leveled her voice. "Why weren't you at the gates?"

The question gnawed at her, and she couldn't move on until he answered. His response determined where her loyalty fell and decided her next move. Once she got off the couch.

She'd avoided the topic for far too long. Just because Blaine rescued her from that hellhole didn't excuse the fact he abandoned her there. She should've asked him earlier, back in the study, but at the time she dreaded his answer. Plus, Slater was there and revealing that epic mess gave him ammunition to use against her.

Blaine shuffled back on the couch and bent up a leg, resting a boot on his knee. "I was there, love.

Albeit rather hidden, but I was there. Then you up and misted before I could get to you."

"You mean before…" She swallowed. "Zath captured me."

"Well, yes, before that. I underestimated Zath's thirst for Ariel power, but I couldn't risk him seeing me."

The lid on her rage exploded. "What?" she yelled. "You're telling me, the reason you didn't help me was because you didn't want Zath to see you?"

Blaine lips thinned, the first time she saw a hint of seriousness in his expression. "He can't discover the powers I possess."

"Are you for real?" She slammed the glass on the table, spilling the contents. "Zath not knowing how powerful you are is worse than him…" The words strangled her throat. Her stomach churned at the mere thought of verbalizing how that monster had hacked off her wings.

Blaine remained silent.

Her heart sank. Why did she suddenly feel like a pawn in Blaine's hellish game of chess?

She pinched her forehead. "If you didn't want Zath to see you, then how did you save me?"

Blaine waved his hand in the air, dismissing her worries but her questions weren't going anywhere. "Oh, I just waited until one of his minions guarded you instead."

By then, it was too late to save her wings. By that time, she hadn't wanted saving.

A more sinister thought sprung in her mind. "Zath said he needed my Ariel powers to heal." She locked gazes with Blaine. "What if he finds me?"

"He's not healed enough yet to rise from Hell. Plus, you're of no use to him now that you're a Fallen."

Her stomach flipped. Sooner or later, her lies would catch up to her. Blaine thought she'd healed, which was the biggest, fattest lie of all. She was far from healed, physically and emotionally. Did that mean light remained in her soul? Did that mean she was still on Zath's capture list? She needed those answers stat, without Blaine knowing why she sought the information.

She cleared her throat. "Zath said Fate made Aric…cut off Zath's wings."

Blaine stood, crossing to a side table to pour another drink. "It's not something that's widely known."

She slapped a palm over her mouth. Zath told the truth. There was no reason for him to lie. She saw his wings regenerating from some form of mutilation but how could Aric be responsible? How could he have done something so barbaric?

Blaine returned and sat on the couch. "It happened when Fate created Hell and imprisoned Zath there. She had to ensure Zath couldn't escape."

Blaine supported Fate's point of view. Of course, he did. "There's never a justification to remove an angel's wings, no matter their crimes." Knowing Aric did exactly that left a bitter taste in her mouth.

"It became Aric's specialty. He gained quite the reputation for it. That Guardian of yours has a wicked side, easily flipped on when your safety is at stake." He sipped his drink. "I'm surprised the light in his soul remains so bright given his…activities."

She knew exactly how the light in Aric's soul

remained bright, because her Ariel powers fueled it. But that wasn't something Blaine needed to know, nor something she'd admit. What concerned her more was the fact Aric engaged in that kind of brutality and she had no idea. He was supposed to be her soulmate. Well…not anymore.

"He's not my Guardian, Blaine."

"Right, yes. You're a footloose and free Fallen now."

Was she? Free from her bond to Aric maybe, but she wasn't sure about the Fallen part. Until her wings returned, she wouldn't know.

Strained silence passed between them while she sipped the liquor, reveling in the heaviness it created in her shoulders and how the drink took the edge off her simmering rage. Perhaps that was why Blaine always had a glass in his hand.

"Listen, love." He leaned forward, forearms resting along his thighs. "I'm going to be straight with you."

About time. Kicking off her shoes, she curled her legs beside her on the couch. "Please do."

"I'm in need of a new evil buddy."

"Really?" She rolled her eyes. Guess the serious Blaine was done for the day.

"I'm kidding," he sniggered. "Kind of…actually no, I'm really not."

"Don't you have enough evil buddies? I just want to forget this ever happened and move on with my existence." *And figure out how the heck I get my wings back.*

"With me, love, you can." He relaxed back on the couch. "Let's just say, I need a few trusted allies and in exchange, you can have all the freedom you desire."

That sparked her interest. Freedom. "What's the catch?"

He winked at her. "All in good time. There's no need to rush. I've already delivered on my promise to give you Fallen power, haven't I?"

Her heart thudded. *Nope.* "Sure. But I would've preferred it didn't involve torture by Zath."

He shrugged one shoulder. "A little mishap. But you can put that behind you now. Your power will continue to develop more and more each day until one day you'll forget you were ever in Hell."

The front door swung open and a gust of wind howled inside, a handful of brown, crispy leaves tumbled down the hall. Slater strolled in, wearing the same black sleeveless robe and skin-tight leather pants that left nothing to the imagination. And she meant nothing.

Slater narrowed his eyes at her, but she refused to lower her gaze.

Blaine stood, still clutching his glass. "I need to take care of a little business, love. The bourbon is on the side table if you care for a refill."

At her nod, Blaine and Slater walked down the hall toward the study. Once out of sight, she massaged the arch of her foot. She'd only wore the heels for a couple of hours and already it felt like she'd scaled up a rocky mountain barefoot. Muscles she didn't know even existed were achy and tender.

Not bothering to finish the drink, she placed the glass aside. Given her lightened mood, the bourbon did its job. Stretching her legs along the couch, she leaned against the armrest and peered around the living area.

Someone had decorated the whole room using a

pallet of deep garnet red, dark mahogany and black, giving a medieval murderous vampire vibe. Perhaps a turn-of-the-century Fallen had the same taste.

Polished bronze candelabras sat atop the two tables. Heavy burgundy drapes hung open over three oversized paneled windows, and an extravagant crystal chandelier took pride of place in the center of the ceiling. The whole house dripped money in a way that stemmed from generations of wealth. Not her taste at all.

She preferred a minimalistic approach to living, one that drew her closer to nature. It strengthened the Ariel magic swirling inside her and soothed her mind and body.

Relaxing her head against the armrest, her mind drifted back to the small log cabin she and Aric had shared in the Heavens. Isolated deep within a forest, it lay nestled amongst tall ancient pine trees, with a narrow stream flowing along one side. On the porch, a two-seater chair swing hung from the rafters. Her chest ached at the memories of curling in Aric's arms, gazing at the wilderness.

She refused to return to the cabin after Aric abandoned her. Instead, she wandered the different realms of the Heavens like a pathetic lost soul. *Exactly what I am.*

Forcing the memory aside, she opened her eyes and swung her legs off the couch to sit up. Enough wallowing. She was once a powerful Ariel, one of the most powerful factions of angels. She wouldn't sit around feeling sorry for herself while pining over an ex-soulmate who threw away their bond.

She made it to the mortal realm and away from

Fate's influence. Once she figured out how to regenerate her wings, she'd have access to her Fallen magic. She'd no longer be labeled weak because her link to Aric drained her power. Finally, she'd take back control.

To do that, she needed information. Blaine said he wanted her help with his plan, and in exchange, he offered her freedom. It didn't matter what it involved. What mattered was he and Slater sat in the study right this second, most likely discussing Blaine's plan.

She wouldn't let them exclude her. If Blaine wanted her on his team, then she deserved the details. Maybe they provided clues she needed for her own plan.

After slipping her shoes back on, she stood. Straightening her shoulders, she embraced her best evil buddy persona and headed to the study.

Chapter Twelve

Aric stormed into the entertainment room, the air charged with tension and fury with each pound of his boots. The room was so quiet, one wrong look in his direction would strike a match and blow the fucking mansion apart. He hurled his leather jacket through the air, and it slapped the back of the couch before flopping to the floor.

No one said a word. Not even when he snatched the bottle of whiskey, screwed off the top and chugged straight from the bottle. EJ, a few steps behind, mirrored his actions, except with a bottle of vodka. Shit got real when EJ skipped adding squished limes and bits of herbs to his drink.

Sitting wasn't an option. With every heartbeat, he forced his legs to stay still, and not bolt out the door to find Willow. Raven had ordered them to meet here, so Aric would give him another two minutes to show before he hauled ass out that door. Leader or not, Raven wouldn't stop him from finding her.

Raine remained silent by the pool table, arms crossed in front of her chest. River sat on the edge of the couch, hands clasped, staring at his shoes. Aric chugged the whiskey to prevent ripping off River's fluorescent palm tree shirt and tearing it to shreds. Who wore a shirt so fucking bright and cheery while his whole world got sucked into a giant black hole?

The air thickened the moment Raven entered the room, arms rigid by his side, dark eyes locked with him. "What the fuck did I tell you?"

Aric held Raven's gaze. "I didn't have a choice."

"Like hell you didn't. There's always a choice," Raven growled. "You failed your fucking Chosen."

Aric recoiled. His Chosen? Why did everyone give a shit about a mortal scumbag who didn't belong in the Heavens? Was Aric the only one who saw that? At what point would they divert their efforts to finding Willow?

Aric had failed her. No chance in hell he'd do it again.

He met Raven's stormy gaze. "I don't give a shit about that Chosen. Fate can have my head for it. I'm dead inside anyway."

"Fuck, Aric." Raven massaged the back of his neck while his onyx eyes changed back to their usual deep blue. Aric's ass was safe for now.

EJ braved an up-close-and-personal and handed Raven a drink. Precious minutes ticked by while everyone waited out the silence, refusing to be the first one to speak.

Screw that. They'd wasted enough time already.

"I'm sorry, man." Aric's shoulders dropped as the gravity of the situation became clear. "I thought I was doing the right thing. Either I took out the Chosen and sent his soul to the Heavens or I handed it over to Blaine." He exhaled a heavy breath. "Guess in the end, it didn't matter."

A muscle in Raven's jaw popped. Maybe Aric wasn't off the hook yet. "Tell me you didn't accept Blaine's deal first."

"I didn't. But I can't say I wasn't tempted."

Raven's expression softened. "Good. At least Fate will see you made the right choice."

Aric clenched his fist. "The right choice? Like hell it was the right choice. If I'd accepted Blaine's deal last week, I could've saved Willow. The result for that Chosen would've been the same."

Raven stared him down, authority booming in his voice. "No, Aric. Allowing a Fallen to take your Chosen's soul is never the right choice. You of all Guardians should know that."

Aric gritted his teeth at the constant reminders. "You wouldn't say that if it was Tayla."

Mortals said never to poke a bear. He never truly understood that expression until now.

Fury rolled off Raven. His hand clenched so tight his knuckles turned white and hairline fractures appeared in the glass. "Don't you dare bring Tayla into this."

Aric stood taller. "It's true." *Poke, poke.* "Think of all the times you screwed up when Tayla was your Chosen. It turned out Fate set up the whole fucking thing. Maybe she's doing it again. What if Fate assigned me that Chosen just so Blaine could harvest the soul at the exact moment Willow walked around the corner?" The theory was a long shot, but it explained why Fate created such a pathetic Chosen.

Raven's head tilted, his brows furrowed. "Why the hell would Fate create a Chosen just so Blaine could take the soul? That's a sick twist even for her."

Now that Raven no longer appeared to want to rip him to shreds, Aric sank onto a barstool with a heavy exhale. "I dunno. Nothing Fate does surprises me anymore."

Raven stared at the brass chandelier hanging in the center of the room, evidently contemplating their next move.

Palm Tree cleared his throat. "How can we be sure Fate is involved?"

"When isn't she?" EJ scoffed from behind the bar.

Raven glanced at Aric. "I'll get in touch with Gabe, see if he knows something. Or at least if he can find out how much shit we're in."

Aric poured a shot of whiskey in a tumbler. No more drinking from the bottle. "No 'we,' this was all me. I take full responsibility and won't have my brothers punished for my screw up."

Raven didn't skip a beat. "No, Aric, we're in this together. We started this mission together, we'll finish it together. Regardless of what Fate throws our way."

Aric downed another shot to swallow the lump in his throat. He hadn't realized how much he longed to hear those exact words. Losing another Chosen sucked, but no way could he shoulder that failure plus Willow's bombshell and lose his brothers. No amount of faith could stop the darkness creeping in if all that happened.

Raine tapped her glossy red shoe on the floor as though impatient for the midnight meeting to end. "What's the plan?"

"I dunno know yet. I'll talk with Gabe first then figure out a way forward," Raven replied.

EJ ventured from behind the bar, holding a short glass stuffed to the rim with lime quarters and vodka. The world righted itself once more. "We could lock Red in the cell in the basement."

Red. The nickname EJ called Willow since the

moment they met. Regardless of the sentiment, no way would they lock Willow in a cell. "Don't be an ass, EJ."

EJ shrugged. "What? We considered doing it to Rave."

Good point. Last year, when a Fallen's talon poisoned Raven and he lacked enough faith to heal, the four of them had considered locking him in a cell forged with Purah until they figured out how to get him back to the Heavens. Returning him to the Heavens was the only way they knew to restore his faith. Thankfully, Tayla's bond did the job.

"How did Fate not see Willow's choices?" Palm Tree asked, full of questions tonight.

Aric swirled the glass in his hand. "That's what I'd like to know."

"I have a theory on that." All gazes snapped to EJ. "I don't think Fate can see or influence a Fallen's path. She's never sent me a vision with a Fallen. Sure, the visions on repeat show this realm engulfed in flames, but they never feature a Fallen." EJ picked a piece of lime from his drink and ate it. "Rave, remember when Fate banished us, you said she mentioned that Blaine had chosen his path and she couldn't bring him back?" Raven nodded. "I think she meant it and wasn't just being a bitch."

Shit. If Fate couldn't see a Fallen, then she couldn't influence Willow's path. "If that's the case, man, she can't help us save Willow. We're on our own with this one."

"Not exactly a foreign concept for us." Raven scrubbed a palm along his jaw. "It doesn't mean Fate isn't involved."

"I know, but what more can we do? At some point,

we have to do what feels right." Aric lowered his voice. "I have to save her."

The room grew quiet and everyone looked at Raven.

"Aric…" Raven cleared his throat. "Willow's a Fallen now. You might not be able to save her."

"Don't give me that bullshit, Raven. We've been in this realm for over three centuries, with the sole mission of saving a goddamn Fallen." Aric slammed his glass on the bar. "You don't need to tell me it's never been done, I know that. But if saving a Fallen is impossible, why the hell did Fate exile us here in the first place?"

Raine pushed off the pool table and stepped forward. "He's got a point."

"And man, it's Willow. I can't let this go."

Raven stared at him long and hard, and Aric could almost see the tennis match of decisions volleying inside Raven's head. "Okay. But under no circumstances will you go rogue and risk more backlash from Fate. If we do this, we do it together."

That was all the agreement Aric needed. "Copy that."

"Right. Now, let's take five to cool our heads so we can plan this right. We may only have one chance. Go get some food, take a shower, whatever the hell you need to do, then meet back in the study."

Raven slid his cracked glass onto the bar before striding out of the room.

****

Cooling Aric's head wasn't an option. Ever since he saw Willow in the shadowy parking lot of SubZero, his body had been lit up like a Christmas tree covered in millions of tiny fairy lights.

No remedy calmed his frantic need to find Willow and return her to his arms. But he'd play by the rules for a little while longer if it meant keeping his brothers on side.

Instead of having a tantrum and insisting they strategize ASAP, he retreated to his bedroom, and found himself under the steamy jets of the shower. Bad fucking idea number four hundred and seventy-two.

Being alone, his thoughts drifted back to Willow. Only now, instead of saving her ass, the thoughts centered more on her ass. The way that navy dress clung to her curves, pressing firmly against her rounded breasts, made him ache to touch her again. Familiar craving burned inside, a need to hear her soft moans when he grazed his chin down her neck, planting delicate kisses along her collarbone.

Desire flooded through his veins. The last thing he needed, and the timing couldn't be more shit. Abstinence wasn't an easy task, especially when his soulmate remained in a different realm, but he'd meant every word of the vow he gave Willow, regardless of how much time and space stood between them. No female, mortal or otherwise, compared to her. Ever.

Instead of giving in to the ache, he slid down the cold, smooth tiles, landing on the shower floor. Water pelted hard against his scalp, spraying in every direction like one of those pop-up sprinklers turning in the center of the lawn.

Leaning his head back against the tiles forced him to close his lids to avoid the water shooting directly in his eyeballs. Bad idea number four hundred and seventy-three. Closing his eyes allowed his first memory of Willow to spring free in his mind.

Aric paused beside a burned tree trunk, mesmerized by the Ariel's movements. The way her delicate fingers brushed the blackened trees, the scorched twigs and grazed over the ash-covered ground. How her magic swelled from her fingertips a moment before tiny shoots of new growth sprouted from the earth. The way she poured her soul into everything she touched, nurturing it back to life.

He'd heard of the Ariel's ability to regenerate nature but had never seen one perform the magic. Yet, the angel herself was what stole his breath. Such beauty and grace.

As though she sensed him, she turned to face him. Her white sleeveless dress unmarked by the ash surrounding her, her fiery red hair falling in thick waves over slender shoulders. Her bright hazel gaze locked with his. In that moment, he knew she was his soulmate, felt the spark of life between their souls as they weaved together.

"Guardian," she said, in a pure angelic voice that nearly brought him to his knees.

He inched closer. "Tell me your name, Ariel."

Tiny stars glittered in her eyes. "Willow."

"Willow," he repeated, as though it branded her name on his heart. "Your magic is beautiful."

"Regeneration is the key to life in this realm. What is destroyed must be reborn. Such as this tree." Her finger brushed the bark of a nearby tree. "A moral will cut down this tree to warm themselves or provide shelter. Some may say then its life is over, but it's transformed into something else entirely. Reborn as something different. That is where true magic lies."

He couldn't speak. Her breathtaking beauty and

the power illuminating at the tips of her fingers kept him spellbound. Never had one angel had such an impact.

New shoots grew taller out of the earth and one curled around her leg like a protective vine. "Lost for words, Guardian?" she teased.

He cleared his throat. "I, ah...I've never witnessed such beauty." In magic or angelic form, he added to himself.

"We each have our strengths."

Crouching, she retrieved a long slim twig and twined it between her fingers as magic the color of a sunset, swirled inside her palms. Her feet glided toward him, close enough that her thunderstorm scent made him dizzy. She peered at him through her long, brown lashes.

Where had all the air gone? And why wouldn't his brain fucking work?

Taking his hand, she gently placed something in his palm before closing it shut. He didn't look, since he was too busy memorizing her features—the tiny dimple on her left cheek, the handful of pale freckles scattered across the bridge of her nose, the stray fiery curl he longed to touch.

"Until we meet again, Guardian."

The surrounding air shimmered with a dusting of glittery orange before she misted away. For a long moment, he stared at the vines she brought to life until the object inside his palm warmed, drawing his attention. Opening his hand, he marveled at the woven band she had made, encased in the same warm, orange glow of her Ariel magic. Without thinking, he slipped it on his wrist. The glow faded, revealing the charcoal twigs weaved together. In that moment, a thread deep inside his soul tightened and locked into place.

Time carried on around him. Flora continued sprouting from the earth as though her appearance in this realm was as standard as the sun rising each morning. Her appearance was anything but standard for him. For the first time since his creation, his heart swelled and sparked to life. All because of her.

"Fuck," Aric groaned, gritting his teeth. His eyes snapped open, his mind crashing back to the present.

His clenched fist slammed the wall beside him, cracking a tile. Hot pain radiated up his wrist. At least it took the focus off the painful memory playing in the comfort of his fucked up head.

Reaching for the taps, he shut off the hot water and sat there like an idiot under icy jets while the crippling agony inside his chest eased a notch. His shoulders sagged and the happiness from the memory gurgled down the drain with the water. His beautiful Ariel wasn't there, instead he faced emptiness in the form of a wall covered with glossy black tiles.

God, he missed her. No, missed didn't capture the way his heart had ached for her for centuries, nor how his soul mourned her every fucking second of the day.

Existing without Willow felt like living half a life; one foot in the present, one in the past with eons of time and space in the middle. Each day, he woke with that stupid feeling of hope that, one day, he could have both feet together again.

Chapter Thirteen

Aric was the last to arrive in the war room, unusual for him. Silence smacked him in the face as he trudged in, telling him the others had waited for him before beginning.

Instead of sitting, he leaned his forearms on the back of a chair pushed in under the table. Everyone wore their standard fighting gear and no doubt strapped to the hilt with weapons. Thank God River had changed into a more appropriate black T-shirt.

Raven sat at the head of the long boardroom table, leaning forward in the chair. "Let's do this. The first task is finding where Blaine is holding Willow."

Aric clenched his jaw. "It didn't look like they held her against her will."

That skidded the conversation to a halt. Pushing away from the chair, he crossed to the side table and poured a drink. Sooner or later, the alcohol would numb the pain.

River remained silent, stuffing candy snakes in his mouth, while Raine, as usual, stood against the far wall. The world would fall off its axis if she ever sat at the table.

EJ fired up a laptop. "Have you sensed her lately, Ric?"

He thought about the night he dreamed of the wildfire. When imaginary flames singed his jacket and smoke choked his lungs, and the piercing screams of Willow sounded so real they haunted him each following day. The dream Blaine had said was of Hell.

Sudden chill struck his core, and the ground felt as though it collapsed beneath his feet. He didn't dream the wildfire. He sensed the exact moment Willow misted to Hell.

How? His soulmate connection with Willow disappeared when Fate exiled him to the mortal realm. Unless…He brushed his thumb over the band at his wrist. It wasn't possible. But the band was the only logical explanation. He knew Willow bound her powers to him with that band, but he assumed that severed also when he left.

Was their soulmate bond powerful enough to still link her to him? Was it powerful enough to pull him to the gates with her, without him knowing?

For once, Blaine could be fucking right. If that was true, maybe Aric had sensed Willow at SubZero. The sadness and resentment flowing through his veins had felt as real as those damn flames. That was probably the moment she severed her connection to the Heavens. And he'd carried on drinking as though nothing had happened.

Funny how things suddenly made sense.

Glass in hand, he traced a small crack in the floorboards with his boot. "Yeah," he croaked. "The other week at the club I sensed her there, but it seemed impossible, so I shrugged it off. I think it was the moment she…" He couldn't say it aloud.

After a pause, Raven spoke, "You couldn't've known, Aric."

Like hell he couldn't. He should've known. Willow

was his soulmate. He vowed to protect her for eternity.

Aric spun and faced the pity-party looks. "I sensed her Fall, and I fucking shrugged it off."

River swiveled the chair to face him. "Do you reckon you could track your connection to her?"

Aric dropped his head. "There's no connection. I didn't even sense her behind me in the parking lot. It must've severed after she entered the gates." Or had he not felt the connection with Willow because he was too consumed with fury at Blaine for bargaining with his Chosen's soul?

The corner of the room lit in a bright white light. "Here we go…" Raven mumbled.

The light faded as Gabe materialized in a navy blue, double-breasted check suit and a matching pocket square. That Archangel had one helluva sense of style. River should take note.

Gabe peered around the room. "Good evening, gentlemen." He nodded to Raine. "And to you, Raine."

Raine rolled her eyes. Pretty sure she'd rather include herself in the "gentlemen" statement than be singled out.

Gabe's gaze settled on Raven. "Where is your beautiful soulmate?"

Raven frowned. "Gabe, it's three in the morning. She's asleep."

EJ snorted. "You wear her out, Rave?"

A smirk lifted the corner of Raven's mouth, but he didn't take the bait. How could they make jokes when Willow's life was at stake?

Aric stiffened, tracking every twitch in Gabe's face. Every slight movement. Either Gabe came to help them, or he was about to rip Aric to shreds for failing to protect a Chosen. Either way, he wanted the answer now. He'd never been good at sitting around waiting.

"Give it to me straight, Gabe. How pissed is Fate?"

Gabe sighed heavily. "It's hard to say, my friend. Fate creates each Chosen using her magic, so when a Fallen harvests a Chosen's soul, it destroys part of Fate's soul. Even for an immortal as powerful as she, it will take some time for her to heal before she can use her powers again."

"Does that mean we've got a grace period before she nukes me?"

Gabe's lips thinned. "How much time exactly, I do not know."

River slapped his hand on the table. "Righty-o, let's not waste a second then."

Gabe slipped off his suit jacket and slung it over the back of an empty chair. "Bring me up to speed on your plan."

Raven cleared his throat. "Aric thinks he sensed Willow's Fall, but that also severed their connection. We don't know where Blaine is or where he might be holding…ah, accommodating Willow. As you know, Gabe, our link to Blaine isn't functioning either." Raven circled his finger around the rim of his glass. "We're kinda in the dark here. Since tracking Blaine through our Guardian connection isn't possible, we've relied on him finding us. Over the past few decades, we've gotten used to him showing up whenever he fucking pleases, before disappearing again. I presume he trots off to Hell whenever he gets bored. We've become a bit complacent where Blaine's concerned."

A muscle under Gabe's eye twitched, so slight the others would have missed it. Aric didn't. Gabe knew something more than he told them, and Aric needed to find out what.

Before he had the chance to ask, Gabe spoke. "I've tasked Cole with tracking Willow's soul. If Aric sensed Willow severing her connection to the Heavens, then the timing is on our side. When an angel becomes a Fallen, their soul remains in Hell until their transformation is complete. After which, they have enough power to mist to the mortal realm." Gabe glanced at him. "The fact only a week or so has passed since Willow Fell, means her transition is still new. That might be in our favor."

Tiny flares of hope sparked inside his chest. "Does that mean we'll have more chance of restoring her soul and returning her to the Heavens?" The question churned his stomach, but he had to know the answer. He had to know their odds.

"I cannot say, Aric. As you know, restoring a Fallen soul is a complicated and delicate process, one which we haven't yet achieved."

Power radiated in the room to Aric's right. He clenched his fist. "Fucking hell, now what?"

Cole materialized beside him, and Aric shot back his remaining whiskey. "Is this it now? Can we get on with it without any further drop-ins? 'Cause I'm sick of seeing you guys mist in and out whenever you bloody well please."

Cole glared at him. "Nice to see you too, brother." He bowed his head slightly at Gabe. "I tracked Willow's soul—"

Aric yanked Cole's arm. "Where?"

"If you let go of my arm, I'll tell you."

At any moment, his rage would explode. He

released his grip on Cole.

The Azrael stepped forward. "I tracked the trail left by Willow's soul."

"How? If she severed her connection?" Raine asked.

"Each angelic soul has a distinct signature, like a fingerprint. I can track that signature across any realm, provided it's not tampered with."

Aric slide his glass on the side table. "Tampered with? What the hell does that mean?"

Cole turned to him. "Since you left the Heavens, Willow's soul misted back and forth to the mortal realm as normal."

"Willow could mist here?" He assumed Fate had confined Willow to the Heavens. If she could mist, why the hell didn't she mist to him?

Cole winced, as though he heard Aric's last thought. "After you left, Fate restricted her movements, as she did for all Ariel. Willow could only mist back and forth from her assigned locations."

When Aric remained silent, Cole continued, "But what's strange is, for the past year, shortly after arriving at the locations, her soul faded in and out. Then when she returned to the Heavens, there was a murkiness to her signature."

"Meaning what exactly?" Was Aric the only one not following?

"Blaine," Raven grumbled. "I bet he met with Willow in the mortal realm."

Aric's body tensed, heat flashed through his veins. If Blaine met with Willow without Aric's knowledge, he'd make him pay. How dare he? Willow was Aric's soulmate for fuck's sake. If anyone met with her in the mortal realm, it should be him. But no, Fate made sure that didn't happen, and Willow had spent the entire time misting back and forth without his knowledge or protection.

Aric slid a dagger from its sheath and flipped it in his hand. "Where was the last place you tracked her soul before she Fell?"

"This is where it gets even weirder. I can still see the trace of her soul."

Aric stepped forward. "Still see? You know where she is?"

Cole nodded. "An old abandoned mansion on the outskirts of town. She must've left Hell before her transition completed because there's still a faint sliver of light remaining in her soul." He lowered his voice. "I can't explain why. But the rest of her soul is full of this black swarming cloud. It doesn't look good, brother."

Time wasn't on his side. He needed to save Willow before that light extinguished completely and blackness filled her soul. No one knew how quickly that would happen.

Did it really matter? Fallen or not, it wouldn't influence his mission to return her to the Heavens. He would save her regardless. He was the damn reason she Fell. He needed to figure out how.

"No way…" EJ swiveled the laptop so everyone saw the screen. "The old Alpine property."

"The bonfire," Raven muttered.

Last year, the Fallen staged a huge bonfire on the Alpine property, luring unsuspecting mortals to blacken their souls. Raven and Tayla had attended, and it became the date from hell. Literally. The Guardians suspected Blaine's involvement in the little stunt, but after a thorough search of the property and the grounds, they found no trace of him or any other Fallen.

Raine screwed up her face. "Why would she hide out in a decrepit old mansion?"

Aric sheathed the dagger. "It doesn't matter why. I'll go check it out."

Raven stood and narrowed his gaze at Aric. "No. You're staying here."

Aric's whole body went rigid. "You can't expect me to sit here and wait. C'mon, man. You know I won't do that."

Raven stared at him for a long moment, his jaw tight. "Fine. But you're taking River and EJ with you."

"Copy that." He could ditch River easy enough, and he'd figure out how to lose EJ.

He wore a track up and down the room as they sorted out the game plan. Raine disappeared for a few minutes and returned with magazines of Purah bullets.

"This is purely a recon mission, do you understand?" Raven stared hard at Aric. "We don't know how many Fallen are there with her. Do not do anything reckless."

Yeah, right. If Willow was there, he wasn't gonna fly home. He'd storm that mansion with guns blazing. "What if she's there and I can save her?"

Raven's expression softened. "At this stage, we don't know if she wants to be saved."

His chest tightened, squeezing the air from his lungs. He hadn't thought of that. Willow didn't look held against her will, nor did she look like she needed him to save her. Come to think of it, with her flashy dress and hair all done, Willow looked like she enjoyed herself.

His stomach plummeted to his boots. What the hell would he do if she wanted this path?

Chapter Fourteen

Willow stared into the empty abyss called a refrigerator. It resembled the stark, empty shelves of a grocery store where mortals rushed to prepare for a hurricane. Only one plastic container sat on the shelf. No staples such as milk, cheese or fresh vegetables. The fridge was as bare as the cupboards she rummaged through earlier.

It took less time than expected for her stomach to rumble for food, but whatever nutrients she found did nothing to dull the tiredness plaguing her. The lack of edible food in the house meant her exhaustion steadily increased until the thought of eating felt like a chore.

She grabbed the lone plastic container, seeking something other than fruit to eat. Lifting the lid, she gagged at the contents. The sight of rotting flesh in Hell looked more appetizing. Giving up, she returned the festering food to the shelf and shut the refrigerator door. The mansion needed major improvements if she remained here for much longer. At least, so she could eat.

She sagged on a stool at the kitchen bench, snatching a bright red apple from the handful she picked during the day. The only food her stomach approved. Blaine didn't even know he had fruit trees growing on the property. Thank goodness she found them, otherwise, compelling a mortal for food became her only option. Unless she wanted to starve.

She bit into the delicious apple and sprays of juice dotted the countertop, soaking through the thick layer of dust. Blaine strolled into the kitchen from the far door and headed straight to the refrigerator, grabbed the container of festering food and a fork off the counter, and took a mouthful. *Gag.*

"Shouldn't you at least reheat that?"

Blaine frowned. "Don't fret, love. It can't kill me."

She shuddered as he swallowed another mouthful. What a way to ruin her appetite. Taking a tissue from her dress pocket, she spread it on the counter and wrapped up her half-eaten apple. Her Ariel magic may be gone, but she'd continue to give nature the respect it deserved. She wouldn't waste the fruit. It grew on a tree created by an angel like her…or rather, an angel like she'd been. Change of topic.

She swiveled to face Blaine, without looking at the food container. "Are you really gathering an army of Fallen or is that a lie you spin to recruit angels like me?"

Last night, Blaine told her of his plan and this morning, she still couldn't get the conversation out of her head. Talk of war and dethroning Zath seemed so farfetched, but now, after digesting the information, could he be serious? Was Blaine capable of such destruction?

Blaine leaped onto the countertop, dangling his legs over the edge, the revolting food in one hand and fork in the other. "Sure am, love."

She motioned to the lack of Fallen in the room. "Then where is your army?"

Blaine took another fork full. She swallowed the

bile rising in her throat.

"As of late, I've kept them hidden in Hell. That brotherhood of Boy Scouts wipes them out quicker than I can recruit replacements."

That sounded like a stupid plan if ever she heard one. "Won't Zath discover your plan to dethrone him if your army is in Hell?"

Blaine chewed another mouthful of moldy food before answering. "Zath's weakness is he's too preoccupied with harvesting the souls of Fate's precious mortals to even notice I'm building an army right under his nose. He's so blinded with rage he can't see the bigger picture. He's not terribly smart like that." He cocked his head. "Zath's weakness will be his downfall."

War raged between Zath and Fate since the beginning of time. No one outside Fate's inner circle knew what happened, but Willow knew their feud resulted in Fate creating Hell to imprison Zath. Oh, and she also now knew Fate commanded Willow's ex-soulmate to hack off Zath's wings to remove his power, just like her.

"Why bother though? By the looks of it, you're fairly set up here in the mortal realm. Well…except for the edible food situation."

Blaine scrapped the bottom of the container before tossing it and the fork in the sink. "Without a purpose, love, an eternity is quite unforgiving." He gripped the edge of the counter and glanced at her. "Speaking of purpose, have you considered my offer?"

If only she could change the subject as quickly and easily as Blaine. Diversion was one of his strengths.

She pursed her lips. She thought of little else while

stuck inside the mansion without her powers or wings. "When you offered to regenerate my powers, this wasn't exactly what I had in mind. I don't understand why you need me. I'm not a fighter like you and Slater, I don't fit in with your army."

"Oh, but you do, love. You fit in perfectly. You'll see." He leaped off the counter. "Anyhoo, I'm heading out for a bit. Slater organized a cell phone for you." He tapped his chin. "I'm puzzled why your telepathy isn't working, considering you're healed."

Damn it. Evidently, Blaine suspected she lied, and he tested her. Her heart rate quickened. If Blaine couldn't read her thoughts, then maybe he wouldn't discover the truth. God, she pitied those mortals who lied, how hard it must be keeping track. Maybe they didn't care if they got caught? But if Blaine couldn't read her mind, how did Zath while she was in Hell? Was he more powerful?

Diverting the focus from her non-existent Fallen powers, she threw a hand in the air. "Great, a cell phone. Another thing to figure out how to use."

The diversion worked, for now. Blaine's throaty laugh filled the room. "Trust me, love, if that backward brother of mine, Raven, can figure it out, you have no worries."

Should that make her feel better? It didn't.

Blaine continued laughing as he exited the kitchen through the same door, leaving her alone in the useless room. In the past twenty-four hours, she'd discovered too many revelations. Her body felt restless, buzzing with energy she couldn't harness but exhausted by the thought of putting one foot in front of the other. She wanted to explore beyond the estate but without a mode of transport the task overwhelmed her.

Because everyone else can fly.

Maybe a long soak in a tub would lift her spirits. After that, she could explore the inside of the mansion, wander the corridors like a lost soul instead of wandering the infinite number of realms in the Heavens.

The same process, yet, so entirely different.

Chapter Fifteen

Aric landed in a dense pine forest surrounding the century-old mansion the Guardians discovered last year. A second later, EJ and River touched the ground behind him.

By the time Raven approved their recon mission, the first tendrils of dawn had crept over the mountains. They wouldn't have the cover of darkness for much longer.

Bundles of energy and adrenaline fired through his veins. His mind a raging mess, deciphering the facts laid on the table: Willow was a Fallen, shacked up with their former brother-turned-enemy, and chose this path because of his actions. When Fate tasked the Guardians with saving Blaine, he hadn't known the consequences meant abandoning his soulmate. But that wasn't what caused his chest to tighten. What if Willow wanted this path? What if she wanted to be with Blaine? Nope. Not going there. Until he heard her answer, he'd continue with his mission and save her, before Fate unleashed fury on him. *Again.*

Keeping his voice low, he addressed EJ and River, "I'll take the east. EJ you swing around the far side, and River, you scope out the rear of the property and see what you can find out. Meet back here in thirty."

"Gotcha." River nocked an arrow in his bow and took off toward the mansion.

EJ nodded before heading in the opposite direction.

Ditching those two was easier than expected. Aric would follow the rules and hang back in the shadows for the moment, but the second he sensed Willow in danger, he'd bust through the damn door.

With only an hour until dawn, he had no time to waste. They still had to fly back to the Guardian mansion without mortals spotting them.

The quick recon he did through the pine forest increased the wariness tingling across his nape, as though Fallen were everywhere, he just couldn't see them. He crept closer, crouching low to remain hidden. Through the thick branches, he spotted the mansion directly ahead—a two-story stone home covered in leafless vines. The blackened stone gave the impression a fire had burned the outside, leaving a dirty layer of soot.

He scanned the overgrown grounds. Nothing.

Returning his gaze to the mansion, a window on the second floor drew his attention. With the curtains closed, he couldn't see inside but something about the room called to him. He noticed nothing strange the last time he searched outside the mansion. What was different now?

While he stared at the glass, a faint sensation fluttered inside his chest, warming his blood—

His heart stopped. He knew that feeling. He held his breath, concentrating harder.

Willow.

He bolted from the tree line, grabbing his daggers as he raced across the lawn. Reaching the wall of the mansion, he softened his steps as he crept around the corner toward the front door. The flutter under his ribs heightened the closer he came to the mansion.

Someone grabbed his arm, jerking him back. He spun around with a dagger raised but lowered it once he saw the culprit. Damn River.

"Were you about to knock on the front door?"

He glared at River. "Nope, I have no intention of knocking. I'm gonna kick that fucker in."

River shook his head. "Rave gave strict orders not to enter."

Aric shrugged off River's hold. This pointless conversation wasted precious time. "Listen, you can either come with me or turn the hell back. I won't hold it against you for following orders. Either way, I'm going in." He peered at the mansion. "I can sense Willow inside, and something isn't right."

River pursed his lips. "What if there's a battalion of Fallen waiting to ambush us? We're severely outnumbered."

He didn't give a shit if they outnumbered them. "Have you spotted any Fallen?"

"No, but that doesn't mean there aren't any."

Case closed. Aric hadn't spotted any either, so they were in the clear. No need to confess he sensed Fallen, he'd deal with that when the time came. "Maybe not. But it's good enough for me." Before River protested further, Aric snuck around the side of mansion.

River huffed before he fell in step behind him. With steady, measured movements, he hunched over, daggers gripped tight, creeping around the front porch toward the door. A few feet from the door, EJ stepped from behind a pylon, arms crossed over his chest.

Are you fucking kidding me?

EJ glanced at his non-existent watch. "You took

long enough."

"Whatever happened to following orders?"

EJ shrugged. "As if. Rave knew you wouldn't do what he said. I figured that's why he sent us with you." EJ nodded at River. "Clearly Sunshine here caught onto your plan to ditch us, too."

Ignoring the intervention, Aric ascended the steps and stood before the oversized double doors.

EJ stood beside him. "There's no one in there, Ric."

"Willow is. I feel her." Aric paused, gripping the brass handle.

EJ groaned. "Or maybe frickin' Fate is compelling you."

"I dunno. But I have to check it out."

"Fine. I'll hang here by the door in case our resident Fallen returns." He stared hard at Aric. "You have ten minutes, Ric, before I haul your ass outta there. Understood?"

Plenty of time. "Copy that." He glanced at River. "You comin'?"

River nocked an arrow in his bow and gave a curt nod.

Aric twisted the doorknob. "Fuck, it's locked," he grumbled to himself. Well, there went their element of surprise. "Let's do this." He sucked in a deep breath and slammed his boot against the door, busting it open.

With both daggers gripped in his hands, he entered the mansion, and proceeded down a narrow hall. River followed close behind. Thick gray cobwebs loomed from the high ceiling as though they remained undisturbed for years. Wasn't this the same mansion bought last year by some hot-shot billionaire from the city? Where had the guy gone?

Running the pad of his finger along a hall table, he grimaced at the track left in the dust. All the mansion needed were white sheets over the antique furniture to complete the abandoned vibe.

Using hand signals, he directed River along another narrow hall while he ascended the stairs, ducking under the cobwebs. On the second floor, he rolled his feet avoiding any creaks in the floor. The burgundy carpet running the entire length of the hall did a brilliant job of concealing his heavy steps.

Each time he came to a door, he tried the knob. If it opened, he searched the room. When he came across a locked door, he stretched his senses to determine if an occupant was inside. Nope, no one.

About three-quarters of the way down the hall, with five rooms cleared and two to go, heat flashed across his nape, followed by that same tickle of awareness. He froze. His gaze darted left and right, anticipating a Fallen to materialize. His palms tightened around the hilt of both daggers. Several seconds passed. When an ambush didn't come to fruition, he exhaled but didn't relax his stance.

He approached the end of the hall, toward the room that drew his attention earlier. A slight draft drifted down the hall, carrying a faint scent of…

His body tensed. The smell of thunderstorms filled his nostrils, mixed with…Lavender? Absently, his feet inched closer to the room. He knew that scent. For countless centuries it had branded his skin.

He stopped in front of the closed door and inhaled again. Her scent was so strong in that particular spot as though she stood right there, on the other side of the door.

Fire ignited beneath his flesh, and the fluttering behind his ribs roared with renewed purpose. Willow was here. He was sure of it.

He gripped the door handle, turned the knob, and swung it open.

****

Willow wiped the condensation from the bathroom mirror, but the humid air fogged the mirror quicker than she could wipe. Through the mist, she turned this way and that, getting a better view of her wild mess of curls. Even after raking her fingers through it, her hair remained full of knots and crazy tangles. She added a hairdryer and comb to her growing list of necessities.

Blaine and Slater left not long ago, and she spent the time figuring out the cell phone Slater left on her nightstand. It proved less difficult than expected, and she even correctly dialed the pre-programmed number "Handsome Devil." Blaine, of course, answered.

After that, she found a room with a claw-foot tub and filled it to the brim with lavender-scented bubbles. But the soak hadn't lasted long. A strangle tingle crept over her body each time her eyes drifted shut, until it became so uncomfortable, she called it quits and got out of the tub. The calming smell still lingered on her skin so that was a plus.

Focusing on the mirror, she inhaled a deep breath and pivoted to glance at her back. She willed her wings to emerge through the twin scars running parallel down her shoulder blades. She begged them. Pleaded. Nothing. The skin didn't part, her new wings didn't unfurl. Once again, the black jagged scars represented nothing but failure.

Her stomach twisted in tight knots. *What have I done?*

Transitioning to a Fallen took an unexpected toll on her. She thought the process would be swift, that new Fallen powers replaced her angelic ones the minute she passed through the gates of Hell. Then Zath captured her. That caused a delay, sure, but her wings should have regenerated by now.

Not accessing the healing powers of the sun was the biggest disadvantage. She could use a boost.

Turning from the mirror, she wrapped a towel around herself and padded out of the bath to grab clothes. She skidded to a halt. Aric stood in the open doorway to the bedroom. Staring directly at her.

Blaine assured her he cloaked the mansion, that she was safe here. How had Aric found her?

She didn't dare move. His body filled the doorway, legs shoulder width apart with daggers gripped tight in his hands. She knew that stance. He readied for battle but the only one to fight was…her.

She staggered back. She was a Fallen now. The enemy Aric vowed to kill.

Would he kill her? She couldn't take the chance.

Heart thudding behind her ribs, she stepped back further. His brows knitted, his eyes narrowed, but his body didn't move.

Hang on…

He stared at her, yet, his eyes lacked recognition, as though he looked through her. She waved and snuck closer, just inches from his face. Her shoulders relaxed when he didn't react. The glamour worked.

Remaining silent, her gaze roamed over his features while her heart sped up for a totally different reason. His whiskey eyes drew her in, melting her heart into a hot gooey mess. With one look, he reminded her how those same eyes once shone with love and adoration. She bit the inside of her cheek, longing to feel the rough touch of his knuckles as he brushed along her jaw. How easily he washed away her hurt without saying a word.

Stupid, stupid, Willow. Their history together didn't excuse what he did.

His arm shot forward. She leaped back, Aric missing her by less than an inch. That was way too close. She had no clue what happened if he touched her. Could he touch her? Would the glamour concealing the entire house break if he discovered she stood right in front of him?

No. If that happened, he not only saw her, but he also saw the horrible scars on her back. He'd see her failures. And the pity in his eyes would break her.

She backed up a few more steps.

At a safe distance, she admired his sculpted body as he searched the room, striding into the bath before returning to the bedroom. The way his black jeans hugged his strong muscular legs caused tingles to dance along her skin. Warmth pooled in the pit of her stomach as her gaze roamed over the dark gray T-shirt stretched across his broad chest. A perfect picture formed in her mind of the abs and firm pecs she knew lay underneath.

God, he was so damn sexy. She fought every ounce of self-control not to grab the lapels of his jacket and smash her lips against his. Ever since she saw him in the nightclub, her body ached to smooth her fingers along his dark stubble. Heat flashed over her body and she bit the inside of her cheek to prevent from moaning.

He caused an ache between her legs, and he didn't even know she was in the same room.

"There's no one here, bro."

She sucked in a sharp breath. Another Guardian appeared in the doorway. She didn't recognize him. Ducking behind the open door, she kept out of sight, just in case. Distracted by her fantasies of Aric, she forgot to remain hidden.

Another close call. One of these days, she wouldn't be so lucky.

She peeked around the door at Aric.

His chest expanded with a long, deep inhale as he peered around the room. "Maybe not. But Willow's been here. I'll never forget her scent." His shoulders dropped. "I could've sworn I sensed her in this room."

Damn her heart for aching at his words.

The other Guardian glanced around, his gaze passing right over her. "Well, she's not here now. I checked the entire lower level and there's nothing but cobwebs and a century's worth of dust. Let's get outta here, before we get ambushed or worse, eaten alive by mutant spiders."

Aric waited a long moment before answering. "Copy that. Let's go."

He turned toward the door but halted midway. His gaze locked on hers. He stepped closer. She held her breath, heart pounding as she stood frozen behind the door. A heartbeat later, his shoulders sagged, and he exited the room.

She waited until his heavy boots faded down the stairs before releasing a silent breath that turned into a quiet sob. Sinking to the floor, her head fell back against the wall.

Why did she let him affect her? She needed a neon sign reminding her of the pain he caused, the reason she Fell. The fact she lost her wings because of him. She couldn't trust Aric. Even worse, she couldn't trust her feelings for him. Each time she saw him, a spark reignited deep in her soul. But he always chose his brothers, and this time was no different. Once again, watching him walk away left her heart a shattered mess.

Chapter Sixteen

Aric split the last log cleanly in two and chucked both pieces in the wheelbarrow, laying the axe on top. He snatched his shirt from the waistband of his pants and used it to wipe the sweat from the back of his neck. That workout was better than any gym and blaring heavy rock into his ears, always lifted his mood.

Shirt hanging from the waistband of his sweats, he pushed the wheelbarrow across the manicured lawn and returned it to the woodshed. Judging by the overflowing log pile, the Guardians had enough wood chopped to last them the next seven winters. At least. He hung the axe on an inside wall and locked the shed.

Music still blaring, he dragged his feet back to the house heading for the shower. Although he wasn't on shift today, he still planned to head into town and wander the streets like he had the last five nights, searching for Willow. Each night ended with him on the rooftop of Blaine's creepy lair.

Tayla waved him over from her spot under a shade tree.

He paused the music and cut across the grass toward her and slipped on his shirt, the earbuds dangling out the neck. No need to poke Raven the Bear again by chatting to his woman while half naked.

He halted at the edge of Tayla's picnic blanket. "Hey, Tayla."

Her head tilted to the side and her eyes narrowed. "Were you cutting more wood? Don't we have enough?"

He hitched a shoulder. "Someone's gotta do it. Plus, it's as good as the gym I reckon."

Tayla laughed. "I think Raven would rather run for three days straight than chop wood."

"You're probably right." *Yeah, great chat, time to go…*

Tayla patted the spot beside her. "Why don't you sit with me?"

He peered toward the house where nothing but a shower awaited him. Talking wasn't his strong point, and he was damn sure that's what Tayla wanted. But without a plausible excuse, saying no just made him an asshole.

Fine, five minutes. He sat on grass beside the rug but didn't get too comfortable.

Tayla slid a bookmark between the pages of her book and closed it. He mentally rolled his eyes at the cover featuring a half-naked guy with a drop of blood falling from his fangs.

He nodded toward the book. "Why are mortals so fascinated with half-naked vampires?"

"I don't know. I guess it's the allure of unearthly creatures living undetected around us. Plus…" She shrugged. "They're hot."

"Don't let Raven hear you say that."

"No need to worry. He's constantly reminding me of his superior hotness."

He chuckled. "I bet."

Their chat wasn't so bad. He stretched out his legs, leaning back on his hands. A light breeze rustled the pine trees, creating a tranquil sound in the background. A stark contrast to the jam session his eardrums usually heard.

They sat there in silence, again, not as bad as he expected. Each time his fingers brushed the blades of grass, his heart ached a little more. Countless times he sat like this with Willow while she wielded her Ariel magic over the earth, regenerating everything from ancient oak trees to single blades of grass. The wildflowers were his favorite. Each vibrant color she created more beautiful than the last. They reminded him of her beauty; her spark for life. They filled his soul with happiness.

"Aric," Tayla straightened, crossing her legs. "I know we haven't known each other long, but I think you need to hear what I'm about to say."

Here we go. Was it give-Aric-advice-week? Willow had become a Fallen and arrived in the mortal realm, and now everyone thought he needed fucking advice.

He stared at a thick blade of grass. Whatever. He'd let them get it out of their system. It didn't mean he'd listen.

"You may think I don't notice, but I do." Tayla paused. "I catch the longing in your eyes whenever Raven pulls me close or whispers in my ear."

He diverted his gaze to the mansion on the opposite side of the lawn. Would counting the bricks be easier than the stained-glass window at the church? More importantly, how did everyone see through his shield?

He didn't reply, so Tayla kept talking. "I saw it the first day we met. Even then, you knew Raven and I were destined to be together, didn't you? I see it in your eyes, Aric. I know it's not longing for me, it's longing for what Raven and I share. That soul-deep connection."

He closed his eyes and remained silent. The giant lump in his throat prevented words from forming. What the hell should he say? *Yep.* He saw the connection between them when he first met Tayla. He knew Raven felt it. Raven just didn't know what it meant. Because it involved Fate, Raven had to choose the path. Raven had to choose Tayla.

He was no stranger to that connection. The soulmate bond had flowed through his veins for over a thousand years. Every time he looked at Raven and Tayla together, it fucking hurt. Their bond reminded him of his screw up. Reminded him of the choice he made to save Blaine. That choice abandoned his soulmate in the Heavens.

He sat up, wrapping his arms around his legs, twirling a blade of grass between his fingers.

Tayla softened her voice. "I don't know Willow, but I do know you deserve that bond, Aric. You deserve happiness and love, and to share that with someone for the rest of eternity. If Willow is your soulmate, then why the heck are you moping around here feeling sorry for yourself?"

He frowned. "I don't feel…" His throat tightened, and he lowered his head, unable to finish the lie.

Yep, he felt sorry for himself. But more so, he ached to find Willow.

He left her in the Heavens to protect her, to ensure she was safe. He had a long list of enemies, one who'd targeted Willow for centuries. When he left, he hadn't known it would be forever.

He thought of Willow every single day, and each decision he made in the mortal realm put him one step closer to returning to the Heavens. He wasn't proud of the things he'd done, but if torturing a Fallen gave him updates on the situation in Hell, then he did it.

Now, all that meant nothing. Three centuries later, he and Willow were finally in the same realm and she couldn't stand the sight of him. Not to mention the added complication of her being a Fallen—the dark angels he'd sworn to annihilate.

"Maybe she's better without me," he grumbled. "I hurt her badly. She'll never forgive me for that."

Tayla fiddled with the tassels on her bookmark. "Do you still love her?"

His gaze snapped to hers. "Of course, I fucking do." He clenched his jaw, reining in the frustration. "Shit. Sorry, Tayla. I'll never stop loving her. She's my soulmate."

Tayla straightened like she was on a mission. "Then you need to fight for her, Aric. Fight to win her back. Fight to save her."

That damn lump returned in his throat. "I'm not sure she wants saving."

Tayla's gaze turned distant. "Trust me, there's no way she can fight the connection or walk away. I would know. I tried, remember? I walked away from Raven and I was a miserable mess." A faint smile brightened her face. "You need to remind her. Remind her how good you two were together, the love you have for each other. It isn't gone, it's been locked away for a really long time."

Why were females so wise? Was it a specific gene Fate included in their creation?

"I can see why Raven keeps you around."

"Someone needs to help Ellen make you guys see sense. Sometimes, I think you all need to lower your tough-guy persona and see what's right in front of you."

"You're forgetting one important factor in this plan of yours, Tayla."

Her eyebrows furrowed. "What's that?"

Heaviness settled on his chest. "Willow's a Fallen. It's not just a matter of reminding her of our history. She severed her connection to the Heavens."

Tayla tilted her head. "Maybe if you win back her heart, it will heal her soul?"

He took a moment to consider her words. Win back her heart? After what felt like an eternity, he and Willow were within reach. Why did he waste time chopping endless amounts of wood when he should be finding her? Sure, winning her back would be easier if she wasn't a Fallen. But he could only play the cards Fate dealt. This time, she sure as hell had a sick sense of humor.

"I can practically hear your brain whirling." Tayla nudged his shoulder. "Find her. And when you do, romance the heck out of her."

He snorted. "Sound advice, only I'm possibly the universe's most unromantic Guardian. Just ask EJ."

"Oh, I don't think that's true." Tayla smirked. "Plus, I suspect you're up for the challenge."

A light-hearted feeling filled his chest, planting a tiny seed of hope. He was up for a challenge and he and Willow had centuries of lost time to make up for.

Aric stood. "Thank you, wise woman."

Tayla smiled, lighting up her hazel eyes. "You're welcome, Aric. Now get a move on, you have work to do."

When he turned to leave, he spotted Raven crossing the lawn on a mission. He cocked a brow at Tayla. "Looks like I'm not the only one on a romantic mission."

Her cheeks flamed as her gaze locked with Raven's.

The ache in his chest intensified. Tayla was right. He did long for that connection. He longed for Willow, to watch desire ignite in her eyes, to wake with her curled between his arms, as they had for more than a thousand years.

When Raven reached them, he gave him a brotherly handshake. "You good, my man?"

Aric faked a smile. "Yep, apparently I need to do some romancing."

Raven arched a brow. "I'm not going to ask."

"Wise move, man. I'll catch ya later." Aric nodded at Tayla before leaving the two lovebirds alone.

As he put one foot in front of the other, heading to the mansion for that long overdue shower, a weight lifted from his shoulders. He now had a clear mission: Figure out this romance shit and win Willow back. The first task was to find her.

Chapter Seventeen

The dagger sliced through the air. Willow's heart soared with hope. This time she'd hit the tree for sure.

On second thought…nope. Another miss.

"Damn it!" She threw her arms in the air. "I can't do this."

Beside her, Slater remained unaffected by her constant failure. He stood there with his shoulder against a tree, arms crossed. "Throw another."

"Why?" Her voice rose. "Why do I need to learn to use a dagger?"

Every muscle in her arm ached from overuse. She couldn't lift another dagger, let alone throw one with any accuracy.

"Because you refuse to use the handgun," Slater replied with a dead-pan expression on his face.

Her hands curled into fists. "I'm not a fighter like you, I told Blaine that. I never will be."

Slater pushed off the tree. "You need to be."

"Why?" she shouted. "So, I can join this invisible Fallen army? Why should I? Blaine promised me powers. He promised me freedom. None of that…"

She sucked in a sharp breath, ceasing her words. Damn it. She almost let slip she still didn't have powers. If Slater knew, he'd know she also didn't have wings. Without them, powers were impossible.

Slater's expression darkened, and he studied her

for a moment. She held his stare. If she looked away, he'd know she was hiding something.

"You need to learn to use the dagger to defend yourself when the Guardians try to kill you."

"They wouldn't…" Would they?

Though the thought crossed her mind when Aric found her in the mansion. Would he have killed her if he saw her?

Sure, she'd severed her connection with the Heavens and become a failed Fallen, but she was once Aric's soulmate. Surely that held weight? The twisting in her gut told her it wouldn't.

Did the Guardians kill every Fallen, or only particularly bad ones? Was there some priority order on the evil scale?

"Yeah, they would." Slater flipped a dagger in his hand. "You're a Fallen now, princess, you're no longer aligned on the same side of this war."

"Don't call me that," she snapped. "How can you be so sure Aric will kill me?"

"Because he's a Guardian. His oath to Fate compels him to kill Fallen." Slater narrowed his dark eyes. "Has he ever broken his oath?"

If she were closer, she'd slap that smug look right off his face.

No, Aric's loyalty to his duty never wavered. None of the Guardians had ever broken their oath. But would Aric really kill her and send her soul back to Hell? Back to…Zath.

She swallowed. Better safe than sorry. She'd fight with everything she had if it meant not returning to Hell.

"Fine," she grumbled.

Slater handed her another dagger. "Keep your arm straight this time."

She gripped the cool blade between her thumb and forefinger, drew back her arm…

Come on, Willow, you can do this.

In one swift motion, she flicked her wrist and threw the dagger, aiming for a tree trunk thirty yards away. She watched the dagger slice through the air, holding her breath in case any slight exhale changed the trajectory of the blade.

Yes…yes…yes!

The dagger slammed into the tree trunk, the handle wobbling from the impact.

"I did it!"

Slater looked unimpressed. "Now do it again."

She glared at him. "Clearly, you can't give out compliments."

When she reached the tree, she inspected the only dagger that hit its intended target. It lodged in the trunk all the way to the hilt.

Finally, she'd done it. Days of training, persistence and willpower paid off.

But the joy didn't last long as another realization struck her. Throwing a dagger at a tree trunk was one thing, but could she throw one into the chest of a Guardian? With her soul at stake, could she throw a dagger at Aric?

She had to. Injuring a Guardian was a small price to pay for her safety. She knew, deep in her gut, that Zath would hunt her down if she returned to Hell, and without Fallen powers, she was no match for him.

Gripping the handle, she yanked the dagger from the tree. She brushed her thumb over the deep cut left in the trunk. If she had Ariel magic, she'd seal the wound and regenerate the bark. But no, she'd given up her powers when she Fell.

From what she knew, when an angel Fell, their powers transformed into darkness—the opposite of their angelic powers. Would her powers regenerate life or would they destroy it? Only Blaine could give her the answer but asking him meant admitting the truth. She wasn't ready yet.

Blaine's motivation still puzzled her. Until she knew why he wanted her on his team, she wouldn't reveal her failure. Once her wings grew back, she'd figure out what that meant for her powers.

After grabbing the remaining daggers off the ground, she strode back to the throwing line. She dropped all but one dagger at her feet. Standing at a slight angle, she gripped the blade and steadied her hand. Deep breath in…hold…throw. The dagger cut through the air and slammed straight into the tree. Closer to the center this time.

She cocked a brow at Slater.

"Better." He turned and walked away. "Tomorrow we start on moving targets," he called over his shoulder.

What? Is he for real?

"Great job, Willow. You're really getting the hang of this," she grumbled to herself. "Gee, thanks, Slater. Nice of you to give me a compliment."

She stared at the dagger protruding from the trunk. Five days of practice and training, and she lodged two daggers in the tree. How the hell would she hit a moving target?

Maybe she should try the handgun option? Nope.

Bullets did more damage and risked killing someone. She created life, not ended it.

Grabbing another dagger off the ground, she straightened and threw again. Repeating the process over and over until the sun sank low in the sky and darkness crept into the forest.

She peered through the tree canopy to the dark purple clouds, grinning for the first time in so long. She'd severed her connection to the Heavens, escaped from Hell, and had a temporary place at Blaine's mansion, which now had a refrigerator stocked with fresh food.

With lightness in her step, she ripped all five daggers from the trunk. Today was her turning point. She'd nailed dagger training and tomorrow she'd work even harder. Once she excelled at defense skills, she'd tackle her next challenge: Demanding Blaine give her what he promised. Power and freedom.

Chapter Eighteen

From behind the attic window, Willow peered across the roof of the mansion to the large shadow slumped on the far side. For the tenth night in a row.

On the first night, she discovered the shadow after faint tingles stirred in her blood. A sensation likening the soulmate connection she and Aric had shared for over a thousand years. She tracked the invisible thread all the way to the attic where she found Aric slumped on the other side of the rooftop.

At first, she'd freaked out. Blaine and Slater weren't there. What if Aric harmed her? Slater had planted the seed so well that thanks to hours of solitude, the thought matured into full-blown fear.

But that tingle in her blood told her otherwise. If Aric wanted to kill her, he would've done it by now. He didn't waste time.

Since that first rooftop sighting, Aric arrived each night at the same time and sat in the darkness until dawn. Tonight was no different.

"He's here again," she whispered.

Blaine leaned forward and peeked out the window. "Poor guy looks miserable."

He did look miserable, sitting there with his legs bent, forearms resting atop his knees, and a bottle of alcohol clutched in one hand.

Blaine gave her a little nudge with his shoulder.

"Go talk to him, love."

Why was Blaine encouraging her? Aric was a Guardian, his sworn enemy. Shouldn't he want to fight him? Though thank goodness they hadn't fought. From what she'd seen of Blaine's powers, Aric didn't stand a chance.

Now she thought about it, Blaine seemed completely unfazed by Aric's repeated visits.

"There's no point talking to him."

"Who knows? You might rekindle your relationship."

She screwed up her face. "Why would I bother doing that?"

Blaine shrugged and without another word, he strolled out of the attic, closing the door behind him. Leaving her alone in the dark.

What a joke.

She didn't want to rekindle their relationship. She'd severed her connection with the Heavens so she could break her tie with Aric. That way he no longer drained her powers as he had since abandoning her. The longer her powers remained tied to Aric through that stupid band she forged him, the longer it took to move forward. Cutting that bond meant her powers became her own again.

Well, excluding the complication where Zath stole them with her wings.

Argh. When would her wings regenerate?

Regardless, she had no intention of mending her connection with Aric. But since the first night Aric arrived on the rooftop, Blaine had insisted she talk with him. It became harder and harder to think of plausible excuses why she wouldn't.

Why didn't Aric get the hint and go away? Why wouldn't he leave her alone? It wasn't enough for him to rip her heart out, but now he had to torture her by turning up every night like he…cared.

She knew that wasn't the case. If Aric cared, he would've come back for her. He wouldn't have left her.

Every night, she hid behind the safety and protection of the paneled glass avoiding the conversation. Climbing outside the window freed her from the glamour Blaine had over the mansion. It forced her to face Aric. Face his disappointment, his lies, or rather his excuses for why he'd shattered her heart.

She couldn't deny climbing out that window was tempting. Because each night Aric arrived on the rooftop, her willpower dwindled away, replaced with desire for his strong arms wrapped around her. Becoming a Fallen would've been so much easier if she didn't see him and he couldn't constantly remind her of the happier parts of their history.

He lifted the bottle to his lips and took a long swig, before setting it beside him. From this distance, she couldn't see his face, but she sensed his sadness by the way his head hung low and how his shoulders dropped with each heavy exhale. The sight of him in pain, regardless of the history between them, made her chest ache.

When she saw him at the mortal club before her Fall, he seemed happy, at peace with living in the mortal realm, content with their separation. Why did he now appear so unhappy?

Had she ruined his fun by arriving in the mortal realm? Heaviness pressed against her chest. Could he have missed her like she had him? She wished for the latter, but that meant he had a heart. He proved he didn't when he abandoned her, throwing away their life together for yet another mission. More proof a Guardian never broke their oath.

She should tell him to go away, put him out of his misery. A courtesy he should've extended to her.

Nearly three weeks had passed since she first confronted him in the alleyway. She'd avoided a conversation with him that entire time, hoping her wings grew back and her powers returned. At least then she could defend herself.

The regeneration of her wings made her a fully-fledged Fallen. Then Aric held no influence over her. He couldn't convince her she'd made a mistake and the pity and disappointment on his face wouldn't affect her. And neither would his smoldering eyes.

She threw her arms in the air. "Damn it."

This was pointless. Aric was the sexiest Guardian she'd ever seen. There was no defense against his hotness. Her Fallen-in-limbo state didn't dampen her desire for him. In fact, with her emotions all haywire, that desire escalated.

Walking away would prove easier if she didn't know the feeling of his rough hands against her skin. The gentle, yet, firm way he cupped her face between his palms and kissed her. The way his rich earthy scent lingered in her pores long after he'd gone.

She exhaled a heavy breath. She needed to step free of Blaine's glamour on the mansion and face Aric. Make it clear she had no intention of reuniting, and he could stop sitting on the rooftop each night.

Facing him would seal the gaping hole left in her

heart so it never reopened. The longer she left the seam unstitched, the easier Aric could convince her she'd made a mistake. Telling him they were over also prevented Slater from stabbing him with a dagger if he discovered him on the roof.

With an hour left until dawn, she made her decision and slid open the window.

"Be strong, Willow. Be strong…" she whispered, as she ducked her head and climbed onto the roof.

****

Noise behind Aric made him glance over his shoulder. His heart flipped. Willow stepped free from a windowsill and stood on the opposite side of the rooftop.

He couldn't move. He remained frozen to the spot as she tiptoed with slow and steady steps in his direction. The serious look of concentration on her face puzzled him, as though she were an acrobat walking along a tightrope hung miles in the air, each step a risk she might slip and plummet to her death. If Willow slipped, she'd just unfurl her wings. She wouldn't splat on the gravel.

Willow halted a few steps away, shifting her weight between her bare feet. She wouldn't meet his gaze, ripping his fucking heart to pieces.

He turned away. "I won't bite," he grumbled to the bottle, taking another chug.

Her soft footsteps approached before she sat on his left, legs curled up beside her, just out of arms' reach.

"Why are you here, Aric?"

Her tone wasn't mad, nor angry, more resigned to the fact this conversation needed to happen. There was a hint of exhaustion there though, and he fought every cell in his body not to scoop her in his arms. Like he had so many times.

Instead, he stared at the gloomy pine forest surrounding the estate. Tonight, the yellow full moon hung low in the sky, creating an eerie glow as the light seeped between the trees.

He didn't have an answer to her question because he didn't know why he sat on the rooftop each night. He sensed her here but never saw her. Did he return in hopes of seeing her? In case one night she spoke to him? Maybe his heart ached to know she was real.

He didn't dare speak. Didn't want to spook her or have her leave again. Her approaching him was progress, and he'd treasure every minute.

This was the first time in over three centuries he had the chance to erase all those hurtful memories between them and replace them with happier ones.

And he was fucking drunk.

"I know you come here," she muttered, so softly it drifted to his ears as though carried by the gentle breeze.

He glanced at her. His vision took a minute to catch up. "Huh?"

"I see you." She met his gaze. "I know you come here every night and sit on the roof."

He held her stare for a heartbeat before the pain in his chest squeezed his lungs so tight it prevented his next breath. More slowly this time, he stared back at the forest. "I feel closer to you here than at the church. My soul keeps pulling me here, and I catch your scent every night."

"Church?"

Each night, he parked his ass on the rooftop,

drowning his sorrows, hoping like hell he wasn't going crazy. The rooftop of this creepy-ass mansion became his sliver of connection to her. He wouldn't give that up.

He took another mouthful of whiskey, swallowing the giant lump in his throat. "For over three centuries, I've searched for a way to be closer to you. A way to reach your soul in the Heavens so you knew I thought of you. So, you knew I didn't forget." He paused, pressing the heel of his hand against the pain behind his ribs. "Mortals light candles inside churches for their lost loved ones. I dunno…it felt right lighting a candle each week for you."

He couldn't look at her in case something in her beautiful eyes told him she didn't care. Instead, thanks to half a bottle of whiskey, the words kept coming. "I caught your scent here a couple of weeks ago. It's the closest I've felt to you since I left. I guess I keep returning, hoping like hell one night I'd see you." He sighed. "And now you're sitting beside me, I don't know what to fucking say."

She remained silent for so long, he glanced to make sure she hadn't left. Nope. Back to staring at the tops of the pine trees as they swayed back and forth like his head.

"What's it like living in the mortal realm for so long?"

God, the pain inside his chest wouldn't fucking stop and hearing her voice made it worse. "Without you…" He met her gaze. "It may as well be Hell."

She scowled at him. "You were the one who left, remember?"

Great. He ruined the moment in less than five

minutes. Why was everything so goddamn hard?

"I don't wanna argue. I just want to be here with you."

He reached out to touch her only to force his hand back. He had to take this slow, otherwise, he risked losing her all over again. Their strained silence stretched into the night.

Grabbing the whiskey, he took another long sip before offering the bottle to Willow. She hesitated a moment then accepted, lifting it to her pale pink lips.

He frowned. Why were her lips so pale? Her whole face looked pasty, duller than the last time he saw her in the parking lot. Though, that night she stood under a streetlamp and his brain had short-circuited. Maybe he didn't notice?

Willow choked and coughed, covering her mouth, before handing the bottle back.

He forced a smile. "You get used to the burn."

She grimaced. "I'm not sure I will."

He placed the bottle beside him and wrapped his hands around his legs, locking his fingers tight so he didn't reach out and touch her. Though he never stopped looking at her. Memorizing how her bright red hair fell in a wavy mess over her shoulders and how the moonlight reflected in her soft hazel eyes each time she glanced at him.

He ached to tell her how much he'd missed her, how much he yearned to be near her, even from a distance. Just having her in the same fucking realm felt like he'd won the jackpot. Instead, some other random shit came out, again, thanks to the damn whiskey.

"I sensed your Fall," he mumbled, the words thick on his tongue. "It kills me that Blaine saved you, when it should've been me."

She twisted to face him, and her gaze locked with his. The world crashed to a halt, as though time stood still holding its breath anticipating her next words. So, did he. He never tired of the feeling when their gazes locked, a completeness he took for granted for so long, before one day it vanished forever.

Her expression softened. "You couldn't have known."

"I should have."

God, he wanted to touch her so bad, press his lips against hers. Taste her. Breathe in her stormy scent one more time. "I've missed you so fucking much. More than you could ever know."

Romance her, Aric. Show her how good they were.

Bracing his weight on one hand, he reached toward her with a trembling arm. When she didn't pull away, he brushed the back of his knuckles along the soft skin of her jawline. She sucked in a breath; her head tilting toward his touch.

His heart flipped. He'd waited so long for this moment, to have her within reach.

"Let me kiss you," he whispered.

Her gaze heated with desire, darkening around the rim. He braced himself for a flash of crimson in her pupils, what happened when a Fallen's emotions heightened. It didn't appear. But he didn't bother wondering why. Her eyes were beautiful no matter the color.

For agonizing seconds, he held his breath, heart pounding, waiting for her answer. One kiss. That was all he asked. All he needed.

She drew in her bottom lip. He wanted this more

than air. Would their lips remember each other and dance together like old lovers? Or would it feel like their first kiss more than a thousand years ago?

He slid his palm around her nape, coaxing her closer. His breaths came fast and heavy and he clenched his jaw to avoid rushing. He wanted her to want this as much as him. He inched closer, hovering at her mouth, waiting. Her stormy rain scent scrambled his thoughts.

Her gaze dipped to his lips a second before she eased her mouth to his. His heart exploded. He kissed her back, as though the universe depended on this moment, pouring all his desperation and longing into her soul.

She tasted of familiarity and comfort. She tasted of heaven. She tasted of home.

He angled her head slightly, gaining better access while she deepened their kiss. Scooting closer, Willow slid her hands under his jacket then up and over his shoulders. He shuddered at the contact, his body overcome with yearning.

Soft moans escaped her mouth and the moment her tongue swept over his, his brain went to mush. He needed more. Needed her straddled over his hips. Needed her all over him.

He slid his hands along the soft fabric of her dress to the indentation of her waist, gripping her hips to lift her onto his lap—

Saltiness entered his mouth, breaking through the fog of lust. A tear? Why the hell was she crying?

A single memory blasted his mind. The last time he'd kissed her, where he'd cradled her head between his hands and showered her with all the love in his heart, while tears streamed down her face. The moment before he left the Heavens and never returned.

He broke their kiss and drew back. Her lips were swollen, cheeks slightly flushed. But what ripped his heart in two were the streaks of tears running down her face.

"Lo-Lo, I didn't mean to—"

She shoved against his chest and stood.

He got to his feet, reaching for her hand. She snatched it away.

"Why would you do that? Kiss me like that? Kiss me like you care!" Her soft, angelic voice vanished, replaced with raw pain.

He stepped closer, but she retreated. "I do care. I love you."

"You left me," she shrieked, tears continuing down her cheeks.

He shoved a hand through his hair. What the hell just happened? With one mind-blowing kiss all their centuries of happiness returned. Now, he'd fucking ruined his chance.

Their kiss hadn't eased his pain, it amplified hers. Made it fucking real again.

Was this their reality? Fate and her twisted games, toying with them. Reuniting him and Willow only to tear them apart.

He screwed up the day he left the Heavens, but he took Fate's deal to protect Willow. To save her the heartache. If he didn't, Fate would have imprisoned him for failing that Chosen and torturing the Fallen responsible. What the hell had she expected him to do?

"I had no choice."

Her nostrils flared. "You're telling me, Fate, the Queen of Destiny gave you…" She shoved his chest.

"Her honored Guardian, no choice?"

"Yes." Why didn't she believe him? "Willow, you know deep inside it's the truth. Fate screwed every one of us."

Her expression tightened. "No. I don't know that. Maybe deception is a skill you've mastered in your time here."

She may as well have smacked him across the face. He stood there stunned, unable to form a reply.

Blaine landed on the rooftop beside Willow, crimson wings spread wide behind his back. Aric glared at the fucking Fallen responsible for coaxing his soulmate from the safety of the Heavens.

Blaine placed a hand on Willow's shoulder as though protecting her. Protecting her from him? Like hell.

"You okay here, love?"

Snap went the rubber band holding his rage in check. He had no control over what happened next when his mind checked out while his body went ape shit. He lunged forward, shoving Blaine backward with so much force Blaine flailed his wings to avoid catapulting off the roof.

"Get the fuck away from her," Aric roared.

Flames ignited in Blaine's eyes. Good, Aric was more than ready for a fight. No one, and he meant no one, laid a hand on his soulmate.

Blaine leaped in the air toward him. Aric ripped a dagger free, gripped it in his palm, steadied his feet, preparing to attack.

Willow jumped between them, arms extended from her sides. "Stop it! Both of you."

Blaine skidded to a halt; bits of broken tiles

tumbled off the roof.

"Get outta the way, Willow. This is between me and that traitor." Aric grabbed Willow's hand, pulling her to his side.

She shoved him away. "I'm not a fragile Chosen requiring your protection, Aric."

Blaine scoffed. "Not that you're particularly good at that."

Aric stalked forward, jaw clenched, murderous intentions consuming his thoughts.

Willow's arm slammed hard against his chest, trying to hold him at bay, but it lacked the strength she once had. It lacked any strength. The rational part of his brain filled with concern for why she appeared so frail.

She glanced at Blaine. "Give us a second, will you?"

"Are you sure, love?" Blaine replied, a cocky smirk on his face.

When she nodded, that motherfucker gave her a royal bow before leaping off the rooftop.

He was done with saving Blaine. He didn't owe that Fallen a goddamn thing. Blaine voided that deal and any remnants of Aric's loyalty when he convinced Willow to Fall. Fate was fucking delusional if she still thought they could save him.

Willow lowered her arm. "Aric, listen to me."

He couldn't. His brain came back online after its trip to Rageland, but it wasn't firing on all cylinders. What the hell just happened? Had Willow asked Blaine to give her a minute like they were suddenly mates? Or lovers? His hands curled into tight fists.

"Aric…"

At the sound of her voice, the engine to his brain

kicked into gear and roared to life. He glared at her, forcing the words out nice and slow to avoid any misunderstanding. "Are you with him?"

Her expression softened. "Don't you get it? This is the choice I made."

She didn't answer the question...

"I asked if you're with him," he growled, unable to contain the sense of possession consuming his body.

She exhaled a long breath. "That's none of your business."

Rageland fast approached again. "Like hell it isn't."

She diverted her gaze to stare at her feet. "I'm a Fallen now. What was between us has ended. You have no claim on me."

Like hell he didn't. Willow was his soulmate until the end of time. That little touchy-feely episode with Blaine only heightened his determination to win her back.

Now that his brain wasn't a heap of mush, he concentrated on the subtle changes in her expression. He considered strategies to win her back. The kiss they shared moments ago confirmed their spark hadn't vanished, quite the opposite. For him, that spark exploded into a raging fire.

He wouldn't give up.

Closing the distance between them, he crooked a finger under her chin, lifting her gaze to his. "I don't give a shit what color your wings are. You're mine, Lo-Lo." He lowered his voice. "And I plan on reminding you just how fucking great we are."

He didn't miss the hitch in her breath, but she held her ground.

Easing back, he admired her warm hazel eyes, the specks of gold around the center. No sign of crimson. Maybe he could save her. Maybe her transition wasn't complete.

Her expression softened but a second later, tightened again. "No, Aric, I'm not yours. Get off this roof and leave me alone."

He shook his head. "I'm not giving up. Ever."

She shoved his hand away. "You already did remember?"

Her words sucker punched him in the gut. He just stood there as she hitched up her dress and climbed back inside the mansion, slamming the window closed behind her.

Chapter Nineteen

As soon as she shut the window, Willow collapsed on the floor of the attic, her legs unable to hold her.

How could Aric do that? Kissed her with so much passion and love it made her heart split into a thousand pieces.

She brushed a finger along the bottom of her lip, recalling the feel of his mouth against hers. Kissing him made her feel whole, connected and loved all in a matter of seconds.

Why? How?

She lowered her head in her hands, inhaling deep shuddering breaths. The last time he kissed her like that, he left the Heavens and never returned. She'd questioned him about the black blood splattered on his clothes and where he headed but he wouldn't tell her. Just told her not to worry. How could she not?

With each passing day, she had worried more. She knew him almost her entire existence, and each mission always returned him home. But that time had felt different. He never came back and never told her why.

Her stomach clenched. Was their kiss a moment ago a final goodbye? She should feel relieved. One less thing to worry about. She became a Fallen to sever her connection with Aric and return her powers, not to reunite with him.

Yet, when he held her, a familiar tingle awakened

inside, like a distant light brightening after centuries of no use. Damn him. How did his soul reach hers when she was a Fallen?

Aric's final words sent a shiver of heat through her blood. He promised to remind her how good they were together. Oh, she didn't need reminding. She knew how spellbinding and passionate their soulmate connection felt.

Before Aric tore it apart when he chose his brothers over her.

She wouldn't let one magical kiss fling her backward. No longer would she allow Aric to render her speechless with his touch. If he re-entered her life, there was a high possibility she'd fall for him all over again. Big mistake. Falling once for a Guardian like him took an eternity to get over. Her heart and soul wouldn't recover if she fell for him a second time.

She must strengthen her resilience, be strong. Tell him to leave the next time he arrived on the rooftop, or better yet, ignore him again. If he didn't leave, she'd send Slater onto the roof to deal with him. Sooner or later, he'd get the message.

She wiped the tears from her cheeks before standing.

This was the path she chose, the one she wanted. Her priority remained regenerating her wings and returning her powers, not reliving old memories of a life with her ex-soulmate.

Straightening her dress, she composed herself, and exited the attic without bothering to look back.

Chapter Twenty

Aric stomped up the stone steps to the church and twisted the door handle. Locked. Shit. Tonight was not a good night to be out on the damn steps. He twisted the knob again, yanked it, and nudged the door lightly with his shoulder. Still locked.

Fuck.

If he shoved harder, he'd bust the door. A standard lock was no match for his immortal strength, but even he had boundaries. Creeping inside a church in the eerie hours of the morning was one thing but breaking in…that crossed the line. Plus, given it wasn't Wednesday, he had no right to barge through that door.

Which left him out in the fucking cold.

Shoulders heavy with the weight of all his screw ups, he turned away and planted his ass on the top step. He crossed his arms atop his knees and lowered his head, concentrating on the numbing coldness.

No matter how hard he tried, he couldn't prevent one horrific memory from rising in his mind. How his choice set this entire train wreck of a path in motion.

He trudged up the steps of Fate's sanctuary, black Fallen blood stained his hands and clothing. He was ready to accept the punishment for the death of his Chosen. When Fate served it, he would stand tall and take it.

His first ever failure.

He'd punished the Fallen more than he should have. He knew that. But he regretted nothing. That asshole deserved every gash, every tear in his wings. Every stab of Aric's dagger.

How Blaine pulled him from his rage was a fucking miracle. For that, he owed Blaine his life. Another second and his soul would've passed the point of no return, blackening until it severed his connection to the Heavens. With Willow's powers bound to him, his screw up would've turned them both into Fallen. The band he wore made sure of that. Her Ariel magic couldn't save them both, and he'd drag her to Hell along with him.

Exactly what Zath intended. Zath sent that Fallen to harvest Willow's Ariel magic like some twisted fucking game. So, he sent Zath a little gift of his own: the Fallen, minus his wings.

If the Fallen had gotten to Willow first…

But the Fallen hadn't. He made sure of that. That Fallen wouldn't come anywhere near his soulmate or any other Chosen, ever again.

He rapped his knuckles on the oversized white paneled doors to Fate's sanctuary and waited for her to grant him entry. When they didn't open, he knocked again, louder this time. Several moments ticked by and he stood there on the steps, waiting.

He scoffed. This must be stage one of Fate's punishment. Any minute now, she'd make it rain and leave him out in the cold. No, she'd make it hail.

Strange sensations tugged deep inside his chest, like tiny, thin bands stretching until they snapped. He rubbed the heel of his hand over his sternum. What the hell? Those sensations only stirred when one of his brothers were in trouble, and he knew they were all accounted for in the Heavens.

After standing there for God knows how long, the sweet scent of cherry blossoms drifted in the air. Descending the steps, he tracked the scent around the side of the sanctuary. He pulled up short when he spotted Fate, sitting on a long marble bench with her back to him.

He approached with slow, steady steps. "Fate?"

She didn't respond nor turn his way, only tilted her head and peered at the bright, clear sky.

He veered around the side of the bench to stand before her. His breath caught. Fate's sapphire blue eyes were glazed with silver, as they did when she wielded her magic. He remained silent. A coil tightened low in his gut when he noticed her puffy and swollen lids, and the flushed cheeks on her ivory complexion stood out like the Fallen blood covering his bare hands.

Fate blinked a few times before her eyes returned to their usual color. She stood and smoothed down the front of her pale-yellow dress.

"Guardian," she said, with a slight nod.

He bowed his head. "Your Grace."

He didn't dare move as Fate drifted past him, halting at the edge of a nearby pond to peer into the murky water. The silence made him edgy. Like the calm before the storm, only Fate never created measly little storms. She unleashed fucking hurricanes.

When Aric couldn't stand the silence any longer, he cleared his throat. "I know I screwed up, and for that I'm sorry. The Fallen threatened the life of my Chosen in exchange for Willow. I protected what was mine."

"Not well enough, it seems," she responded.

Guess he wasn't out of the war zone.

Fate turned to face him. He straightened his shoulders, ready to accept his punishment. The quicker he accepted his punishment, the sooner he returned to Willow.

"Blaine saved you, did he not?"

He nodded. He'd forever owe his brother in arms.

Fate exhaled a heavy breath. "Very well."

He frowned. Hang on. Where was the catch? "I don't understand."

"Fate," Raven's voice bellowed from inside the sanctuary, full of crippling agony.

Fate turned to the building as Raven screamed her name again.

"You will understand soon enough, Aric." Her gaze dropped momentarily before she lifted her chin, regaining her composure. She glided toward the sanctuary, radiating her queen-of-the-fucking-universe power.

"Wait." He rushed forward. "That's it? I'm free to leave?"

He must've missed something. Fate wouldn't let a Guardian who'd just failed their Chosen walk away with nothing but a little chat. Waiting wasn't one of his strengths. He'd rather Fate dish out her punishment so he could get on with it.

Without slowing her stride, Fate replied, "No, this is only the beginning, Aric. Now it is time for you to repay Blaine. Now you must honor your oath to your brothers, and to me."

He paused, still confused. What the hell was going on? Instead of roasting his ass, Fate gave him a cryptic message about repaying a favor to Blaine and honoring his oath as a Guardian? Something was wrong.

As Fate opened the side door and entered the sanctuary, she glanced over her shoulder. "And so it begins."

In that moment, her words made no sense, didn't answer his many questions. But they sure as hell caused the hairs on his nape to stand to fucking attention.

He scrubbed his face with his hands, coming back to the present. It began all right. The nightmare of his existence, his torturous hell in the mortal realm, the heartbreak he caused Willow. It all began in that single moment. The moment Blaine severed his connection with the Heavens.

After Fate entered the sanctuary, Aric had bolted inside. The sight brought him to his knees; Raven, kneeling before Fate, and Gabe standing to the side with his head hung low.

In that moment, he connected all the dots and signed up for a rescue mission. Only back then, he'd misread the fucking fine print.

Chapter Twenty-One

Willow tiptoed up the stairs to the attic. Tonight, she'd put an end to Aric's visits and his hope of reuniting.

He'd made his intentions crystal clear, but she'd also made a decision. He wouldn't like it, but that didn't matter. She wanted her power and freedom, and to get it she needed to remain strong. She wouldn't let her desire for her ex-soulmate sway her.

Since their kiss three nights ago, Aric arrived on the rooftop at the same time without fail. Each night, her soul pulled her to the attic but instead of engaging with him, she stood behind the window under Blaine's glamour like a coward, watching Aric until he left at sunrise.

He lured her toward him without even knowing, made her remember how committed he was just by arriving each night. Though she remembered the other side of their not-so-happy love story—the part where, without warning, he ripped the bliss out from beneath her feet.

Their beautiful kiss the other night reminded her of the moment he left. In the far corners of her mind, she knew he wouldn't return. She'd felt it in her soul but held onto the hope anyway.

How many times would she let him drag her under? How much longer would she be a doormat? It didn't matter how many glorious centuries they shared. What mattered was when it came down to it, he chose the Guardians over her.

Nudging open the door to the attic, she slipped inside. She sensed Aric arrive a few moments ago but took her time wandering to the attic so she appeared less desperate. Because she wasn't. She was only impatient to end this charade.

Creeping across the room, she paused at the paneled window and glanced at the spot where Aric usually sat. He wasn't there.

Her heart ached a little at his absence, which was silly. She didn't want him there.

She stepped back from the glass with heaviness in her chest. It didn't matter. She'd just wait until he returned. Because he would, he'd proven that night after night. Why would tonight be any different?

Unless…She bit the inside of her lip. He'd given up?

If Aric changed his mind, then even better. It saved her from breaking the news to him.

As she turned away from the window, something fluttering on the rooftop caught her attention. She eased closer to the glass, narrowing her gaze. Where Aric usually sat was a piece of paper held down by a rock, the edges flapping in the breeze.

Another cowardice action by Aric. He couldn't even tell her face to face. Some things never changed. At least this way she avoided his whiskey eyes mushing her brain, until she forgot what to say. *Win-win.*

Break-up via a note was the smarter option. Not that she and Aric were together.

Except for that kiss…

Smoothing her hands down the front of her dress, she straightened the non-existent creases. The sooner she read the note the sooner she put all this behind her.

She lifted the window and climbed out onto the rooftop. Easing one foot in front of the other, she crossed the roof, maintaining a line of sight with the note so she didn't see how far she'd fall if she slipped on the dewy tiles. Without wings, the thought of falling made her nervous. From this height, the injuries would take weeks to heal, if not longer given the time it took to regenerate her wings. They were taking forever.

When she reached the note, she tucked the hem of her dress in behind her knees and crouched. The rock held down a thin piece of parchment and a single bright yellow wildflower—one she knew bloomed in this region once the snow melted.

Where did he find one so early?

Placing the rock aside, she lifted the note to read it.

Lo-Lo,

Each year when these wildflowers bloom, their vibrant color reminds me of your beauty. I meant what I said. I'm not giving up. Come meet me and I'll show you…

Underneath Aric's name, he'd scribbled a location. Given the directions he gave, he assumed she'd navigate by air.

Nope, she traveled by foot nowadays.

Meeting Aric somewhere foreign wasn't the smartest idea, and it wouldn't aid her defenses. The easier choice was to walk back inside and pretend she hadn't found the note. Pretend it blew away in the wind. That way, when she didn't show, Aric would come here where she had the advantage.

He couldn't sway her with his swoony words or looks while standing on the roof. There was also no risk of getting naked here when she shared the accommodation with two Fallen. But at some remote location? Ugh, she wouldn't even think of that.

She scanned the neat cursive writing, making her heart ache. Aric wrote her notes all the time when they were together. He'd place them beside their bed if he'd left before she woke.

He may have broken her heart, but he still deserved to know she ended their commitment when she Fell. Every minute she delayed telling him was another minute he remained hopeful of their reunion. For this charade to stop, she'd have to go to him. Afterward, she could move on with her plan.

She was sure the connection between her and Aric prevented her wings from regenerating. That was the only thing that made sense. Even though she hadn't seen it, she knew Aric still wore the band she gave him, tying his soul to hers.

Zath had cut off her wings, but her new Fallen wings should have grown already. Her connection with Aric held her back. By any means necessary, she needed to retrieve the band from him to complete her transition.

With the note and flower in one hand, she ducked inside and made her way down to the ground level. On her way out, she grabbed the cell phone Slater gave her. After a few goes, she figured out the map function and punched in the location.

She groaned. No way. The place was in the middle of a forest. A blink of an eye if she flew. A trek and a half by foot.

Another damn reason to get her wings back. Another painful reminder of her failure.

Bone deep exhaustion and lack of powers took its toll on her strength and soon she wouldn't be able to lift a dagger, let alone throw one. She needed this nightmare to end. The sooner the better.

Holding the phone face up in her hand, she followed the little blue line down the road and into the night.

Chapter Twenty-Two

What's taking her so long?

Aric paced back and forth in front of a secluded log cabin, eyeing the dark clouds. Willow should've arrived hours ago. He'd left the note on the rooftop in the same spot he sat every night. Their connection stirred the moment he arrived on the roof, and he knew she was inside the mansion, though he couldn't see her. But he didn't need visual confirmation. Knowing she came to the attic each night told him he could still win her back. If she didn't want to see him, she would've stayed away.

Damn it. It only took a short amount of time to fly from Blaine's creepy mansion to here. He searched the clouds again. Maybe she didn't see the note? Was the rock not heavy enough, and the note blew away? Maybe she got lost? He wrote precise directions on the bottom so she couldn't get lost, but perhaps she misread them?

Unless…she got hurt. In the absence of their full soulmate connection, he had no way of knowing her location or if she was injured. He unfurled his wings. He should fly to her, make sure she'd found the note. Make sure she was safe. But if she went another route, he might miss her.

"Argh."

He swooped to the sky and hovered high above the

roof of the cabin searching for Willow. All he saw was an endless line of pine trees in every direction and low, misty clouds. Even in the darkness, he could spot a pair of crimson wings from a mile away.

His heart sank, a tight knot forming in his gut. *She's not coming…*

"Damn you, Fate." He sneered at the Heavens.

He blamed Fate for this whole disaster. Fate screwed him under the guise of redemption, when she signed him up for a failed mission of a different kind. Had he known, he wouldn't've agreed. Then he wouldn't be stuck in this hell zone on loop for fucking centuries. Instead, he and Willow would be together, curled up in each other's arms back in the Heavens. Fate was to blame for tearing him away from his soulmate and he'd never forgive her.

He lowered his head, staring at the cabin roof. At what point did he acknowledge Willow wasn't coming?

Drifting down to the grass, he stood in front of the cabin. A simple one-bedroom timber structure with a porch along the front and a two-seater swing hanging at one end. Off to one side, a narrow creek flowed year round, with giant forest pines surrounding the edges. The spot was so damn similar to the place he and Willow shared in the Heavens, right down to the colorful wildflowers that bloomed by the riverbanks each spring. When he'd stumbled on the location, he assumed Fate had sent him a sign that he and Willow would reunite. So, he built the cabin for her and waited.

It turned out to be a cruel joke. For almost a hundred years, the cabin sat dormant, waiting for Willow.

With heavy steps, he trudged up the steps onto the

porch. Spending the night alone required a helluva lot more whiskey.

****

Distant cursing woke Aric from his nap on the porch swing. He jolted upright and grabbed a nearby dagger.

"Not again," a female voice grumbled.

Not any female. *Willow.*

Sheathing the dagger, he leaped the porch railing and bolted into the forest toward her voice. When he found her, he skidded to a halt. The sight took his breath away and not in a good way. Her tangled hair had twigs and bits of pine needles stuck in it, her cheeks were flushed, and she winced with every step.

He offered his hand. "Are you all right? It looks like you've walked for hours."

She stormed past him, ignoring his offer of help. "Well…I haven't. That would be ridiculous."

He glanced at her bare feet, covered in dirt and mud. "Where are your shoes?"

"I threw them away. I will never understand why mortals insist on wearing such painful attire."

Snapping out of his confusion, he hurried to catch up with her. "Where did you land?"

Her step faltered. "I don't know." She waved her arm out to one side. "Over there somewhere."

Something in her tone hinted she lied, reminding him she was a Fallen, no longer an Ariel. But why bother lying about where she landed?

Exiting the forest, he led her toward the cabin. His gut tightened, anticipating her reaction. When they curved around to the porch, she halted. His heart thundered behind his ribs. Would she notice? Would she care?

"The cabin…it's exactly the same," she whispered.

He reached for her hand and this time she let him. "I built it decades ago, thinking one day we'd be together. I thought we could use it as our home away from home."

Her shoulders dropped. "Aric…"

"Don't say it, baby. Please. Just give me tonight."

Willow drew in her bottom lip, something she often did when making a decision. She came here when he thought she wouldn't. That meant something. Plus, his romantic plan had only just begun.

"At least sit and rest your feet." He bit the inside of his cheek to stop from smirking. "They look like they've walked enough for one night."

She glanced at the cabin then back at him. "Fine. We have things we need to discuss anyway."

That didn't sound good. Shit. Convincing her to stay might be harder than he thought.

Once on the porch, he motioned to the chair swing. "Take a seat while I get us a drink."

She nodded and padded to the chair. Warmth spread through his chest. He'd ached for this moment for so many years and now he never wanted it to end. He had to lay all his cards on the table, had to show her he didn't forget. Had to prove he was sorry.

With lightning speed, in case she left, he threw together some food, poured her a glass of wine and himself another whiskey. Using his ass to open the door, he backed onto the porch and found Willow curled up on the swing as she had thousands of times in the Heavens. The sight made his chest ache worse than ever.

After placing the platter on a small side table, he passed her the glass.

"Thank you."

She smiled, but it didn't reach her eyes. Nor did it lighten the dark circles underneath. God, she looked like she'd walked non-stop for the past week.

Sitting beside her, he used his boot to kick off a gentle swing. Several moments passed in silence, interrupted only by the wind rustling between the pines. If he drowned it out, he could concentrate on the steady beat of her heart still in time with his.

After a long sip of whiskey, he placed his glass on the side table and lifted her legs, twisting her around so she sat lengthways on the seat with her feet in his lap. With slow, firm pressure, he kneaded her soles with his thumbs just the way she liked.

She sank further into the seat with a heavy sigh. "That feels so good."

"Anyone would think you walked here."

Her face blanched, but she quickly recovered. "No, I just landed in the forest and stepped on every twig and rock between here and there."

The slight twitch under her eye told him she lied again. He didn't call her on it though, instead, he continued massaging, content with having her close after so long. It amazed him how easily they slipped into a comfortable rhythm in each other's company. If only it lasted.

"Why did you ask me to come here?"

Without pausing her foot rub, he shrugged a shoulder. "I wanted to show you the cabin. Prove to you I didn't forget."

She drew back her feet to sit cross-legged. "Things

aren't the same with us anymore. I'm no longer the same Ariel you fell in love with, nor am I the same angel you claimed as your soulmate." She looked away, her voice softening. "I'm no longer an…angel. What we had is over."

She'd said that already, but it didn't matter. He wouldn't give up until his last breath.

God, he well and truly sucked at this romance shit. All he could offer was his heart, because no words expressed his love. No words justified what he'd done. But he had to try. This might be his only chance.

He twisted to face her, laying his arm along the top of the seat. "For centuries, I've wandered this earth. Wandered, Willow. Not explored, not enjoyed, not experienced. Wandered. I've existed in a fog so thick I barely knew what was happening around me, consumed with the sole mission of returning to you." He paused, trying to find the right words. "My body was in this realm, but my heart, my soul, remained in the Heavens with you. On the fucking ground at your feet." He took her hand in his. "I never once forgot you. You're my life, Lo-Lo, my entire existence."

She glanced away, drawing in her bottom lip.

He squeezed her hand. "Look at me, baby." When she did, he continued. "I know I fucked up. I should never have agreed to Fate's deal. But believe me, I had no idea she'd exile me."

There, he'd said it. Now he hoped she felt the spark between them, and it was enough for her to forgive him.

Chapter Twenty-Three

With the pad of her fingers, Willow wiped the tears from her eyes. Aric said the words she'd waited so long to hear. But hearing them now made it too painful.

"Why would Fate do such a thing?"

He let go of her hand, the loss of contact like a slap in the face, so quickly she ached for his touch.

His gaze became distant. "I…screwed up with a Chosen. It seems I have a knack for it," he muttered the last part under his breath.

Her brow creased. "Why would she banish you from the Heavens?"

He took her hand again, interweaving their fingers. "I fucked up bad. Zath sent a Fallen after you because he needs Ariel power to regenerate his wings."

A shudder ran through her. Oh, she knew all about that and didn't care to relive the memory. Knowing that Zath hunted her for centuries made her stomach churn.

Using his thumb, Aric drew small circles on the back of her hand. "I wouldn't let him find you. To bait me, the Fallen he sent threatened to harvest my Chosen's light instead." His hand squeezed hers. "He made me choose between you and my Chosen. You and my oath. A choice I never thought I'd have to make again."

Her heart split into two. Aric had protected her against Zath, choosing her over his oath to protect his assigned Chosen. All this time she thought his duty came first.

She swallowed the lump forming in her throat. "You sacrificed a Chosen to protect me?"

He didn't respond, but it didn't matter. She caught the answer in his tightening features. All this time, she'd hated him, and he'd protected her.

His thumb drew lazy circles. "After, I couldn't let the Fallen take the Chosen's light." He peered toward the dark forest. "I severed his wings, so he had no power when he returned to Hell."

She bit hard on the inside of her lip to prevent gasping. Blaine was right, Aric had tortured Fallen. Was that Fallen his first one after Zath? How many Fallen had he mutilated?

His gaze returned to her. "Blaine found me and pulled me back from the edge. Another heartbeat and my soul would've been beyond repair. I thought because of our connection, I would drag you to Hell with me. I couldn't do that." His chest rose with a deep inhale. "When I went to the sanctuary for my punishment, Fate was a mess, though at the time I didn't know why."

She remained silent, processing his words. The last time she saw Aric in the Heavens, she'd questioned him about the black blood on his hands, but he'd told her not to worry. Then he'd kissed her as though he'd never see her again. Her heart squeezed tight at the memory. In his own way, he'd said goodbye before Fate punished him.

"When I entered the sanctuary, I learned Blaine had saved me right before he severed his connection with the Heavens. Raven had already made a deal with

Fate to bring him back." His lips thinned. "EJ and I couldn't let Raven go his own. I owed Blaine my life."

"Why didn't you tell me?" she whispered.

He lifted his gaze to hers. "I didn't want to disappoint you. I thought Fate would send me to Tartirim as punishment. If that happened, I'd rather that you remembered our last kiss than my actions with that Fallen. Instead, Fate offered me a chance for redemption. When I agreed, I thought we'd mist to the mortal realm as we had millions of times before, grab Blaine then return home. I'd return to you and everything would be back to normal. But that didn't happen. We didn't realize she'd banished us until we arrived and could no longer mist."

The pain in his voice shattered another piece of the protective armor surrounding her heart. Without knowing his side of the story, she'd imagined countless scenarios for why he'd abandoned her, and each one ended with him choosing his brethren over her. Would it have made a difference if she knew the truth? *Absolutely.* But finding out now was too late.

He wiped a tear from her cheek. She leaned into his touch.

"I know it hurts, baby. Trust me, I know how bad it hurts. But I need you to hear this. I can't stomach the thought of you thinking I'd forgotten about you."

This was not the conversation she'd planned. This version raised way too many feelings that cut deep. Regardless, she'd made her decision based on the information available at the time. Regrets were pointless. She had to move forward with her plan and end her connection with Aric so she could regenerate her wings. Then she could set herself free.

She drew back from his touch. "There's nothing you can do to change the past. You chose to go on the mission with Raven and chose the Guardians over us."

He squeezed her hand, refusing to let go. "I had to save Blaine. He was a brother to all of us, and we vowed our lives to one another. I owed him, Willow. Blaine saved me from an eternity in Hell. He saved us both."

When Aric scrubbed a palm over his stubbly jaw, she spotted the band around his wrist. Back then, he'd wrongly assumed her Ariel powers weren't strong enough to save him. They were. Through the band, her powers continually fueled the light in his soul. Aric's soul would never blacken, no matter how dark his actions. But because of Fate, the regeneration no longer flowed both ways, and her powers faded.

He brushed his knuckles along her jaw. "We didn't realize how far Blaine Fell. Christ, it took a century just to track him down, and even then, the timing was pure luck. The Guardian link between us severed when he Fell." His thumb brushed over her bottom lip causing tingles low in her belly. "We didn't even know where to look."

Another chip in the armor. Each second she sat on the swing with him, her willpower dwindled away. Soon, there'd be nothing left, and he'd lure her in with his words and those whiskey eyes she couldn't avoid.

She shook her head, attempting to clear her thoughts. The wine scrambled her emotions and heated her blood.

"Aric, it doesn't matter now. You made your choice, and I made mine."

In less than a heartbeat, he gripped her hips and

slid her toward him. She sucked in a sharp breath. Only a sliver of air separated them. Those damn eyes melted her into a gooey mess.

His hands cradled her jaw. "Fate abandoned us, but never think I abandoned you. To abandon is to forget, and I could never forget you."

Oh, damn him…

She smashed her lips against his. Or did he kiss her? *Who cares?*

Their kiss was fast, hot and wet, and full of pent up emotion. More intense than the night on the rooftop.

Trickles of life seeped inside her as he swept his tongue over hers. He tilted her head to deepen their kiss, sending swells of pleasure between her legs.

She came here to tell him she'd ended their relationship so she could take back the band and focus on regenerating her wings. Kissing Aric wasn't necessary for that conversation.

Oh, but it felt so good.

As though she were as light as a feather, he lifted her onto his lap, straddling him on the chair. A possessive growl rumbled deep inside his chest when she raked her fingers through his thick black hair.

Quickly their kiss turned frantic, filled with longing and hunger. All reasoning and sense flew out the window. Lost in the sensations overtaking her body, she rocked against the hard length in his jeans, seeking release of the tightly coiled tension in her core. His hands squeezed her thighs, pressing her harder against him.

She scraped her nails against his scalp. It felt so good to touch him again, to taste him, to inhale his rich masculine scent.

His hands slipped underneath her dress making her breath hitch. Too lost in the moment, she didn't want to stop. His rough palms heated along the outside of her thighs causing a delicious ache to burn in her core. She knew how skillful his hands were, and she had been without for far too long.

She could touch Aric for eternity. Clench his perfectly formed biceps, graze her fingers along his well-defined chest. The way their mouths moved together as one sent her floating on a cloud of desire. Nothing compared to kissing him. Every time his lips touched hers, it felt as though they were made for each other.

Every nerve ending along her skin sizzled, her blood heating to the point of boiling as moisture pooled at the apex of her thighs.

He groaned as he brushed her damp panties. Desperate for more, she raised her hips and he slipped his hand between her legs. Without slowing their kiss, he tugged aside her panties, venturing closer to her aching peak.

"Aric!" she gasped, the moment his fingers brushed her core.

"God, I've missed you," he moaned between breaths.

She missed him, too. By the throbbing ache between her legs, she'd missed him touching her as well.

His finger found her bud, stroking in a light and steady motion, completely the opposite to wild desperation happening between their lips. She grazed her hands down his shirt to the waist of his jeans and unbuckled his belt.

Aric drew back, breaths fast and heavy. "Lo-Lo, I don't wanna rush this."

The dark primal look in his eyes said differently. Before she could protest, he took her mouth again in another possessive kiss.

Somewhere in the far corners of her mind, she registered a faint voice urging her to stop. This was a mistake. Being intimate with Aric made it harder to walk away. But, oh goodness, she couldn't stop.

Not because of the orgasm that built inside, nor the fact she'd been without any touch since he left. What kept her kissing him was the yearning that consumed every cell in her body. As though her soul had lain dormant for centuries and only now awakened. The spiritual connection they once shared crackled and sparked to life, and she felt it threading back together as a glimmer of light seeped into her soul.

Aric groaned, stroking her, his other hand squeezing her hip. She clenched his shoulders, climbing higher until she teetered on the edge, needy for release. As though he read her mind, he slipped a finger inside her and she fell apart.

"Aric," she cried.

Her core pulsed with such intensity it made her dizzy. All her bottled tension and anger fizzled out in a rush.

As the final pulses of her orgasm ebbed, Aric withdrew and wrapped his arms around her lower back, holding her tight.

She leaned her forehead against his, their heavy breaths colliding between them.

"I love you, baby."

Another crack in the wall that protected her heart.

"I've missed you," she admitted aloud for the first time. She drew back and found a smug grin on his face.

"Have you now?"

She slapped his shoulder. "Don't get all cocky."

His eyes darkened, and he swept a wayward curl from her face. "I said I'm not giving up on us. I'll fight to win you back until my very last breath."

Her chest tightened, recalling the reason she met him tonight. "What if I don't want you to fight for me? What if I'm done?"

He shook his head. "Too bad. I lost you once, and I ain't going through that shit again."

She exhaled a long breath—relief or resignation, she didn't know, but it eased some of the pain behind her ribs.

"I know I hurt you, I see that. But don't give up on us, Lo-Lo." He brushed his knuckles along her jaw. "You're the only one for me."

Leaning in, she kissed him again, a soft, slow kiss, one that made her insides reignite. Massive cracks appeared in her protective wall. Soon, it would fall in a heap.

She had to hop off him. Her brain didn't function being this close to him. Now that the euphoric feeling of her orgasm faded, the reality of their situation crashed front and center in her mind. She was a Fallen. He was a Guardian.

She scrambled off his lap to stand.

He followed, standing so close she inhaled his scent of well-worn leather seeped in rich earth. Close enough, she noticed the faint jagged scar on his cheek and the dark rim circling his irises. Being this close didn't lower her heart rate. It raised it through the roof.

With a gleam in his eye, Aric lowered his head to whisper in her ear. "I haven't forgotten the sound of your moans when I'm inside you."

Her knees quivered.

"And I most certainly haven't forgotten your taste."

Oh no, she was in big trouble now. Vivid memories of all the tricks his tongue preformed replayed in her mind while heat pooled between her legs. Great. Now her breaths quickened.

How did she respond? The Fallen part of her wanted to scream, "No way, buddy, you lost your chance with me, but thanks for the orgasm." But the other side of her, the side somehow still connected with Aric melted like a marshmallow over a flaming fire.

Which half would win? Which path should she choose?

He eased back, and his sexy grin set her heart flipping inside out. She fisted her dress to stop from clawing off his shirt.

She cleared her throat. "There's no point in saying things like that. We can't be together. Tonight was a momentary lapse of judgement."

He cocked a brow. "We're destined to be together for eternity. Reminding you of how good we are is only stage one." He kissed her, lingering for a moment. "Meet me here at the same time tomorrow."

Before she responded, he trailed a finger along her jaw then strolled off the porch with a sexy swagger in his step. *Damn him!* She watched like an enchanted princess as he unfurled his majestic black wings and soared to the sky, leaving her a hot, flustered mess on the porch.

Her chest tightened as she tracked him until he disappeared in the clouds. He said he didn't care about the color of her wings, but what would say if he knew the truth?

She wasn't an angel or a Fallen without her wings. After that bastard mutilated her, she was nothing.

Turning away, she peered inside the cabin. Maybe she should stay here for the night rather than enduring the long walk back to Blaine's mansion. She sighed, glancing at her swollen feet, because she'd stupidly thrown her shoes into the forest a mile into the walk. The shoes hurt so much they could live out their existence lost in the abyss.

They weren't the cause of her frequent stopping along the way. The exhaustion she fought since arriving in the mortal realm doubled in intensity. A few times on her way here, she almost collapsed on the side of the road. No amount of rest helped. And after that little moment with Aric, her muscles were so relaxed she could fall into a deep sleep and never wake.

She glanced at the porch swing and the awful ache in her chest returned. Aric had gone to great lengths to replicate their cabin in the Heavens and staying here brought back all those memories. She wasn't ready to face them, yet, the cabin made her feel a slight sense of peace for the first time since she escaped Hell and she wasn't ready to leave. She should rest before walking all the way back.

After a quick search inside, she found a throw rug and curled up with it on the porch swing. She pulled the throw high around her neck, inhaling Aric's scent as her lids slid closed. For the first time in an awfully long time, Aric leaving didn't rip a hole in her heart. Instead, his departure tonight felt like a turning point, the beginning of a new chapter rather than the end of one. But at what cost?

Chapter Twenty-Four

Aric lowered a wrapped shoebox on the roof of Blaine's mansion and slipped a note and wildflower between the ribbon. Tonight, he felt a swell of certainty knowing Willow would climb out the attic window and find his little gift before she met him at the cabin.

This romance business had become his new favorite pastime.

It felt so good being with her again, breathing in her stormy scent, spoiling her. Imagining her bright hazel eyes sparkle with excitement when she opened the shoebox made him all giddy. Maybe he'd buy her a new pair of shoes every day for the rest of eternity.

Straightening, he glanced at the box. He bought the best, comfiest pair of shoes in town—her feet would thank him. With a grin a mile wide, he took to the sky heading to SubZero.

A low cloud bank gave him the freedom to fly straight over the rooftops undetected. Tonight, the lights in the center of Summit Creek shone brighter like they called to him, welcomed him to town, and filled his chest with a warmth he hadn't felt for centuries.

He veered to the left, spotting the dark empty parking lot at the rear of the club, before touching down on the gravel. Once again, he had an uneventful shift. If more Fallen didn't venture out of the shadows, he and the other Guardians would be out of a job. He'd have to take up knitting or some shit. Though, he could do this romancing gig fulltime and live a long and happy existence.

After his shift he could move onto the second part of his evening, the best part. If all went to plan, that part would have a lot more action.

His boots crunched the gravel as he headed up the alley to the entrance. Fallen sightings had decreased over the past few months. At the bonfire last year, there were more Fallen in town than Guardians with run-ins every night. But now? Their absence made him suspicious. Where the hell had they gone? Unless they were…hidden?

He wanted to ask Willow last night, but the thought gave him an uneasy feeling in his gut, like by asking, he used her for information. Eliciting knowledge from her because she was…one of them.

Could their situation be anymore screwed?

He hadn't told his brothers about his little rendezvous with her at the cabin. He didn't know why. Maybe he feared Raven would tell him to end their meetings? Or more accurately, Raven would tell him to end her. He and the Guardians all took the same oath to destroy the Fallen in this realm. That was before she became one.

Exiting the narrow alley, he turned right and arrived at the entrance to SubZero. The Guardians met at the end of each shift to debrief. Usually, they caught up at the mansion, but tonight EJ wanted to meet at the club. After he reported in, he'd fly to his cabin to, hopefully, join Willow.

His blood heated at the thought. God, no wonder he couldn't keep his head in the game tonight. The taste of her mouth with her scent plastered over his skin, made his mind a scrambled heap. All he thought about was seeing her, kissing her, hearing her scream his name.

They were so perfect together before Fate stepped in and blew their fucking world apart. Now, he and Willow were finally in the same realm again, and he wouldn't let the chance slip away to make up for their centuries of lost time. He vowed an eternity to her, and he didn't go back on his word.

Entering the club, he jogged down the metal staircase with lightness in his step. One drink with his brothers, then he was outta there.

Arriving at the table in the VIP section, Aric fist-bumped River and EJ.

"How goes it, bro?" River asked.

Aric turned a chair around and straddled it. "Nothing on my end. You?"

River shook his head. "Not a single Fallen."

He glanced at EJ.

"Same. I spotted Slater and he frickin' smirked like he was invincible." EJ sipped his drink without choking on chunks of lime. "In the absence of any other Fallen, I wonder if Blaine would retaliate if we took out Slater? I feel like we're going frickin' redundant down here."

He scanned the club for a waitress but didn't spot any. "He might be a little pissed considering Slater's his baddy sidekick."

Being Blaine's sidekick was a risky move given he usually stabbed them in the back.

River peered into the neck of his beer. "Well, that went down super-fast. I'm gonna order the next round at the bar. The floor staff are run off their feet tonight. Plus, then I can bust out some mid-week moves on the way." River pushed away from the table and stood.

"I reckon the DJ's about a hundred years too young to know any sappy eighties love songs," EJ said, stifling a laugh.

River glanced at the DJ then back at EJ, a mischievous grin forming on his lips. "Challenge accepted."

"Oh, great," EJ groaned under his breath.

"At least you didn't wear that ridiculous palm tree shirt," Aric retorted.

"Don't knock it 'til you try it, bro."

Aric exaggerated rolling his eyes. "Thanks, but I think I'll pass."

River strolled toward the bar, waving his arms above his head in time with the music.

"Only the cool kids can pull it off anyway," he chortled, knowing damn well Aric could hear him.

"Cool kids my ass. There's nothing cool, or manly, about wearing a yellow shirt covered with tiny palm trees."

EJ raised his glass in the air and laughed. "I'll drink to that."

A neat whiskey arrived at the table, together with another vodka for EJ, sent by River, who had made it to the bar. God no! Now he weaved through the crowd on the dance floor, beelining for the DJ. If that woman played a row of eighties love ballads, he'd down the whiskey in one go and high tail it outta there.

EJ tipped the limes from his finished glass into his new one. "Give me the latest on Red."

How much should he tell? EJ was his comrade, his brother in arms, he trusted him with his life. Hell, he'd take a Purah bullet for the guy. But could he trust EJ with his plan to win back Willow's heart regardless of the color of her wings? How the hell would EJ respond?

Before he formulated an answer, EJ sniggered. "Have you romanced the hell outta her yet?"

Fucking hell. How many people knew about his conversation with Tayla? "Clearly, Raven can't keep his mouth shut."

EJ chugged his salad-bar. "Nah, River blabbed. I think he heard it from Raine, who heard it from Ellen…"

"For fuck's sake," Aric groaned.

EJ shrugged. "Red's arrival in the mortal realm is hot gossip in the house."

"Well, it shouldn't be." Aric glanced at the dance floor and found River front and center, waving his hand to get the DJ's attention.

"I hope you know what you're doing, Ric. Like it or not, Red's a Fallen now, and we both know how hard it is to save one."

Trust EJ to give him the zero-bullshit speech.

Aric swirled the whiskey in his glass. He knew how tough it was to return Willow to the Heavens; he didn't need the reminder. Every day for the past few weeks, he woke with the hope this nightmare was all some sick joke. Then reality crashed in and snuffed out the light.

"Why does Fate insist on making the path so fucking twisted?"

"If the path was easy, Ric, it wouldn't be fun. Look at it this way, having her in the same realm is a lot frickin' better than having you pining over memories for centuries."

"Except she's a Fallen. Which hasn't stopped me

from wanting her. God…" He raked a hand through his hair. "I can't get her outta my head."

EJ leaned back in the chair, turning to face him. "Has your rooftop stalking worked?"

Raven needed a serious reminder of the brotherhood code, specifically not sharing every fucking detail with the entire household. "I'm not stalking her."

EJ raised a brow.

Maybe he stalked her in the beginning, but that was before she climbed out the window and talked to him. Before she kissed him back. He wasn't stalking her now; he was in full romance mode.

"I made progress last night. Baby steps." He scrubbed his jaw. "It's like she's ignited this fire inside me that burns hotter the more I think about her. It's like…"

"Nothing's changed?"

He studied EJ, whose ice-blue eyes glowed under the colorful lights. "Exactly."

EJ picked a basil leaf from his tumbler and ate it. "Is it weird seeing her with crimson wings?"

Aric swallowed, trying to loosen the lump parked low in his throat. "I dunno. I haven't seen her wings yet." He paused, searching for the right words. "Something just doesn't feel right."

"How so?"

"I can't put my finger on it. I don't get that sensation when I'm near her, like I do when I'm near a Fallen, including Blaine. With her, all I feel is a pull through the connection between us. I thought because she's a Fallen I wouldn't feel it, but I do." He pushed the empty glass into the center of the table. "To be honest, she doesn't look well. Her skin's all pasty and shit, like she needs a serious boost from the sun. Blaine, Slater and every other Fallen doesn't have that problem, so why is she different?"

"Ask her. If she's talking to you and not decapitating you, then it couldn't hurt."

He exhaled a long, heavy breath. "I don't wanna spook her, you know, in case it's all a dream that suddenly ends with her leaving."

His phone vibrated in his pocket at the same time the home screen on EJ's lit up on the table. He read the group text from Raven before returning the phone to his jeans.

He frowned at EJ. "What could be so urgent that Raven and Gabe need us to hang tight at the club?"

"Dunno, Ric. But I hope Gabe doesn't expect jazz music and cocktails, 'cause it ain't that kinda club."

Shit. His gut twisted into a knot. Gabe never appeared in public, let alone at a venue packed with mortals. The Archangel only ever misted to the Guardian mansion or on the grounds. There must be something going down.

River placed a fresh round of drinks on the table, and he sank into a chair. Before they spoke, the rear exit door swung open and Raine entered the club with Raven and Gabe a few steps behind. If they hoped for a discreet entry, they failed. Raine always turned heads when she walked through the club, male and female, but Raven and Gabe stole the show tonight. Those two projected the power and strength of a military tank plowing through an entire army. Mortals scampered out of the way as they strode to the table.

He couldn't sit any longer, unease and uncertainty

swirled together in the pit of his stomach like a boat caught in rough seas. He stood behind his chair gripping the backrest.

Raine sat next to River, but she remained silent. Nothing out of the ordinary. Raven and Gabe halted a step away from the table. With a flick of Gabe's wrist, he paused time. Man, he missed having powers. In a split second, the noise of the club vanished, mortals stilled, some with their arms in the air or drinks at their lips. Using power in a public place proved this conversation with Gabe wasn't a pep talk. It was serious.

Gabe slung his suit jacket over the back of a chair.

Aric couldn't take it any longer. The eerie silence, the waiting, the foreboding.

He peered across the table at Raven. "Raven, what's going on?" No time for small talk. "Is it about Willow?"

Raven's expression hardened. "I'll let Gabe explain. But listen carefully."

He mentally counted down from twenty. Either that or lose his shit at Gabe because he remained so goddamn calm. *Seventeen...sixteen...fifteen.* His clenched fists ached, shooting wild bursts of pain up his forearm. *Fourteen...thirteen...*

Gabe grabbed a glass from the center of the table and downed the whiskey. Gabe drinking? Things were even worse than he thought.

Three...two...one... "Right. Now that you've had a drink, can someone tell me what the fuck is wrong?"

Gabe pivoted his way. The grim expression on his face said it all.

"It seems there was an interruption during

Willow's Fall."

"What kind of interruption?"

"A ripple between the realms."

What the hell? "Was it Fate?" It wouldn't surprise him if she threw another twist.

"Perhaps. I have been unable to reach her since I discovered the information."

Was he slow or was Gabe drip feeding him? "What does this have to do with Willow's Fall?"

Raven stood, leaning on the back of the chair. The tension at the table made his legs jumpy.

"It seems the ripple caused Willow's soul to become stuck in Anahel, while her physical form remains in the mortal realm."

The big-ass knot lodged in the back of his throat plummeted to his gut. "Anahel? How does that happen? I thought only mortal souls get stuck in the in-between?"

He'd heard souls wasted away in Anahel because they couldn't enter the Heavens. They were held back by a loved one in the mortal realm or a sense of unfinished business. The longer they remained there, the more their soul withered away until it no longer existed and drifted into the ether. Some angels believed Fate transformed the soul's essence into power only she could wield.

Gabe's gaze moved around the table before returning to Aric. "I know of it occurring before with immortals. Where a connection is so strong it causes a rift to open in the realms, preventing the soul from returning. Or in this case, progressing. I believe that connection held Willow's soul back from entering Hell."

Held back? He shoved his fingers through his hair. What if the dream he had of Willow's Fall wasn't actually a dream? Blaine had said he'd described Hell. The dream was so vivid, he'd sworn he stood right in the center of a blazing inferno. He'd heard Willow, reached for her, called her name even though he hadn't seen her.

"Could our bond be strong enough to mist me to the outer realm of Hell and prevent her soul from entering? And cause a rift in the realms, flinging her soul into Anahel?"

Gabe nodded. "I believe so."

Because Willow severed her connection with the Heavens, she didn't have enough light to reenter.

It all made sense. Why her skin was so pasty, why she looked exhausted all the time. He staggered back from the table. If her soul remained in Anahel she'd...die.

He stared hard at Gabe. "How do I fix this?"

Gabe's lips thinned. "You can't, my friend. Only Willow can. She must choose and only then, once her decision is final, can her soul depart Anahel."

Raine jammed a throwing star onto the table. "Choose between light and dark."

"While her soul is in Anahel, she is neither here nor there. I suspect your connection is what holds her there. To release her, you must let her go, let her leave the mortal realm. After that, her physical form will reunite with her soul and enter the Heavens. Or Hell, if she chooses." Gabe's expression softened. "The longer she remains in Anahel, the quicker her soul will deteriorate, until there is nothing left. But Aric...the choice must be her own."

Deep down he knew that.

Let Willow go? No fucking way. He couldn't let her go. He'd just got her back.

The thought of everything he put her through made his stomach churn. She wanted the pain to stop, yet, he kept causing it. Then, making him more of an asshole, he'd interrupted her Fall and flung her soul into Anahel. All because he held onto hope.

Regardless of her choice, whether she chose light or dark, he had to let her go.

Raven rounded the table and squeezed his shoulder. "If her soul is in Anahel, my man, that means she hasn't transitioned to a Fallen. There's still hope."

That fucking word again. Hope.

"I'm kinda losing hope, man," he grumbled.

"I didn't think you ever gave up." River leaned back in his chair. "Weren't you just talking about wooing her back? If Willow needs to choose between light and dark, then show her the light." He raised his open arms in the air like he praised Fate.

Raine scoffed. "From what I hear, you need to up your game. Not every girl likes handpicked flowers and ballet pumps."

Aric scowled at Raine. "Hand-*grown* flowers. And I'm damn sure by now I know what Willow does and doesn't like."

"Have you tried getting naked?" EJ lifted a shoulder. "I find that always gets a positive response."

This wasn't a fucking joke. No, he hadn't tried getting naked; he was warming up to it. But sex didn't erase all the pain he caused.

Ignoring all the not-so-helpful advice, he turned to Gabe. "If I convince her to choose light, how do you know she can reenter the Heavens?"

Gabe inclined his head. "If she chooses the Heavens, I'll make sure she's granted entry."

Aric stared at the table and contemplated his options. If Willow returned to the Heavens, she'd be safe, and her soul would heal. It saved her and prevented her becoming a Fallen. If she chose Hell…nope, not going there.

Lifting his head, he gave a curt nod to Gabe. With another wave of his hand, Gabe lifted the freeze on time and the club bustled back to life. Music blared from the speakers, and mortals resumed dancing as though a grenade hadn't landed in his lap.

Convincing Willow to return to a place she fled, a place that held so many painful memories, would be his toughest mission yet. But he had to try. Choosing Hell wasn't an option.

Chapter Twenty-Five

Tiny caged butterflies fluttered deep in her belly as Willow climbed out the attic window onto the roof. She'd sensed Aric arrive a few minutes ago and raced up the stairs, but he'd left before she saw him.

She padded to the spot where he usually sat and found a rectangular box wrapped in a bright yellow ribbon with a wildflower and a rolled note. A smile filled her face as she slipped the note free and read it.

Lo-Lo,

I'm counting down the minutes until I see you again. After I check in at the club, I'm all yours. See you at our cabin.

If the walls around her heart were still there, they would've crumbled into dust. She rolled up the note and opened the box. Her breath caught. Underneath a layer of delicate white tissue paper were a pair of pretty bronze shoes.

Oh, Aric. Forever winning her heart through his subtle hints of love.

Placing the box down, she slipped on the shoes. A perfect fit. Her feet would still hurt after walking to his cabin, but the thoughtfulness made her heart swell and ache at the same time.

Last night, he'd poured out his heart to her, the reason for his exile and the fact he hadn't given up hope after all these centuries. When he'd kissed her again, something inside fused back together, like their bond also hoped for their reunion. She had, too, for many years until that hope morphed into resentment.

In one night, he made her feel whole, worthy, loved. One single night reignited her love for him, mended her broken heart and repaired their fractured bond as though eons of distance and time had never separated them. But part of her still held back. The part he knew nothing of, and she feared once he did, he'd reject her. The thought of severing their bond forever now confused the hell out of her.

He'd told her he wouldn't give up, but he would when he found out about her wings. Every time she lied it ate away at her. She had to tell him the truth before he figured it out himself. If he was serious about not giving up, then he deserved to know exactly what he fought for. Knowing she kept a secret from him made her sick in her stomach.

Tonight, she'd tell him.

She slipped the note and flower inside the box and closed the lid. When she left the Heavens, she promised herself a fresh start. If she wanted Aric in her new life, then owning her failures was the first step. Tonight, when she met him at his cabin, she'd come clean. No more lies.

After climbing back through the window, she dropped the box in her room before making her way downstairs. His note said he'd meet her at the cabin after checking in with the other Guardians at the club. But she couldn't wait. She needed to tell him now before she lost her nerve. Instead of going straight to the cabin, she'd surprise him at the club, and then, if he still wanted her, they could continue their night together.

Grabbing her phone, she programmed the club's address into the map and headed out the front door.

"Good evening, love."

Blaine stood beside the town car, dressed in the same worn leather jacket and black jeans. Did he own anything else?

"Are you heading into town?" she asked. Driving took less time than walking and kept her new shoes intact.

"Sure am. Would you like an escort?"

She rolled her eyes at his protective tone. Escort? She wasn't a mortal teenager needing an adult watching over her safety. She'd mastered the use of a dagger. Remembering to bring one when she went out was the problem.

"I wouldn't mind a lift to that mortal club."

He opened the door for her with a smirk on his face. "Apparently, it's the place to be tonight."

Whatever, she didn't care for seeing anyone else but Aric. She knew by now if the other Guardians saw her, they wouldn't harm her. They had always protected her as though she were one of them. Thinking Slater could convince her otherwise made her feel silly.

"Sure." She tucked her phone into her dress pocket and slid into the car.

****

By the time the driver pulled up in front of the club, those butterflies had broken out of the cage and fluttered like crazy. How would Aric react when she told him? Would he still feel the same or would he walk away forever?

Regardless of his reaction, she had to tell him.

Lying didn't sit right. They had been together for so long, he deserved to know the truth.

"I have a few matters to take care of, love. I'll swing back a little later."

She dismissed Blaine's suggestion with a wave of her hand. "I'll be fine. I can find my way back." The last thing she needed was Blaine showing up while she told Aric about her wingless situation.

Without waiting for his reply, in case he insisted on returning, she exited the car and strode across the road. Lost in thought, she didn't register the warmth stirring in her blood until she reached the entrance of the club at the same time Aric exited. Her heart flipped at the sight of him and suddenly all the words she hoped to say disappeared.

He halted a few steps from her. "Hey." His gaze dipped to her feet. "You're wearing the shoes. Do you like them?"

"I love them. Thank you." She did a little ballerina pose, giving him a better look.

He smiled, though it didn't reach his eyes. Something was wrong, and those butterflies became creepy crawlies scratching under the surface of her flesh. Why did it feel like a giant canyon had opened between them? Last night, he touched her at every opportunity and now he remained an arm's length away.

Mortals surrounded them, wandering the street and lining up at the entrance to the club. This wasn't the place to ask him what was wrong, nor the place to tell him about her wings. They needed privacy. "Is there somewhere we can talk?"

She twirled the ribbon on her dress around her

index finger. She wore this one because she knew Aric liked the color, which was also why she left her hair down even though the tight curls drove her crazy.

The tension between them was suffocating. She had to get this over with, tell him the truth so they could move forward.

His chest rose and fell in a deep breath, and she braced herself for bad news. "Fly with me to the cabin."

Her mouth went dry. She should have met him there. Now if she said no, he'd think she didn't want to, resulting in her confession in the middle of the street. "Let's go for a walk first."

"Look at me, I don't care what color your wings are, you don't need to hide them from me. Their color isn't the reason I love you."

Her chest tightened. There wasn't any way around it, she needed to tell him now. She stepped closer. "It's not that. It's just…"

Without another word, he took her hand and led her into the parking lot at the rear of the club. Thank goodness Blaine had gone. Telling Aric in public was bad enough, she didn't need Blaine interrupting the conversation.

As soon as they were out of sight, she pulled back her hand. "Aric—"

"It won't change things, I promise you. Show me your wings, Lo-Lo."

Her stomach plummeted all the way to her shoes. Darkness smothered her.

Show me your wings, little pet…

Bile rose in her throat as the memories surfaced. *Zath's manic laugh…his hot, foul breath tingling her nape…the scrape of metal against stone the moment before searing pain ripped through her wings…*

She gagged. Her chest heaved in and out. She clawed at her arm, but the pain spread, consuming her entire body. The acidic stench of sulfur fired through her nostrils.

A familiar voice cut through the panic, and she registered the hazy figure of a male towering in front of her.

She staggered back. Sucked in gulps of air.

The figure reached for her. "What's wro—"

She shoved the hand away. "Get away from me!"

"Lo-Lo, it's me." Concern edged his voice, but he didn't move closer.

She fisted her hair, sorting the mess of reality verses nightmare. "I can't…"

Smoke filled her lungs. She coughed, spinning in a tight circle. Where was she? She spotted flames in the distance and backed away. Wait. The orange glow weren't flames, it came from a streetlamp.

The haze cleared, unveiling a dark parking lot. No Zath prepared to sever her wings. No torturous screams. No Hell.

Her gaze found Aric and gradually his features came into focus. His shoulders were tense, brows drawn tight. Her heart rate steadied as his whiskey eyes drew her in, easing her back to reality.

"What's going on?" He curled a finger under her chin, lifting it. "What the hell just happened?"

For a moment, it felt like she was right back in Zath's hellhole before he hacked off her wings. She wasn't though. Instead, Aric stood in front of her with a protective stance that made her believe he'd kill anyone who harmed her.

He brushed his knuckles up and down her arm. Soothed by his touch, her breath steadied, and her pulse slowed to a normal rhythm and stopped hammering in her ears. Soft waves of reassurance flowed into her veins, as it always did with him.

But it wouldn't last. She had to tell him before things went too far. She knew she'd slip one day because of the lies she told. Today was that day.

Lifting her chin, her gaze locked with his. "I can't...fly."

His shoulders dropped. "Why?"

Now or never. Tears burned her eyes. They'd both made choices that damaged the other, but her choice forced them on to different sides of the war. Aric had walked away from her, then she'd done the same by becoming a Fallen.

Telling him the truth meant they could move past this, either together or separately. This moment could snap the final sliver of connection between them, a thread she'd held onto wishing things were different or fuse it back together.

She stared at him, summoning every ounce of courage. "I don't...have wings."

His brows knitted. "What do you mean?"

She stepped out of his reach. Having him touch her made it too damn hard to concentrate. "Zath..." *Gag.* "Captured me when I Fell. He...severed my wings." She inhaled a deep breath that hurt like hell. "They haven't grown back."

Muscles popped in Aric's jaw. "That fucking bastard." His voice a low menacing growl, making the hairs on her neck stand at attention.

She fought back a sob. "I'm sorry I kept it from

you."

His hands curled into tight fists. "If he ever shows his face in this realm, I'll rip his limbs off one by fucking one."

"It won't change anything. It wouldn't bring my wings back."

In one step, he closed the distance between them and wrapped his arms around her, squeezing tight.

She rested her cheek against his chest, listening to his strong heartbeat as silent sobs quaked her body.

"I'm so sorry. This is all my fault." He kissed the top of her head.

She drew back. "No. This is my mess. I wanted to leave the Heavens, to have a fresh start, to stop the pain, but somehow along the way I failed."

His lips formed a thin line and the hurt in his eyes nearly brought her to her knees. He cupped her face between his hands. "Listen to me. You didn't fail. I failed you. I'll fix this."

She shook her head. The only thing she knew that fixed this was him giving her back the band. That stopped him syphoning her light, allowing her to heal. It sounded like a good plan in the beginning, but that was before he kissed her. Before he tore down the walls around her heart and let her love him again. That was before she gave herself hope.

If Aric gave the band back now, it was the end, and that hope would shatter along with her heart.

"This isn't something you can fix. If there was another option to regenerate my wings, I would've found a way by now. Trust me, I've considered everything."

"If I may…" Blaine sauntered down the alley

toward them. "I know exactly how to fix your little mishap, love."

Chapter Twenty-Six

Trust Blaine to interrupt his moment with Willow. That Fallen appeared every time he wished he wasn't there, and it grated his fucking nerves.

"Piss off, Blaine. This is between Willow and me."

From out of the corner of his eye, he saw EJ and Raven skid to a halt at the end of the alley.

Stay back, he mentally told them. He didn't need more of an audience. They could all stay the hell away.

Willow, however, welcomed Blaine's arrival. Her eyes lit like he was her fucking savor. "You know how to regenerate my wings? How?"

Blaine wasn't the only one. Aric suspected he also knew how but kept that to himself for the time being. Did Blaine know Willow's soul was in Anahel? Had Blaine kept that to himself hoping she'd waste away in the ether so Aric couldn't save her? Or had Blaine waited for this exact moment just to rub it in his face?

Blaine stepped closer and gave her a royal bow. *Asshole.* "A quick little trip to Hell and back will fix that pesky problem of yours in no time."

Go back to Hell? No fucking way. Willow was heading back to the Heavens. "She's not going to Hell," he growled.

Blaine faced him. "How do you propose for her to regenerate her wings?"

He had a plan. It would hurt like fucking hell, but

he'd do anything to save Willow. Anything.

He got right in Blaine's face. Now was not the night to test his patience. "I will be the one who fixes this."

Blaine acted unfazed. "On the contrary, friend, as of the moment Willow Fell, she's under my protection."

He shoved Blaine in the chest, but he didn't budge. "Was she under your protection when that fucking asshole hacked off her wings?"

Beside him, Willow balled her fists, slamming them down through the air. "Stop," she screeched. "Stop it! Both of you."

His gaze snapped in her direction, but he never got a chance to speak.

"I never wanted this." Her voice rose. "All I wanted was for the pain to stop. I wanted my powers back. I wanted my existence back after you…" She shoved her finger into his chest. "Took it from me. You promised me forever. Held my heart in your hands then you crushed it into a thousand pieces. You abandoned me in the Heavens and took the link to my powers with you."

He recoiled. "Wait, what? I didn't take your powers. You linked them to me when you gave me your heart with this band." He raised his wrist.

"Yes. Then you left, and the powers no longer worked both ways. Each time your soul needed light, it drained it from me until my powers deteriorated so much, they no longer worked. I became a joke, a failure within the Ariel."

What the fuck? He'd syphoned her light since Fate exiled him and given none in return?

Him refusing to let her go got her into this mess.

He'd held on, keeping the band on his wrist while in the mortal realm, clinging to the last remaining thread tying their souls together. Instead of holding onto his soulmate, he drew light from her powers every day and flung her soul into Anahel when she cut her connection to the Heavens. Then Zath severed her wings as revenge. She'd gone through enough.

He raked his fingers through his hair as it all made sense. She'd walked to his cabin last night because she couldn't fly. That was why her feet hurt so much. He'd made her fucking walk all that way to see him.

Now who's the asshole?

"I had no idea. If I'd known, I would've given the band back before I faced Fate. She never said a damn thing."

Her expression softened. "It doesn't matter now. What's done is done. I just want my wings and my powers back. I'm sick of looking in the mirror and seeing nothing but horrific black scars."

"There's another option, Lo-Lo. Return to the Heavens, where you'll be safe."

Blaine scoffed. "You can't expect her to return there. An Ariel without wings or powers? Could you imagine how they'd treat her?"

She shook her head. "I can't do it. Fate would imprison me in Tartirim for an eternity just because I betrayed her."

He was losing the battle fast; he saw it in her eyes. The way they hardened when she spoke of the Heavens and the way they lit when Blaine gave her another option to regenerate her wings.

Stepping closer, he tugged a crazy curl of her fiery hair. She'd worn it down tonight, just the way he liked it, and that showed him she still cared. "Come to our cabin with me. Let's talk about it."

He needed to convince her to return to the Heavens, not Hell. If he let her go, and she went to Hell, she'd become a Fallen. For real.

"No, Aric. There's no point in talking. Returning to the Heavens isn't an option. My powers are still linked to that band you wear and if I return, I'll be in the same situation as when I left."

That wasn't true. He knew all the facts now and could save her. For her soul to escape Anahel, he needed to let her go. If he didn't cling to their connection, then her powers could return. Easier said than done.

"Returning to Hell puts you in more danger. Zath won't think twice about torturing you, Willow. He's as evil as they come."

"Then perhaps you should accompany her?" Blaine suggested. "If protecting Willow is important to you, then you shouldn't let her go alone."

Fucking Blaine. He'd underestimated Blaine's ability to be as manipulative as Fate. If he said no, he looked like he didn't care about her. If he said yes, they both became Fallen. Either way, her soul escaped Anahel, but at what cost? He couldn't save her and return her soul to the Heavens if he was a Fallen, too.

Damn it.

A weight the size of a boulder pressed on his gut. He had to do this. Now that he knew the truth, the damage holding on caused her soul, he couldn't continue. Their reunion was magical while it lasted, and he wouldn't give up hope they'd be together again, but now wasn't that time.

He'd rather her think he broke her heart than for her soul to die.

He locked his gaze with Willow's, summoning all his strength. "I'm a Guardian, I would never choose Hell."

For the first time since Willow gave him the band more than a thousand years ago, he removed it from his wrist and handed it back to her. In that moment, he saw her heart crack into a million pieces, shattering at his feet. And his soul died along with their connection.

Tears pooled in her eyes, but she didn't let them fall. "I'll never come first for you." Her breath shuddered in and out.

His words lodged in his throat. "You'll always come first." He reached for her hand, but she stepped back. "Fate has paved a different path for us right now."

Her hands curled into fists. "Fate can go to Hell. No. She can go…ugh! I don't care where she goes. Somewhere else. Because I'm going to Hell. I'm regenerating my wings, becoming a Fallen and getting my powers back." She wiped her eyes and turned to Blaine. "Will you take me?"

He nodded without even a glance at Aric. "Of course, I will. It would be my honor to protect you in the absence of your soulmate. Slater's across the road, love, he'll take you home. I'll meet you there and we'll sort out the details."

It took every bit of self-control Aric possessed not to punch Blaine across the parking lot. He was so done with that Fallen.

"Fine," she snapped.

He remained deathly still, so he didn't reach out and touch her. This was the only way he could save her soul. *Let her go.* "I'm sorry, Lo-Lo."

Ignoring him, she lifted her chin and strode down the alley toward the street, still wearing the shoes he'd bought her because he thought romance was the answer. The shoes he wanted to see her wear tonight. When she reached the road, instead of stopping her, EJ and Raven stepped aside and let her pass. Absolutely no help at all. If anyone should've had his back…

His soul ached to chase her, stop her from leaving, but that would only make it worse. She thought he chose his oath over her, as she'd thought since he left the Heavens. That was better. If he told her the truth, she might stay in the mortal realm just so they remained together. This wasn't their destiny, he saw that now and the sooner he let her go, the sooner her soul healed.

He always chose her, and always would.

"Ouch," Blaine sniggered.

The words snapped his last shred of self-control. He pivoted lightning fast, fist clenched, and smashed Blaine square in the face.

"I don't know why I agreed to save you," he roared. "You're beyond redemption."

Blaine smirked through the black blood pouring from his disfigured nose. "I don't seek redemption, friend."

He shoved Blaine's chest, sending him stumbling backward. "I'm not your fucking friend. A friend wouldn't destroy my soulmate."

Blaine straightened and wiped off the blood with the back of his hand. "I saved her, remember? I went to Hell and brought her here. Me. I saved her from an eternity of torture by the Fallen you mutilated."

"You think I owe you or some shit? News flash,

asshole, you made her leave the Heavens in the first place."

How long did it take for Blaine to coax Willow from the Heavens? How long did it take for him to turn her?

He glared at the Fallen, once a Guardian he'd lay down his life for. The Fallen who had pulled him back from the brink when his soul teetered on the edge of darkness.

The Fallen he'd once considered a brother.

He shoved Blaine again. *Fight back, goddamn it!*

"You knew," he growled. "You knew she was already in Hell when you offered me that deal."

Blaine half shrugged. "Technically, she wasn't in Hell. I'd already retrieved her by that point."

Red blotches clouded his vision as Rageland zeroed in. "Are you kidding me? You're just as manipulative as Fate."

"Fire must be fought with fire as the saying goes. Plus, I was curious to see how much she meant to you. What you'd give up for her." Blaine scoffed. "It's no surprise you didn't fold. You've always been so loyal to Fate."

I was this close…

He gripped the front of Blaine's shirt and twisted the fabric in his fist. "You had better protect her."

Blaine narrowed his eyes, unconcerned at the blood dripping down his shirt. "If you're so concerned, come with us. You can protect her from Zath."

He shoved Blaine away. "You're fucking crazy."

"So, I've been told." Blaine shrugged. "It was your fault Zath took her wings. It only seems fair for your help to regenerate them."

Stick the knife in a little further why don't you?

"I won't let him become a Fallen," EJ growled, suddenly behind him.

Shit, he'd forgotten about EJ and Raven.

Blaine cocked a brow. "What? A Fallen like his soulmate?"

Silence. Dead fucking silence. Even the wind ceased blowing and club music paused between songs.

Blaine unfurled his crimson wings. The wings Willow would soon have.

"I'll let you mull over your decision for twenty-four hours. Think of it this way, if you accompany Willow to Hell, you keep your girl and end up on the winning side." He winked. "We were once an unstoppable team."

Without waiting for his reply, Blaine shot into the night and disappeared among the clouds.

Aric didn't give a shit about winning the goddamn war between Zath and Fate. He also didn't give a shit whether Zath held a grudge against him until the end of time. The only thing he gave a shit about was saving Willow's soul.

Chapter Twenty-Seven

Aric landed on the roof of Blaine's lair two hours later. He'd flown back to the Guardian mansion and listened to Raven, EJ, Gabe, the whole damn household tell him he'd made the right decision. He'd saved Willow's soul. Blah, blah, blah.

Had he though? Or had he pushed her to the point where she fled to Hell instead of listening to him?

Without that band, he felt hollow, lost, like a piece of him had gone MIA back in the parking lot, never to be found again. Would Willow have listened if he told her the real reason he gave the band back? Would it have changed her decision?

He needed the answers to those questions because he couldn't bear knowing she chose Hell for the wrong reason. That she chose Hell to spite him.

Pacing in a tight circle on the roof, he hoped she sensed him there. Could she sense him? Because the second he took off that band, he couldn't distinguish any of the haywire emotions raging in his blood.

He stretched his neck side to side, a series of pops released some tension. He'd lost count how many times he'd considered busting in the front door. That dumbass move wouldn't give him answers nor do him any favors. Plus, he guessed the mansion was cloaked, so he wouldn't find her anyhow.

Why the hell was he here? This wasn't letting her

go.

That stupid emotion of hope, that's why. Nothing good ever came from the feeling. He had hope when he and his brothers stood before Fate in her sanctuary, ready for their mission. Hope flooded him the moment he misted to the mortal realm, prepared to bring Blaine home. Then in waltzed reality. Fate had tricked them. Saving Blaine would take longer than they all expected. But over the centuries, he never lost hope of returning to Willow, even as their mission grew more and more hopeless.

Then that damn hope trickled in again when he'd sensed her at the club. Hope she'd found a way to him, hope they'd reunite, that their lives returned to how they once were.

Fucking hope. Though, after a while, hope felt the same as numbness.

The first sign of dawn blanketed the horizon with a fiery glow. The cool night air gave way to a pre-dawn chill, as though the weather reminded mortals to stay in their comfy beds for a few hours longer before the sun warmed things up.

He hadn't even made it to bed. If he made it in time, he could stop Willow from returning to Hell. He could save her—an act Blaine had robbed him of the first time she Fell.

Blaine gave him until tomorrow night before he and Willow made their field trip to Hell. He had less than twenty-four hours to convince her to go to the Heavens instead.

Back to pacing. Each time he considered leaving, a ray of light seeped inside his soul and urged him to stay. Maybe Fate's almighty powers were back up and running. Or perhaps the connection between their souls remained even without the band on his wrist. Maybe each time he came here he gave Willow a sliver of his faith.

That last thought kept him on the rooftop, and he wouldn't leave until she spoke with him.

Whatever it takes.

A familiar *swoosh* sounded before the thud of heavy boots landed on the tiled roof behind him.

"Piss off, Slater," he growled without bothering to face him.

"Time for you to go, stalker."

He spun. "Stalker? Is that her term or yours?"

Slater didn't respond.

God, he couldn't be more arrogant, standing there with his arms crossed over his bare chest, a low-slung pair of leather pants hanging on his hips. He narrowed his gaze on the uncovered hellfire scars wrapped around Slater's wrists. There were too many to count. From what he'd heard, it took decades of torture to form scares that deep. He'd seen the thick coiled black marks on Fallen before but never took much notice.

Slater deserved the scars. Served him right for forsaking the Heavens and breaking his oath as an Azrael. Every Fallen deserved the torture...except Willow.

He turned away. "I'm not leaving until she tells me to herself."

"You'll be waiting a long time. She's not here."

His heart thudded. Had she left already? Was he too late? No, he'd know if she became a Fallen. He may not sense her in his blood, but he knew in his heart she hadn't left.

"Must be nice to lie, asshole," he sneered.

He'd had enough lies for a lifetime.

A slight smirk hinted on Slater's lips. "It must suck having to tell the truth all the time."

God, he itched to punch that smug look off Slater's damn face. Fate forbid the Guardians from killing Blaine, but nowhere in the fine print did she mention not killing his sidekicks. Slater was a Fallen. He had no right existing in the mortal realm. He should skip back to Hell, away from Fate's precious mortals, away from the Guardians and in a different fucking realm from his soulmate.

He unsheathed a dagger and twirled it between his fingers. "Tell me, Slater, why did you turn your back on the Heavens?"

Slater's gaze shot to the dagger then back to Aric. "I'm still an Azrael." That smirk returned. "Just for a different side."

"For Zath you mean?"

The Fallen shrugged one shoulder.

Aric prowled forward. "What did Blaine offer you to convince you to leave?" He gripped the hilt of the dagger. "Was it worth the torture while he left you in Hell?"

He didn't know exactly when Slater Fell, but it happened sometime between the Guardians' exile and when they first spotted him in the mortal realm a few decades ago. By those scars, Slater was in Hell a long fucking time.

"You here for a chat or are you going to throw that dagger?"

His patience thinned by the second. "You don't want me to use this dagger." He eyed the thin scar on

Slater's pec where his dagger lodged the last time they fought.

Slater's eyes darkened further, and he caught the slight adjustment in Slater's stance as he prepared to fight. Good. He was done playing Mr. Nice Guy. His only focus right now remained seeing Willow and Fallen assholes kept getting in his goddamn way. The sooner Slater left, the sooner he got back to pacing on the roof like a loser.

Dagger held low and tight, he lunged at Slater, delivering a quick stab to the Fallen's exposed side. Served him right for never wearing a goddamn shirt. Slater grunted but sidestepped his second swing. He didn't wait, launching another swipe of the dagger. Slater blocked the jab with his arm, knocking the dagger from Aric's hand. It flung through the air before tumbling down the roof and over the edge.

All the shit crammed into his head slowed his reflexes. It didn't matter. He didn't need a dagger to fight. He'd fought plenty of Fallen long before discovering knives.

Fist curled, he spun as quick as lightning, punching Slater's jaw. Slater's head flung to one side and his footing faltered.

"Fuck!" Slater spat oozy black blood onto the roof.

The Fallen's pupils changed to bright crimson, matching the wings unfurled behind his back. A feral growl rumbled in the night.

About time. He wanted a fight and now he'd get one.

Slater engaged, reaching him in one leap. Arm curled, Slater swung his fist. Aric ducked. Weight planted on one foot, he whirled around, and side kicked

Slater in the ribs. The sickening crunch of bones echoed in the night. The Fallen landed on his back, commando rolled, then launched himself to his feet in one swift maneuver. He leaped forward and jabbed his elbow in Slater's cheekbone. Slater grabbed his forearm and twisted it so viciously he backflipped. Using the momentum, Aric twisted in the opposite direction as he landed, freeing his arm. Before he righted his balance, Slater yanked the back of his jacket and hurled him through the air. His body thudded on the other side of the roof, punching the air from his lungs, then skidded toward the edge. His arms failed, trying to stop from falling off the roof. At the last second, his hand gripped the edge just as he was about to unfurl his wings.

Shit, that was close.

Clinging to the gutter, he swung his legs and launched himself back onto the roof, landing on his feet. Red blotches dotted his vision. Slater helped Blaine convince Willow to Fall. He deserved to rot in Hell for the rest of eternity.

He charged at Slater, shouldering him in the chest and tackling him to the ground. But his reflexes were all over the place and instead of landing on top of Slater, he over calculated and ended up on his back. Drawing his knees in tight to his chest, he leaped back onto his feet.

Slater reengaged, matching each of his blows with one of his own. Adrenaline raced through his veins, his warrior body primed for battle. If only it wasn't diluted with concern for Willow.

Slater punched his jaw. His head snapped to the side. Pain exploded in his skull making his vision blur. He fought against it, swinging a side kick aiming for

Slater's shattered ribs.

The world flipped. One second he twisted, next his back slammed against the roof. Air exploded from his lungs. His vision momentarily blacked out. Slater's knee dug into his chest, preventing any movement, and the Fallen Azrael locked his hands around his throat. He gripped Slater's forearms, tugging to break free. Blood pounded behind his eyes.

Slater glared at him, eyes blazing crimson. "Unless you're here to accept Blaine's offer, get the hell off the roof."

He grunted, struggling with words thanks to the pressure closing his windpipe. "I'm not going…anywhere…until Willow tells me to leave."

Slater tightened his grip. Pressure throbbed inside his head.

Centering his weight, he flung his legs in the air, but the move lacked enough momentum to kick the back of Slater's head. Tiny white specs appeared in his vision, and he braced for them to morph into blackness.

Not a moment too soon, Slater released his hold and the pressure on his throat eased. Air rushed into his lungs as the weight lifted from his chest.

Slater stood, towering over him, seeming unfazed by the nasty purple-ish bruise darkening his ribs and the thick black blood oozing from the gash in his side.

"I told you, idiot. She's not here."

Aric rubbed his throat, surprised to find his head still attached. He rolled to one side and peeled himself off the roof. Pain pulsed in his jaw, but he got a better deal than Slater.

Slater peered at his stab wound then glanced around as though looking for something to wipe the blood.

He straightened his jacket. "Maybe next time you should wear a shirt."

Slater wiped the blood with his hand, then cleaned it on the thigh of his leather pants. "And where's the fun in that?"

He slid a hand inside his jacket but came up empty. Damn it. Slater flung his dagger off the roof. He'd better find it before Raine kicked his ass, too.

Slater turned to leave. "She made me drop her off on the side of the road, halfway up the mountain."

He gaped. "You left her in the middle of nowhere?"

Slater smirked. "She can hold her own in a fight. I trained her," he said over his shoulder before he leaped off the roof.

In a split second, Aric ripped off his jacket, unfurled his wings and shot into the sky.

Chapter Twenty-Eight

Willow curled her legs beside her on the porch swing at Aric's cabin and peered at the surrounding pine forest. Morning light filtered through the branches, glistening in the misty fog. The colors shimmered, reminding her of Ariel powers, the warm orange glow pulsing between the trees. It called to her, eased the churning in her stomach, and gave her a sense of peace.

She'd stared at those trees until the sun lifted passed the horizon and rose on a new day, waiting for Aric. She came here for a final goodbye; closure Fate had stolen from them when he left the Heavens. But Aric hadn't returned, just as he hadn't back then. With no other way to contact him, she'd settled on the porch, prepared to wait for as long as it took.

The band held in her palm felt cold and empty, and absent of Ariel power. Just like her soul. He gave it back, and in that moment ended their bond, but she needed a goodbye. In the parking lot, she'd been too stunned to formulate words.

I never expected him to walk away.

A *whoosh* made her jump off the chair. She spun just as Aric landed on a grassy patch beside the cabin. The fierceness of his body a stark contrast to the delicate day awakening behind him. The second he touched the ground, his stormy gaze locked with hers.

The sight of him twisted her heart into mega-sized

knots, tightening until it felt as though it stopped beating. She saw him only a few hours ago, but somehow it felt like a lifetime. So much had happened since then.

He approached the cabin with slow steps. "You're here."

More of a statement than a question, like he wondered if she were real.

"I…" What? She came to say goodbye but now that she stood here, goodbye seemed too hard. Willow didn't want to make this hurt; she wanted it to be sweet and beautiful, like it once was between them.

She gravitated toward him as he ascended the timber steps onto the porch. She stopped short. "What happened to your face?"

He rubbed his swollen jaw. "It doesn't matter."

A strangled moment passed between them. He must have fought with Blaine after she left. She was so sick of them competing for alpha male status around her. Even more reason to say goodbye, so Blaine could return her to Hell and stop tormenting Aric. She and Aric would be no more but at least she'd have powers and her wings back. She could finally start again.

He stepped closer. "I spoke with Gabe," he said, his voice gravelly and thick.

Her shoulders dropped. "It doesn't matter what Gabe said, I've made my decision and you've made yours."

"Just hear me out. I need you to know why I took off the band."

Her chest fell with a heavy breath. "I didn't come here for an explanation."

"I need to give you one." When she sighed, he

continued. "Before you arrived at the club, Gabe came to see me. He told me your soul is stuck in Anahel."

Her eyes burned. Of course, why didn't she piece it together herself? She'd wrongly assumed she hadn't completed her transition as a Fallen, not that her soul was frozen in a wasteland. It all made sense now. The reason she felt like a ninety-year-old mortal, her lack of energy, no powers, why her wings wouldn't regenerate.

He took her hand in his. "My connection to you is keeping you there. When you Fell, I diverted your soul."

She squeezed his hands. "Don't blame yourself. I knew the consequences when I tied my powers to you."

Why didn't she listen to the other Ariel? At the time, it felt so right. She had wanted to give him her soul, her body, every part of her. If she had listened, none of this would've happened. If she had listened, their bond would've severed when he left.

"That choice made our bond even stronger. Your powers held us together, against impossible odds." His gaze dipped to the floor before returning to hers. "To save your soul, you needed to choose a path. Hell isn't your only option. There's still time for you to choose the Heavens."

She let go of his hands. "No. There's nothing but loneliness waiting for me in the Heavens. I won't go back there. When I Fell, I promised myself a new start, and that's what I'm doing. Both my options will be hell but at least this way, I get a clean slate."

His shoulders stiffened. "Gabe can help, tell Fate you made a mistake."

"Aric, stop. Please. I came here to say goodbye."

Their gazes locked. In that moment, time stood

still, pausing and waiting for his next move, as though their fated paths had led them to this fork in the road. She stared into his whiskey brown eyes. Eyes that reminded her of the forests she had once created with the touch of her fingertips. Eyes filled with so much history and love she couldn't bear to look away.

"I don't wanna let you go," he whispered.

The knot around her heart twisted tighter. "You have to."

Before he said anymore, she cupped his face, coaxing his head down as she rose on her toes. When their lips met, she kissed him with everything she had. Let all her fears and regrets vanish as his tongue swept over hers.

She leaned in, roaming her hands over his shoulders as he drew her closer. He tasted like her own personal realm of the Heavens, rich and earthy, full of happiness and joy. Kissing him felt like home.

Without breaking their kiss, he hitched up her dress and lifted her, anchoring her legs around his waist. He groaned when she squeezed her thighs, pressing her core against his hard length.

Sex couldn't fix the issues they faced, but for them sex had always been more. It wasn't just the satisfaction of joining their two bodies; it joined their hearts and she wanted that feeling one last time.

Cradled in his arms, he kicked open the door and carried her inside. Being near him shouldn't feel this good. Touching him shouldn't feel this good. Without the band on his wrist, she shouldn't feel anything for him. But…she did.

Beside the bed, he lowered her legs to the floor and brushed his knuckles along her jaw. "Tell me you don't want this, and I'll stop."

When his thumb trailed over her bottom lip, she licked it, drawing a possessive growl from his chest. Her body swelled with heat. Once again, his eyes seduced her, consumed her insides until they hummed and burned with desire.

They had danced around this moment for weeks. Well, no longer. She wanted him, wanted to feel him inside her again, and wanted his scent branded on her skin before she walked away.

Instead of replying with words, she yanked him to her. Their mouths collided, hands fumbled, tugging at clothing. He drew back and ripped off his shirt while she clawed at his belt.

"Wait." He stilled her hands. "Slow down, baby."

Umm, nope. Slowing down meant processing thoughts and making decisions she didn't want to make. She wanted to be with him without all the baggage, without the weight of the universe hanging on her shoulders.

"I need you, Aric," she whispered.

Holding his gaze, she stepped back, toed off her shoes then reached under her dress and slid off her panties. Aric's eyes darkened.

"Please don't make me beg."

In one swift movement, he lifted again, locking her legs around his waist.

"Lo-Lo," he growled. "You never need to beg."

He strode to the nearest wall and eased her back against it. Her head tilted to one side as he nuzzled her neck, his stubble grazing along the sensitive area under her earlobe. She moaned, raking her fingers through his short black hair.

"Lo-Lo, I wanna slow down," he groaned. "I wanna savor this moment."

"Don't stop." She tugged his head to meet his gaze. "Don't you dare stop."

She needed this. They both needed it.

One of his arms supported her weight while the other unbuckled his belt and unzipped his jeans, shoving them down to his knees. His shaft sprung free and rubbed against her core causing tingles to bloom at the apex of her thighs. She rolled her hips, sliding along the outside, sending her body into a spin.

This would be fast and hard, but she didn't care. They didn't need to reacquaint themselves with each other's body. He already knew all the spots and moves that made her burn, ache and scream for more. After such a long absence, once he slid inside, she'd probably lose the ability to think. Exactly what she wanted. Without thought, she wouldn't remember that her soul withered away in a wasteland or that she'd return to Hell in less than twenty-four hours.

Without the ability to think, she could be in the moment with him. They'd waited too long for this day and it would be their last.

She scraped her nails along his scalp. "Now, Aric."

Positioning himself, he eased deep inside her.

"Oh my fucking god," he groaned.

She gripped his nape and pulled him down for a hard, all-consuming kiss. Their tongues collided. With her dress hitched up to her waist, he slid in and out while she clawed at his shoulders. Her blood hummed with desire for the Guardian locked between her legs. The angel she gave her soul to. Centuries of longing, built-up sexual frustration, their need for one another, rolled together and crashed over the surface like a monstrous tsunami.

He gripped her thighs, holding her in place as he pounded harder and faster. Tremors of anticipation danced along her flesh, building in intensity until she hovered on the edge of release.

A sheen of sweat covered his biceps, and she gripped his muscles as they contracted with each deep thrust. She didn't want this to stop. She wanted it to last forever. For centuries, she'd imagined what their reunion would be like, and finally, it happened.

Buried deep inside her, he kissed her, flinging her over the edge.

"Aric," she screamed.

Her core clenched around him as waves of pleasure exploded inside her. One more thrust sent him spiraling over the edge with her.

"Mine," he growled, climaxing inside her.

A blast of blinding white light shot through her soul, but she was too drunk on desire to pay any attention. Just another thing to process and now wasn't the time.

Aric buried his head in the crook of her neck while their heart rates steadied. She breathed in his scent, mixed with the heady desire and sweat, causing her chest to ache. She couldn't unpack those emotions now either. Right now, she'd enjoy the moment.

Once their breaths slowed a notch, she placed her hands on either side of his face and lifted his head to meet her gaze.

"Now you have my permission to slow down."

A sexy grin curled on his lips and she swore his chest inflated. "Copy that."

She lost herself in his eyes as he carried her to the foot of the bed. The adoration mixed with the primal expression on his face, made her quiver with need all over again.

He lowered her wobbly legs to the floor as though she were a delicate wildflower and slid her dress over her breasts—

She stopped his hands. No. She couldn't be naked. He couldn't see…

What the hell was she doing? She side-stepped, yanking down her dress.

His brows knitted. "What's wrong?"

Revealing how Zath hacked off her wings was one thing, but showing him the black, horrific hellfire scars left behind was a different thing entirely.

Aric moved to pull up his pants.

"We can still be together. I just want to keep my dress on." She forced a smile. "It's sexier that way."

He stilled, studying her so intently her insides quivered. "It is sexy. But you said I could slow down, and that involves my mouth on every inch of your beautiful skin. Leaving your dress on makes that difficult."

He took off his boots and slid down his jeans and boxer briefs, shoving the clothing aside with his foot. He stepped into her space, his erection between them, hard and thick, impossible to ignore.

She remembered the sight of his perfectly sculpted body, but now he stood naked before her, the memories faded, replaced with new ones in vibrant color. Her hands roamed his defined pecs, over the droplets of sweat along the hard-ridged muscles of his torso. She grazed her nails up his strong, muscular arms, pausing at his shoulders.

He leaned closer, pushing against her hands to whisper in her ear. "I want you naked with me."

Those damn butterflies exploded in the pit of her stomach, which was stupid. He'd seen her naked plenty of times before, too many times to count. Why should now be any different?

Because this time *was* different. She was different. Her body was different.

"Lo-Lo, look at me."

Her gaze lifted to his. God, she acted so stupid. They were just having the sex she'd craved from the moment she saw him in the club. Whether Aric found her attractive was a moot point. It didn't matter.

Yet…it did.

He crooked a finger under her chin, tilting it upward. "Tell me why you won't take off that dress."

"It's just…" She stared at her toes. Her body had changed so much, inside and out, since they were last together. Seeing disappointment in his eyes would ruin the moment. It would break her beyond repair. "I'm not the same angel you gave your vow to so long ago."

He smoothed his knuckles along her jaw. This was meant to be just sex, a pause in time to say goodbye. Yet now, standing at a crossroad, her heart told her something different.

She lifted her gaze to his.

He stroked the back of his hands up and down her arms. "You're beautiful. Every time I see you, my heart still skips a beat." He curled a strand of her hair around his finger. "Every time the sunlight catches your fiery hair, it still takes my breath away. It's been like that since the moment I first laid eyes on you back in that forest, and it'll be like that till the end of time." He released the curl and cupped her face in his hands. "There's nothing more beautiful to me in this universe than you."

She needed to rebuild those damn walls around her heart. Though, they were now redundant; long ago Aric had found a ladder and climbed over the top.

Damn him for making this that much harder.

She swallowed. "No. What I mean is…when Zath cut off my wings, he didn't do it…neatly."

His expression hardened, but he remained silent.

"Without my powers, the scars didn't heal." *Inhale…exhale.* "At all."

There went the muscles in his jaw again. What a way to ruin the moment.

After a few precious heartbeats, Aric murmured, "Show me."

She shook her head. That required strength on a whole new level, strength she didn't have.

"It doesn't matter what the scars look like." Aric slid up the hem of her dress, pausing at her waist.

She bit the inside of her lip. "I don't want our last moment to be like this."

He planted soft kisses along her forehead, inching her dress higher. "It won't change how much I love you."

Her pulse skyrocketed, but she let him continue lifting the dress. Half wanting to believe his words, half wanting this moment finished. The sooner he saw the scars, the sooner he left. The sooner she went to Hell, the sooner she healed.

He lifted her dress over her head, dropping it on the floor beside his feet. She lowered her gaze, stomach churning under the weight of his stare. She stood naked before him for the first time in centuries, and all she thought of was his reaction. What he would think when she turned around and showed him.

Inhaling a deep breath, she slowly pivoted to face the bed. The sharp inhale of Aric's breath confirmed he saw her scars. The hideous scars that represented nothing but sickening horror and torture.

She remained still, waiting for him to speak, to react, something. Anything. When his lips brushed over one scar, a sob quaked in her chest.

He trailed delicate kisses along the length of the scar, before repeating the gesture on the other. The sorrow in his touch, made her heart shatter.

"I'm so sorry you went through this."

She couldn't blame him anymore. Forgiveness was the only way she moved forward. To do that, she also needed to forgive herself. She made a choice that day, and even if now she would've chosen differently, she had to own her decision, because remaining in the past literally killed her.

She faced him and the pain in his eyes nearly bought her to her knees.

"Lo-Lo, I wish I had—"

She held a finger over his lips, silencing him. She was done with talking. "Don't think, just be with me here and now, in this moment. Let our bodies be together as one."

A single moment in time. That was all she asked for and something she could give.

Having him inside her felt like a piece of her soul returned home, a piece that had been missing for countless centuries. A piece she never thought would be found.

He'd promised to remind her how good they were together, and he'd more than succeeded. Being with Aric was as magical and heavenly as she remembered, more so, after centuries apart. But it didn't change their situation. She needed to leave Anahel to regenerate her wings—an absence she felt more and more each day. She needed to complete her transition as a Fallen and save her soul.

Heaviness pressed against her chest, but she wouldn't change her mind. They had the chance to say goodbye, to tie up all those loose ends before they went their separate ways.

This moment in time gave them closure.

Easing onto the bed, she scooted up to the pillows. The mattress dipped as he crawled between her legs, eyeing her with a dangerous glint in his eyes like he wanted to stake his claim on her. Again. The thought tingled her core, her breasts aching for his touch.

Propping herself up on her elbows, she tracked his rough hands as they roamed from the tips of her toes, along the outside of her legs, all the way to circle at her hips. His heavily lidded gaze dipped to the apex of her thighs.

"I wanna taste you again," he said, his voice thick and husky.

He didn't wait for her reply. The second his hot tongue touched her core, she sucked in a sharp breath, her eyes rolling back in her head.

"Oh my goodness."

A low satisfied moan rumbled in his chest. His tongue circled in slow, delicate motions, round and round, up and down while his thin line of stubble grazed the insides of her thighs. She clenched the bedding. Alternating between fast and slow motions, Aric nipped and licked until she went crazy with need.

She whimpered the moment he drew back. His onyx eyes glanced at her from between her legs, searing her with a red-hot gaze.

"Let go, Lo-Lo. Be in the moment."

His tongue lapped again at her core, and a shattering climax ripped through her body. Her back arched as swells of heat rolled over her skin while his tongue delivered skillful strokes, drawing out every shudder.

With a moan, she collapsed back on the bed, panting.

Aric trailed hot kisses up her middle until he reached her achy breasts. "You make me crazy," he murmured.

Another crack.

Circling her nipple with his tongue, he flicked and sucked the bud, making a shot of pleasure rip through her middle. When she once again hovered on the edge, writhing with need, he positioned between her legs, his shaft halting at her entrance.

Forearms braced on either side of her head, he peered down at her. She grazed her nails along his strong, muscular arms, over the tattoo of a tree etched on his right bicep.

"Tell me about this," she rasped.

Anything to keep this moment going so it wouldn't end.

His eyes locked with hers and in that single moment she forgot where they were, forgot about her soul wasting away, forgot that their time together would soon end.

"It's a Willow tree." He smoothed the back of his fingers over her cheek. "Not only does it brand your name on my skin, but the falling leaves and sprouting regrowth represent your Ariel magic."

Every ounce of breath escaped her lungs. She never imagined the significance would be so…sexy.

He shivered, though the look in his eyes was pure heat. "You've always had a thing for biceps. It seemed fitting."

A slow smile lifted on the corner of her mouth. "I can't help it, they're my favorite part."

He cocked a brow, rolling his hips, sending another wave of tingles through her middle. "Your favorite?"

"Well…one of my favorites."

"Tell me the others," he whispered hotly against her ear.

A moan was all she managed as he slid deep inside her. His all-consuming gaze never shifted from hers as he steadily rocked inside her. Her hands never ceased roaming, exploring his powerful naked body for the final time. Not once did words escape their mouths.

Her climax gradually built, and the tight expression on his face told her he hovered on the brink too, holding on for her. This was the final time their bodies would be joined as one.

Right before she fell apart, the air shifted between them. Aric slowed the pace, brushing his fingers along her jaw. His expression filled with so much adoration it created a crippling pain in her heart, and she struggled to breathe.

"Lo-Lo," he murmured. "I don't want this to be goodbye."

She bit the inside of her cheek to prevent the tears spilling down her face. Instead of answering, she slid her hands around his nape, pulled his mouth to hers and kissed him soft and slow.

She couldn't bear watching him fall apart in front of her. Nor could she tell him the walls around her heart had long ago crumbled.

The taste of him and her, swirling together with a hint of whiskey, sent them both crashing over the edge. Her core clenched his length as his body shuddered on top of her with each pulse.

She didn't want this to be the end; she didn't want them to end. But goodbye was all she had left to give.

Chapter Twenty-Nine

Aric leaned against the doorframe and peered back at Willow, asleep in their bed. Her fiery red curls splayed over the pillow, the deep rise and fall of her chest.

The sight made his heart clench.

He'd convinced himself if he reminded her how good they were together, revived the bond between their souls, then she'd choose to return to the Heavens. She'd choose *him.*

He should've known better.

The hurt inside her, the hurt he'd created, ran too deep. It would take him centuries to repair the damage and once again, time wasn't on his side. She'd already chosen Hell and only came here to say goodbye.

Fate should've given them this last time.

He saw the sadness in her eyes. He felt it in her touch. Her soul needed to get out of Anahel one way or another and she needed to do it now. He couldn't blame her for choosing Hell. For centuries, she'd thought he'd willingly abandoned her. A few hours of pleasurable bliss wouldn't change her mind. He couldn't imagine how lost she felt without wings and the thought of Zath ripping them off made his fucking blood boil.

That wasn't the worst of it. This entire screw up traced back to the moment he cut off that fucking Fallen's wings because he threatened Willow and his

Chosen's soul.

Even if he could go back in time, he would still destroy that sonofabitch. The only thing he'd change would be removing the band before Fate exiled him. Better yet, he would never leave Willow's side. He would have made his own twisted deal with Fate and taken Willow to the mortal realm with him, rather than leaving her in the Heavens where he assumed protection wasn't necessary.

He didn't have the power to time travel, so there was no point looking back.

Over the course of the day, they'd talked about what Gabe had said and he'd tried harder to convince her to choose the Heavens. Deep down he knew she never would, and he had to let her go for good.

As she'd lay curled up by his side, he kept coming back to the fact their bond prevented her soul from healing. Removing the band should've destroyed the connection between their souls, but the more they'd made love, the more he felt it strengthen. The more he never wanted to leave her again.

Light seeped into his soul from hers. In any normal circumstances, that secured their ancient bond, strengthen it, but in this situation, it caused her soul to anchor more firmly in the desolate realm of Anahel. He couldn't hold her back any longer.

It didn't matter what color her wings were or whether she had any. He loved her soul and that would never change, regardless of the realms separating them.

Snatching the cell phone from his back pocket, he sent a short text to Raven requesting the night off. No further details because…he had no clue what to say. He'd never requested a day off in his entire existence, so if Raven declined, he was gonna be pissed. He needed more time, and this was something he had to do on his own.

The phone binged a second later with Raven's reply. *Yes.*

Raven probably assumed he requested the night off to drown his sorrows here at the cabin. Not completely incorrect, but not entirely correct either.

His gaze drifted back to Willow. Deep in slumber, she rolled onto her side facing him. Did she subconsciously sense the choice he was about to make? Did she sense the path he was about to choose?

He was wrong earlier. His fork-in-the-road moment wasn't when he stood on the rooftop with Willow, waiting to see if she kissed him or not. The fork in his two paths was this exact moment. He knew Fate had paved the paths for him, and he hoped she fucking knew what she was doing. The path he'd chosen flipped his entire existence upside down. If Fate bet on him choosing the other path instead, then he was well and truly screwed.

Under the light of the moon streaming through the open windows, Willow's pale skin held a grayish undertone. Her cheeks were more sunken than yesterday, and the circles under her eyes were darker. He wasted time standing here staring at her.

Willow's pulse quickened. He needed to leave before she woke up and talked him out of it. He knew she would disagree with his choice, but he couldn't let that sway his decision.

With one final glance, he eyed the nightstand where he left a bright yellow wildflower on top of a note he'd written. She'd find it when she woke and by then, his plan would be in motion.

His heart ached as he turned away and walked out the door, gently closing it behind him. This was the price he paid to prove she came first. *Always.*

Chapter Thirty

Aric lit a tealight candle and placed it on the stepped platform. He lost himself in the tiny flame as it stood tall in the still air. No breeze, no movement. Frozen in time, just like Willow.

He brushed over the space on his wrist where the band had been. The skin no longer warmed, more evidence that although he felt light in his soul, Willow's Ariel powers didn't fuel it.

Back to staring at the flame. Willow was his heart, the whole reason he woke each morning. Without her, how could he move forward? His love for her made him whole. Their two souls beat as one for so many centuries he no longer recalled a moment without her in it. Nor did he remember the boring existence he lived before she entered his life.

Lost in the flickering of the flame, his mind drifted back to the moment they started their life together. The moment he gave her his heart.

He'd searched every realm in the Heavens since their first encounter in the mortal realm, consumed with the need to see Willow again, hear her angelic voice, touch her ivory skin. The band he wore around his wrist warmed with her magic, pouring into their bond like a steady stream. A magnetic connection he'd never experienced drew him to her, like a beacon of light brightening the closer he came.

He exited the forest and skidded to a halt. His legs refused to work. Willow was there, and the sight made warmth spread through his damn chest. He was too much of a dumbass to turn and walk away, save himself from whatever was going on inside his stupid heart. Save himself from the inevitable crippling pain he'd experience if he lost someone like that. Someone who consumed his every waking moment.

The other part of him was too damn mesmerized by her fiery red curls tangled between bright, colorful wildflowers. She lay on her back beside a narrow stream, staring at the clear blue sky. The yellow dress she wore blended with the flowers as though she were one of them, right down to the white crisscross stitching and intricate lace along the capped sleeves.

Her delicate hand brushed over the petals, waving through the flowers like a wispy breeze, making his breath catch. The same warm orange glow from his band trickled between the stems, pulsing from the earth.

She rolled her head to the side and glanced at him. His stupid heart squeezed so tight it might shrivel up and die.

She smiled, brightening her hazel eyes. "Are you just going to stand there?"

Without further thought, he exited the pine forest and lay down beside her. She moved closer, weaved her fingers between his and rested her head against his shoulder. Peace and contentment flooded his veins and the band illuminated as bright as the sun.

Fate had created his soul for hers. In that moment, his heart claimed her as his soulmate, and he knew he'd follow her to the ends of the universe.

He kissed the top of forehead before closing his

eyes, listening to the chirping birds and the gentle trickle of the flowing stream. While they lay there, he conjured a simple log cabin over to the far side, complete with a swing hanging on the front porch. The cabin would be theirs forever. Because he'd never let her go.

Aric opened his eyes, coming back to the present. He'd worn that band on his wrist every day since the moment she gave it to him. It kept him strong for all those years, kept the light in his soul glowing bright when all he wanted to do was give up. Made with Ariel magic, it never deteriorated.

Being without the band was like being without her.

Her magic enabled nature to be reborn, transform and regrow, yet now, when she needed that ability the most, she didn't have it. Ariel powers wouldn't regenerate her wings, but without her wings, she had no hope of her powers returning. Only now, without the band on his wrist, he understood how empty she felt without them.

He'd give her life now, as she had given it to him back then. She was tougher than he gave her credit for and now he needed to step up to the plate. Do this for her.

With a heavy heart, he turned away from the flame and trudged out of the church for the final time. He wouldn't be welcome back here again.

He slipped out the doors, softly latching them closed behind him, and inhaled a deep breath that burned all the way down his throat. Was he really doing this?

With slow thuds, he descended the stone steps, and crossed to the gravel parking lot.

"Meeting here is slightly weird, if you ask me," Blaine's voice came from behind him.

Turning around, he peered at the roof and found Blaine perched on the edge, his unlaced boots dangling over the side.

"I didn't think you'd come," Aric replied.

Part of him had hoped Blaine wouldn't show, deciding for him.

Blaine slid off the roof and landed on the gravel before strolling over to him. "Leaving a note under my front door is a tad old-fashioned but intriguing all the same."

Without the ancient bond they'd once shared as Guardians, a note under the door of that creepy-ass mansion was the only way to reach Blaine.

For long moments, Aric stared at the first twinkling of stars appearing in the early evening sky. Was Fate looking down at him? Would she try to stop him? Was this part of her twisted plan?

"Anytime now. It's not like I don't have places to be," Blaine said, kicking the gravel with his boot.

Where should he start? He turned to Blaine. "Tell me exactly what Willow needs to do to complete her transition and regenerate her wings."

Blaine shrugged. "It's simple, really. She needs to return to Hell for the powers to take hold and fill her soul. To erase the light you kept clinging to."

Another fucking reminder he caused this entire screw up. "Are you're sure it will work?"

Blaine frowned as though Aric spoke another language. "Is that doubt or plain dumbness speaking?"

Aric sighed. "What's involved?"

"I'll mist her there, drop her off and return to bring

her back once the transition is complete."

"What about Zath? What happens if he finds her while she's there? Will he hunt her? Will he be waiting for her?" He raked his fingers through his hair. "You said you'd protect her."

Blaine half smirked, but in a blink, it disappeared. "I offered you that job, remember?" He exhaled an exaggerated breath. "Listen, because we're friends, how about I stay with her for a while? But if Zath raises his ugly head, I need to skedaddle."

That wasn't good enough. He didn't trust anyone to protect Willow, not even Blaine, and that was saying something. Although he was a Fallen now, Blaine had been one of the most lethal Guardians ever created.

He swallowed, moistening his dry throat. The decision should be easy, Willow's soul was at stake. Then why was it so goddamn hard?

He glanced back at the church. Protecting Willow was his duty, no one else's.

"I'll go with her. To Hell."

Blaine's face lit with triumph. "Ah, the loyal Guardian finally caves."

Aric clenched his jaw to stop from punching that smug expression right off Blaine's face. "I'm not caving. It's because I'm loyal that I'm doing this."

"Whatever you say."

His gut twisted in a knot. "Will you take me with her or not?"

Blaine tapped his chin, making him wait for an answer. "I'll take you with her…on one condition."

Another fucking deal. He should've known. "What's your price? A Chosen soul?" He threw his hands in the air. "No, wait, you already took that."

"Oh, Aric, always so bitter. My price is simple and easy: Swear allegiance to me when you Fall."

His stomach plummeted to his feet. Now shit got real.

Misting to Hell with Willow destroyed the light in his soul, he knew that, but giving his allegiance to a Fallen was another thing entirely. Even if that Fallen was once a Guardian he'd considered his brother. But not anymore.

When he Fell, his allegiance went to Willow and her only. Not Zath. Not Blaine.

"I want no part of your twisted game with Fate," Aric snapped. "What's between you two has only ever caused me fucking pain. I'm doing this for Willow and for no one else."

Blaine narrowed his eyes. "My plot against Fate is no twisted game, friend. It's a bloody battle of revenge. The bloodiest." Tiny flames lit inside his irises. "How dare she sit all high and mighty on her ice-queen throne, controlling everyone like her personal minions. Fate needs to be taken down. She deserves exactly what's coming to her."

Aric saw the hatred in Blaine's eyes, heard the bitterness in his tone and it scared the shit out of him. Was this what Willow had felt toward him? Is this what Willow would become after an eternity of separation?

No way would that happen on his watch. He couldn't force Willow back to the Heavens, so he'd stand by her side while she went to Hell. He wouldn't leave her again. Ever. They signed up for an eternity when their souls bonded, and that was exactly what they'd have.

If he held her in Anahel, then he'd get her out. And

he'd stand beside her every step of the way. Now was the time for him to sacrifice for her.

He exhaled a long, heavy breath. "I accept your condition, but I have one of my own."

Blaine waved his hand in the air for him to continue. "You return both of us to the mortal realm once our transition is complete. We're a package deal. Where one goes, so does the other."

That prevented Blaine from throwing him in the Infernal Pits for the hell of it and taking Willow back to the mortal realm without him.

Blaine inclined his head. "Very well. A package deal, it is."

There, he'd done it. Now, he totally understood the mortal phrase "a deal with the devil," and it made his stomach churn.

Too late now. He lifted his chin. "I need time to get things in order."

Blaine looked unfazed. "I assumed as much. You have until sunrise. Meet me at my place and we'll set out on our adventure."

As Blaine turned away and sauntered off into the night, a heavy weight pressed against Aric's chest.

Shit. *What the hell have I done?*

Chapter Thirty-One

Willow leaned her head back, so the firm jets of the shower massaged every inch of her scalp. The shower had nothing other than a bottle of manly-labeled shampoo, so she skipped washing her hair and made do with just a rinse. The soap smelled like Aric and she couldn't help but lather a little on her hands just so the scent lingered in the humid air.

The smell reminded her of their many hours tangled between the sheets as the day had faded into night. Making love to him was as blissful as she remembered. Made for each other, their souls and their bodies had always fit together perfectly in every way.

Gosh, she'd missed that. She'd missed him.

He'd left her a note and again she wondered where, and how, he found a wildflower when in this part of the realm, all the flowers had long died off for winter. The note asked her to stay but she couldn't. If Aric returned before she left, he'd convince her to stay longer, then one day would turn into a week, which would turn into a year.

Witnessing the sorrow in his eyes when he realized she was saying goodbye was hard enough. Now, each additional moment only deteriorated her soul a bit more until, soon, it wouldn't exist.

They might find each other again someday. She hoped that were true. But she had chosen to Fall and now was the time to complete that transition. Solidify her decision. Save her soul.

Her wings were important but the hollow feeling inside was more than that. Even without the band on his wrist, she still sensed Aric's absence, and it still felt like it bound her soul to him. Removing the band should've severed that connection, but instead, it made the gaping hole in her heart larger. Like a single thread still held on, fighting against the darkness, refusing to let go. Is that what stopped her from leaving the minute she rolled out of bed?

The fact her wings hadn't regrown, and her soul remaining in Anahel, represented her countless failures. She'd failed Aric for so long because she believed he abandoned her. When she turned her back on the Heavens, she failed Fate. Then she failed herself for being too weak to fight Zath when he sliced off her wings. By returning to Hell, she took back control and her failures no longer defined her.

The door to the bathroom swung open making Willow gasp.

Aric stood in the doorway, wearing black jeans and dark gray Henley, bracing his arm on the doorframe above his head, with a takeout bag dangling from his other hand.

Damn it! She was so stuck inside her head and enjoying the shower that she lost track of time.

"You're still here."

His voice held a hint of surprise like he suspected she'd leave before he returned. Her chest ached a little knowing she should have. Nothing he said could convince her otherwise.

To avoid the conversation while trapped in the

shower, she nodded at the bag hanging from his fingers. "I hope you brought dinner. Or is it breakfast? I have no idea what time it is."

He glanced at it as though he'd forgotten he even had it. "Yeah, there's a great Thai restaurant in town. I thought you might be hungry." His gaze slid back to her with a wild, dangerous glint that wasn't there a second ago. "May I join you?"

The air thickened. Her stomach did a flip while moisture instantly flooded her core. How easily he seduced her without even touching her.

He stood there, waiting for her answer. She should leave, but he kept drawing her in as only a soulmate could. Making her forget all the reasons she should.

Saying no and exiting the shower was easier, but instead she nodded.

Her heart sped up as he placed the takeout bag on the vanity top, removed his boots and approached the glass door. His eyes darkened making her shift under the weight of his molten stare.

She ogled his golden, tanned skin as he lifted his shirt in a slow and precise motion, as though giving her the chance to flip off the water and run out of the bathroom. Pity her legs wouldn't work. Or her brain. Every muscle across his torso twitched and bulged as he shucked off the rest of his clothes, tossing them aside with his foot.

The second the glass shower door opened, nippy air rushed in and danced along her skin. She backed against the tiles as he entered, closing the door behind him.

"I really thought you'd be gone," he mumbled, consuming the space around her.

"So did I," she said, aloud or inside her head, she wasn't sure.

His fingers grazed up and down her arms making goosebumps sprout over her flesh, though she was anything but cold. Every nerve inside her body sizzled.

"I can't get enough of you." His deep voice rumbled in the confined space. "For over a thousand years, I took having you for granted, not knowing that with one choice, Fate would rip us apart."

Her head leaned back against the tiles. She should leave. It prevented them both from reliving centuries of pain when their paths forced them in opposite directions again. But how could she when the words he spoke were the truth? They had both taken each other for granted. She was just as much to blame as him.

He inched closer, his smoldering gaze peering down at her, seeping deep into her soul. Rough fingers circled her hips making a hot tingle race down her middle.

"I've missed having you in the shower," he growled, nudging his erection against her middle.

She rolled her hips a little to tease the tip. Wasn't she going…somewhere…?

He tilted her chin up with his thumbs. She stared at him, lost in the moment, lost in his eyes as their warm breaths collided between them. Her breath quickened, anticipation fluttering in her belly like those damn butterflies had returned. She would remember this moment for the rest of her existence. The love in his eyes, the warmth of his touch, the steady drum of his heart in time with hers.

His gaze dipped to her mouth and without another word, he lowered his lips to hers. A hint of whiskey met her tongue as he kissed her, slow and gentle, as though savoring every taste. How easily they fell back into a familiar rhythm. How easily they forgot their relationship had an expiration date.

All day he pleasured her in ways she missed, yearned for, and in a way only he could touch her. Now she wanted that for him.

Flattening her palms on his firm chest, she pressed him back slightly. Once there was enough space between them, she squatted, supporting herself with her back against the tiles.

"Lo-Lo, you don't have to—"

She wanted this. If only the moment could last forever. If only they could.

Aric sucked in a sharp breath when she licked along his shaft, his hands braced against the tiles above her head. His reaction caused a familiar stir deep inside her belly. Giddy on the sensations, she ran her tongue along the length before circling the tip.

His hips bucked.

Gripping the base with her palm, she worked her way around the head before gliding his thickness inside her mouth. She eased him all the way in and back out, grazing her teeth gently along his skin the way he liked.

With her other hand, she gripped his ass, setting a slow and steady rhythm. Through wet lashes, she glanced at him as his groans deepened. The vulnerability in his eyes as he watched her take him unwound the last of her restraint. If she ever had any.

"Baby…"

His strangled voice broke her thoughts and she eased back, stroking his shaft with her hand. His tight muscles contracted with each stroke. His hips bucked.

She needed more from him, but it wouldn't be enough. They could make love one more time, three more times, it didn't matter. It wouldn't change the situation. Nor would it change their paths. Eventually, it would all end.

"I want you inside me."

Cupping her face, he guided her to stand. "Good. 'Cause that's exactly where I'm heading."

He lifted her with ease, locking her legs around his waist. Wrapping her arms around him, she held on tight, held onto this last moment with everything she had.

The shower sprayed over his shoulders, pooling water between their bodies until it cascaded over her hips. The air became so thick and humid dizziness washed over her. He must've sensed it, because with one hand he fiddled with the taps, cooling the temperature. A pointless exercise given the heat their joined bodies made.

Taking advantage of his distraction, she rocked her hips, rubbing her core along his hardness.

He growled, tightening his grip on her thigh. "Any more of that and this show will end before it begins."

"That's never slowed you down before."

His grin set her whole damn body on fire.

"Damn straight."

Lifting her, he nudged his head at her entrance and gently eased inside, filling her. Soft moans escaped her lips as he steadily rocked his hips. Her eyes rolled back from the swell of pleasure rushing over her skin. The heat between her legs and the coolness of the tiles against her back created a muddle of sensations.

"Aric…"

Water splashed over her hips as though they were back in the Heavens, underneath a waterfall. She wasn't going to last. Already her core tingled, hovering on the edge, more intense each time he thrust. Lowering his head, he grazed his stubble along her neck sending tiny tremors of pleasure straight to her center.

"Let go, baby. Fall apart with me," he rasped against her ear.

That was all it took for her to spiral over the edge, her core pulsing and clenching as intense light ripped through her body.

He squeezed her thighs, holding her in place. "I want you to be mine, Lo-Lo. Forever."

"I'll always be yours." In her heart, she told the truth. She was his, would always be his, if Fate hadn't gotten in the way.

"Just as I'm yours."

He kissed her as they climaxed together, claiming every cell of her body right to the gaping hole where her soul had once been. Bright pulses of light traveled through her blood, and for a moment, she could have sworn the light came from Aric. How? Their connection ended when he took off the band.

For precious moments afterward, he held her until their breaths slowed and their heartbeats steadied. Easing back, he nipped at her bottom lip before lowering her legs. She stroked her fingers up and down his arms, her heart clenching when they brushed his tattoo. Each time they made love just made it harder to say goodbye.

He cupped her face in his palms. "As much as I wanna continue this, there's something waiting for you on the porch and dinner is getting cold."

Her heart skipped. Really? Nothing could be better than this. "What is it?"

A mischievous grin lit his eyes. "It's a surprise."

Without waiting for her reply, he washed, rinsed and exited the shower as fast as only a male could. Ugh! This surprise had better be good.

She gave her hair a final rinse and squeezed the excess water from the ends before turning off the taps. After insisting on drying her, Aric wrapped a towel around his waist—*sigh*—and snatched the bag of food off the vanity top.

"I'll meet you on the porch. If I stay in the bathroom any longer, we're gonna end up back in that shower."

"Wouldn't that be a good thing?"

His eyes darkened, and the look would've melted her panties if she wore any.

"The thoughts swirling in my head are anything but *good*."

Heat flashed over her skin. Her breath quickened. Deciding between having his hands roam over her body and the surprise on the porch was absolute torture. Alas, her tummy growled, becoming impatient and deciding for her.

"Food it is," he said over his shoulder, exiting the bathroom.

Why did she keep prolonging the inevitable? Her plan was to leave before he returned, but something deep inside kept her here and the damn thing prevented her from leaving.

After dressing, she followed the sweet smell of stir-fried meat out to the porch. Her breath caught as she stepped out the door. Not because of the bitter air or the flurry of snowflakes falling from the night sky. But because of the tiny flickering tea-light candles scattered along the length of the railing, with shot glasses of wildflowers positioned between each one. Her heart swelled. He'd created the perfect setting for a romantic date.

Aric sat on the porch swing in jeans and that damn form-fitting shirt, gently rocking back and forth. Beside him, a takeout food container and a glass of wine sat on a small table.

"Aric…" she whispered. "This is beautiful."

The hole in her chest widened.

He lifted a shoulder as though he didn't care, but the drop in his chest and slight part of his lips from a long exhale told her otherwise. She knew him too well.

He patted the cushion beside him. "Come and eat."

Once settled on the swing, he draped a thick blanket over her legs and passed a container of meat and noodles. She dug in. Each mouthful an explosion of delicious flavors, so much better than the foul leftovers in Blaine's fridge.

"Have you thought any more about returning to the Heavens?"

Date night had an ulterior motive.

Why didn't he understand that she couldn't go back there? Her soul wasted away in the Heavens just as much as it did in Anahel. Not wasted but it sure felt that way. Why didn't he get that?

"There's nothing more to think about."

He turned to her and the pain behind his eyes made her chest ache.

"I just want you to be sure."

Of course, she was sure. She'd thought about this a

thousand times. Then why did his words make that hole even deeper? Another mouthful of noodles didn't help because now they tasted like soggy cardboard.

"I need to know this is definitely what you want."

She placed the container on the table and pivoted to face him. "I can't stay in Anahel and waste away to nothing. Surely, you don't want that either?"

Maybe turning the tables on him would work. He said himself their bond held her in Anahel, but would he really want their connection to make her soul wither away and die?

He lowered his head. "No, I don't."

While he took a slow draw of whiskey, she stared at his gorgeous face. The thin dark beard trailing his strong jaw, the slight cleft in his chin, his full bottom lip.

"When will you go?" he asked, his voice rough.

"After I leave here, I guess. Blaine said he'd take me when I was ready, but I can't keep delaying it. I don't know how much time my soul has left."

He nodded, staring toward the flickering candles scattered over the railing.

Goodbye sex was so much easier than this conversation. How did she feel so loved and whole one minute, and the next, feel like she was making the biggest mistake of her existence?

"I'm scared, Aric," she muttered.

He curled an arm around her shoulder, drawing her closer. Which made it so much harder.

"I'm scared about going back. What if Zath captures me? What if I'm not strong enough to get back to the mortal realm?"

He placed his glass down and took her hand.

"You're so much stronger than you think."

Her eyes stung. "I know I pretend to be confident and tough like you, but inside, I'm really not."

That brought a grin to his face. "You're braver than you give yourself credit. Not every angel could go through what you did and come out the other side." His face softened. "Although it kills me that I wasn't there to protect you, I'm proud of you. I'm proud of how you took a stand to leave the Heavens, even though I would've preferred you didn't. I'm proud of you for holding on while you're stuck in Anahel and for returning to Hell even though it terrifies you."

Letting go of her hand, he brushed the back of his fingers along her jaw. "You're full of strength and courage, Lo-Lo. You'll make it back to the mortal realm. I know you will."

She swallowed the lump in her throat. "How? How can you be so sure?"

"Because I'm coming with you."

She recoiled. "What? You can't be serious?"

His steady gaze held hers. "Deadly serious. I've already made a deal with Blaine to ensure he takes me with you. We'll mist there together."

"No!" Her voice rose a notch.

She scooted out from under his arm as though the lack of physical contact would snap Aric out of his idiotic plan. "A deal with Blaine? What did he make you sacrifice?"

His lips thinned. "It doesn't matter, baby. The only thing that matters is that we're together."

This was her mess and she wouldn't drag Aric into it. She couldn't allow herself to get all dreamy about a future together. If he went with her, he'd become a

Fallen, too. He'd give away his whole existence, everything he'd ever known. He'd break his oath to Fate and his brothers.

As much as she wanted him, had longed for the moment he chose her, this wasn't the right way. "Blaine does everything for a reason. If he agreed to take you, then he's up to something. No, Aric. I won't let you do this."

He took her hands and squeezed tight. "It's already done. I was wrong earlier, thinking I could let you go. I can't. You're the only one for me, Willow. Where you go, I follow."

She shook her head, the lump in her throat tightening. "You don't understand what you're doing."

"I understand perfectly. Listen to me. Here we are again, as history repeats itself and this time, I'm not fucking it up. This time I'm choosing you. If it means going to Hell to heal your soul and regenerate your wings, then I'm coming. I've failed you too many times. I won't do it again." He cupped her face with one hand. "I would Fall for you, Lo-Lo, every single day."

"Don't say things you don't mean," she whispered, her eyes filling with tears.

His stare didn't waver. "I can't lie."

Would he truly Fall for her? Was this really happening?

She eased her lips against his, poured out all her love for him, told him all the things she wanted to say but couldn't find the words.

They would be together again, their souls no longer existing in different realms. They'd no longer be on opposite sides of the war between the Heavens and Hell. Returning to Hell could break their bond, but she had faith a new connection would form if they transitioned together. She would have everything she'd ever wanted back in her arms.

He drew back, admiring her face. "I've gotta go see Raven, but I wanted to tell you beforehand, so you didn't leave without me."

"Okay. But before you go, tell me where you keep finding the wildflowers. I thought you couldn't mist?"

He grinned liked he just won the lottery. "When we make it through this and come out the other side, I'll show you."

A future. They once again had a future together.

"Is this really happening?"

He kissed her forehead, lingering for a moment. "Sure is, baby. Wait for me here, okay? We'll go to Blaine together at sunrise."

She nodded, too overcome to speak. Thoughts of the deadline on their souls raced through her head; these were their last moments together in the mortal realm and she wanted to spend every second with him. The unknown on the other side scared her but having Aric by her side gave her the strength to face the gates of Hell, the strength to risk Zath capturing her. The strength to step forward. Aric gave her the strength only a soulmate could.

"How much time does that leave us?" she purred, tossing the blanket aside to straddle his hips.

He hardened against her core. She unbuckled his belt and jeans while his hot palms slid underneath her dress. He groaned when they reached her bare hips, his eyes darkened, heated.

"Take all the time you need."

Chapter Thirty-Two

Aric touched down on a patch of dewy half-dead grass in a secluded open space on the side of the mountain. This place was the first location he'd thought of to request a meeting when he texted Raven earlier.

They all had their own hideaways, a place they checked out, got away from things for a bit, a place of their own. He had the cabin on the outer edge of the Guardian's property and Raven had this place. EJ…who the fuck knew where he went but given it was forbidden to bring a mortal to the mansion, his chill-out pad was likely the club. Raine and River, he guessed, hadn't been in the mortal realm long enough yet to need a timeout space.

No surprise he beat Raven here, given tonight was Raven's night off. He relaxed his wings behind his back and glanced at the home screen on his phone, three o'clock in the morning.

He and Willow had taken their time on the porch swing.

Focusing back on the task at hand, he surveyed the vacant space. He'd scoped out the place a handful of times when Raven had gone off the radar and he and EJ found him and hauled his ass back to the mansion. Nine times outta ten, one of them found Raven here.

He never understood Raven's fascination for the spot. There wasn't anything special here. It had a kick-ass panoramic view of the Snowy Mountains, but zero appeal. Ugly large gray boulders closed in one side and thick bushland surrounded the other. Nothing to sit on, nothing to sleep on, there weren't even any lights, well, except for some glass lanterns hanging around the perimeter that weren't there the last time he'd visited.

He grinned to himself. To think Raven made fun of him for being romantic. Raven too had a sappy side.

Speaking of Raven...

The Guardian swooped down and landed beside him. "Why the hell are we meeting here?" Raven grumbled. "Couldn't we meet at the mansion or that whiskey bar?"

Straight to business. Good, the sooner they got this over with, the sooner he got back to Willow, the sooner he...

Swallowing the lump in his throat, he stared into the dark night, focusing on the shadowy mountains looming in the distance, caving in around him.

"I didn't wanna run into the others."

Raven, folding his jet-black wings behind his back, stepped closer. "Is something wrong? Is it Willow?"

Yes. No. Kind of...

"Yeah, man." He raked a hand through his hair. "I went to see her. Well, she came to the cabin. I thought I could convince her to return to the Heavens. I thought maybe she chose Hell because I gave the band back." He paused as the weight of all his choices caught up with him. "It didn't work. Her final choice is Hell."

Raven swore under his breath. "I'm sorry, my man."

Aric paced in a tight circle, his boots wearing a track in the patch of grass. Shit, this was so much harder than he'd expected.

"I should've brought bourbon with me," Raven muttered from his right.

Aric pivoted and found Raven standing beside a massive boulder, his arms crossed with a who-do-I-need-to-kill look on his face.

"Yeah," he grumbled. Back to the track in the grass. "Maybe."

His insides coiled in a tight knot. Telling Raven that Willow had chosen Hell was a helluva lot easier than confessing his own intention. That required more balls than ever.

What if his backup plan didn't work and he and Willow were stuck in Hell for the rest of eternity? What if Raven abandoned him?

Raven cleared his throat, pulling him back to the present. "Tell me what happened."

Aric kicked at the stupid grass again, digging up dirt with the toe of his boot. "What made you so sure you could save Blaine?"

Raven's brows furrowed. "I dunno. I convinced myself he could never completely forsake the Heavens. That there would always be a shred of light left in his soul. The fact there are still flecks of black in his crimson wings, after all this time, tells me there's something different about his Fall. He didn't transition like the others. That alone makes him worth saving." Raven's gaze grew distant. "Plus, he's my brother. I have to at least try."

Back to wearing track in the grass where the only sounds came from his boots crunching the dirt and forest creatures skittering deep in the woods.

How the hell did he tell Raven? The Guardian he'd

treated as a brother for more than millennia, the Guardian he'd give his life for. The Guardian he'd swore an oath to when he agreed to save Blaine.

Now I'll need saving.

"Don't do this, Aric."

Shit. Aric stopped dead in his tracks. Spun to face Raven. "Whadda you mean?" He acted dumb even though he knew Raven must've heard his thought.

Raven pushed off the boulder. "You think I don't know why you're meeting me here? I'm not stupid. I know what you're about to do." He shoved his hands in his jeans pocket. "I won't let you. I won't let another brother of mine Fall, especially when I can prevent it."

Fuck. He'd never meant to make this harder for Raven. He didn't want it to feel like Blaine Falling all over again. But he had to do what was right for Willow. He wouldn't be without her again and there was no way he'd leave her unprotected.

In the Heavens she was safe, out of danger, out of reach of the Fallen and Zath. But in Hell she didn't have those same protections. Protecting her was his job, goddamn it. He wouldn't fail again.

"I have to. I won't let her do this alone."

"Gabe could force her back to the Heavens."

Aric shook his head. "Gabe said *she* has to choose. Not me, not you, not Gabe. Willow."

Now, Raven carved up the dead grass with his shoes. "We'll figure out another way. I'll request a meeting with Fate."

His fists balled. "Like hell you will. Fate will make it worse. She'll make Willow return just so she can lock her in Tartirim for the rest of eternity."

Raven stilled. "I used to think the same, and hell,

maybe Fate is a bitch. But Aric…" He narrowed his stare. "I have a feeling she's up to something and sending us to this realm is one piece in her twisted puzzle. I don't think she'd intentionally hurt us."

"She fucking banished us," Aric sneered. "She would've known it wouldn't be easy saving Blaine, but she sent us anyway. She made each of us fucking *choose* a path without knowing the consequences."

He kicked a stone off the edge of the mountain and watched it coast through the air before it lost momentum and plummeted into the valley. Fate had better have a plan, and that plan had better be a step ahead of Blaine. If Fate had a moment of weakness, Blaine's revenge might just take her down, ending the universe as they knew it.

"I don't want Fate involved any more than she already is."

Raven took a moment before answering. "Fine. But I need more time to figure out another way to save Willow before I end up having to save both your asses."

"Sorry, man. Blaine gave me until sunrise. I need to respect her decision." He exhaled a deep breath. "And I need you to respect mine."

He sat on the grass with his arms crossed atop his bent knees. Exhaustion took its toll. He couldn't remember the last time he'd slept or lay under the sun's healing rays—earth magic he'd soon lose.

"I should've brought the fucking bourbon," Raven grumbled, planting his ass beside Aric.

"Yep."

Silence passed between them, as though they'd reached a stalemate—neither of them conceding but neither willing to let the other win. Heaviness pressed against his chest when he thought of Raven losing another brother. But he'd vowed to stick by Willow. He'd vowed his love and protection to her when they joined their souls.

He'd failed her once by abandoning her in the Heavens. He wouldn't abandon her again.

Even if that meant breaking his oath to Fate and turning his back on his brothers. This time he chose Willow.

He picked at a piece of grass. "Can you honestly say you wouldn't Fall for Tayla?"

Raven exhaled a long breath. "I'd do it in a heartbeat."

That was the answer he hoped to hear. The answer he needed to hear, to confirm he wasn't going bat-shit-crazy.

"Tell me you have a plan."

Aric scoffed. "When am I ever without one?"

Raven remained silent as he filled him in on his dodgy deal with Blaine. The details regarding exactly how shit went down once they arrived in Hell were still foggy; he needed to sort that out with Blaine before they left. The king of surprises wouldn't blindside him.

After a few moments, Raven spoke. "I'm glad you added the package deal condition. It'll be easier to keep track of you both if you're together. Plus, it'll prevent him from double-crossing you once both of you arrive in Hell."

"Provided he keeps his word."

Raven glanced upward at the sky. "He may be a Fallen, but he's never gone back on his word. His hatred isn't directed at you, or any of us for that matter. Otherwise, he would've tried to take us out decades ago. I think having us in the mortal realm keeps him amused or something. Like he'd be bored if we weren't here."

Aric sighed. "Maybe. But man, Blaine's got a serious grudge against Fate. He didn't give me any details, but he's out for blood. I hope she's prepared."

"I suspect she's been preparing for a while."

They sat like that, side by side on the ground until Aric felt coldness seep through his jeans. One part of him wanted to stay like that for longer, frozen in time, no battles, no Fallen, no plans that sent him and Willow to Hell. Just two brothers, sitting on the edge of a mountain enjoying each other's company, without the weight of this world heavy on their shoulders.

But that wasn't reality. The battles, the Fallen and the plan for a screwed up field trip to Hell existed, and he needed to face them head-on.

Grabbing his cell from inside his jacket, he checked the home screen—shit; the time was later than he thought. He needed to get back to Willow and prep her on the plan before they ventured off at sunrise…just over an hour left.

He stood and brushed off the dirt and grass before offering a hand to Raven. Raven accepted, and Aric pulled him up.

He cleared his throat. "I guess this is it. Tell the others not to be too pissed and keep a fucking leash on Raine, so she doesn't hunt my ass down and hang me from a tree." He took a set of keys from his pocket and dropped them in Raven's open palm. "Don't let River touch my bike."

Raven nodded, pocketing the keys.

Jesus, he sucked at goodbyes. "Tell EJ…" His

throat tightened making it impossible to speak. Dirt or some shit got stuck in his eyes causing them to water.

"I will, Aric." Raven squeezed his shoulder, staring hard into his eyes. "I'm gonna bring you both back, you know that don't you?"

His gaze locked with Raven's while unsaid words passed between them. Raven's look vowed he wouldn't give up on him and confirmed there was light at the end of this nightmare. He and Willow just had to make it through the darkness. The look communicated exactly what Aric needed.

He gave Raven a curt nod. "I'm counting on it, man."

Chapter Thirty-Three

Willow should be excited. Ecstatic even. Finally, she and Aric had their happily ever after and nothing came between them. Eons of space and time no longer separated them. They were together again, on the same side of the fence in the war raging between Fate and Zath. They were no longer impacted by the fighting between the Fallen and Guardians.

Fate no longer controlled her destiny, her movements and her choices. She had everything she hoped for when she Fell. So why was there a sour taste lingering her mouth?

Blaine assured her she'd only return to Hell for a short period, long enough for her soul to completely blacken. That was all it took. Now Aric would be there to protect her from Zath. It didn't matter if her Fallen powers were instant or how strong they became; she was no match for Zath. He was one of the most powerful angels before Fate imprisoned him in Hell.

What held her back then?

She was ready to become a Fallen. This was the path she'd chosen, the path she mapped for herself. But that was before she saw Aric again and heard his side of the story. A side vastly different from the version she'd played in her mind since he'd left the Heavens. She never considered her version was wrong.

She'd been so wrapped up in resentment, she never

once stopped to consider how Aric felt. Blaine had ensured that. Each time he met with her, Blaine reminded her of the hurt, using it to his advantage and she'd let him. Her bitterness blinded her until she didn't see that ceasing the pain also meant giving up. Giving up on what she believed, on the vow she'd given to the Guardian who loved her more than anything. It meant giving up on her soulmate.

Now, as she stood at a crossroads in her path, she thought twice about whether Fate truly couldn't influence her destiny. Because once again, she faced a decision between right and wrong, good and bad, light and dark.

Did Fate have control over Anahel, too? Or could her soul remain tethered to Aric even though Zath syphoned her remaining light?

She twirled the band in her fingers. Was a soulmate bond more powerful than her Ariel magic?

The timber stairs outside creaked, interrupting her internal torture. Expecting Aric, she padded to the front door, swung it open, and stepped onto the porch. The candles had extinguished long ago, leaving only the light from the low yellow moon illuminating the foggy night.

Aric wasn't there. Instead, EJ perched on the top step, his gaze distant, a grim look on his face.

His palms rubbed over his stubble, before glancing her way. "Hey, Red."

He'd called her that since the day they first met, way back when she and Aric became one. Her chest tightened. Why did everything feel so comfortable? So familiar? Like she wasn't about to become a fully-fledged Fallen, which included the instinct to kill the

Guardian sitting in front of her.

Why was everything so damn complicated?

EJ patted the space beside him on the step. "Join me for a minute?"

She crossed the porch and sat down, wrapping her arms around her knees. "It's been a while."

She was terrible at small talk and awkward silence, and right now was as awkward as it came.

"Yep. Three hundred and seventy-two years, give or take." EJ lifted a shoulder. "I'm kinda losing count these days."

Had it been that long? She peered at EJ while he stared toward the mountain range. He still wore a dark gray beanie with strands of dirty blond hair poking out from underneath, but the rest of his attire had hardened since she last saw him in the Heavens. He wore frayed black jeans, torn in more places than not with a white tee that stretched over his broad chest, failing to conceal the tattoos inked across his shoulders and down his arms.

Perhaps the Guardian's exile had taken its toll on them all in different ways.

EJ cleared his throat. She couldn't remember him ever having an issue with conversation.

"You know, Red…Fate sent me the weirdest vision earlier."

Her heart sank. *Oh no, please tell me she doesn't know.*

"The vision was of Ric." EJ paused and glanced at the sky. "Hellfire surrounded him, his eyes glowing red…crimson wings splayed wide behind his back. You get the idea."

She bit the inside of her lip so hard a metallic taste

seeped onto her tongue.

"I thought to myself, that can't be right. Ric isn't losing his faith. He's releasing your soul from Anahel. Even without the band, the light in his soul would be over-flowing after that sacrifice."

EJ swiveled her way and his ice-blue gaze locked with hers.

She held her breath, dreading his next words. Not daring to turn away, not daring to speak either.

"Then I thought, what could possibly make Ric become a Fallen? You found each other again, reunited and got all freaky, despite your soul being stuck in Anahel. He gave the band back to save you." Another painful pause. "Then it hit me. What would Ric do to prove his love for you?"

She turned away as the air vanished from her lungs. "That's between Aric and me."

"I know, Red. I'm not judging your decision. Who knows what I'd do if my wings were hacked off by that psycho? I also don't know what I'd do if my soul was stranded in Anahel. But what I do know is this: For the three hundred and seventy-two years, I've had this curse, never once has Fate sent me a vision of the future where I could change the outcome. That was her sick little twist. I could see the future but never change it. I have no control over when the visions come, and it eats away at me each time I get there too frickin' late. But you know what?"

The hardness in his expression made her scoot backward a little.

"This time she didn't torture me with a vision in real time. This time she sent it early, with enough time to do something about it. You catch my drift?"

A knot formed low and tight in her gut, churning around inside the swarm of emotions. Fate knew and sent EJ here to stop her.

"You think I haven't thought about this choice a million times?"

He sighed heavily, his shoulders sagging. "I'm not saying you haven't. All I'm saying is that I hope you understand what you're asking of Ric. 'Cause he may have been exiled from you, but he never once forgot about you. He's fought beside us every single day, determined to save Blaine so he could fulfill his deal with Fate and return to you. Ric stepped up on F-Day back in the Heavens and stood beside Rave, as a brother, a friend, a Guardian."

His gaze grew distant toward those mountains again. "He hasn't been the same without you, and I know your separation took its toll, but he never gave up. And there were so many times when he could've."

She lowered her voice. "I have to leave Anahel. My soul dies a little more each moment I remain stuck there. Soon, there'll be nothing left. I can't stay here forever, EJ. I have to make the choice."

He draped one arm over his knee. "I know. I also know you can go either way. Up or down. You have the power to choose. What you're asking of Ric, what you're choosing for yourself…it can't be easily undone. If it could, we would've saved Blaine the minute we got here."

She stood and descended the steps, pacing the narrow gravel path. EJ was right, she knew. Becoming a Fallen wasn't something she could easily undo, otherwise, Aric would've returned to the Heavens centuries ago.

What was she asking of Aric? Was she so selfish she'd make him Fall just so they weren't apart again? So, she didn't return to Hell by herself? The thought of going back there alone made bile rise in her throat but the alternative split her heart in two.

Blaine could take her to Hell. But deep down, she didn't want to lose Aric and his determination to keep her safe would send him after her anyway.

Was becoming a Fallen worth making Aric sever his connection with the Heavens? With his family? Break his oath to his brothers?

"Our wings don't define us, Red. Our soul does."

She pivoted to face him. "How can you say that? The fact that we have different colored wings differentiates us from each other."

She felt broken without her wings. A failure. They connected her to immortality, to her powers and made her whole. They would only regenerate once her soul left Anahel.

EJ shrugged. "It doesn't matter what color our wings are, or if we have none. What matters is what's in our soul." He leaned back against the banister. "Mortals do it all the time."

"Do what?"

"Keep living. They lose a piece of themselves in a tragic accident, in battle or a horrific attack, and they get back up and keep living. Christ, mortals even have dedicated sporting events these days to prove their courage and determination to keep moving forward. You don't think they'd want to go back in time and prevent it from happening? Sure they would, but they can't. They don't throw away their life because of an obstacle placed in their path. Instead, they adapt and keep on living."

"That's not the same, and you know it. I'm not just choosing whether to get my wings back or what color they'll be. I'm choosing not to die in Anahel."

"Really? Because I think you're afraid to return to the Heavens. I think you're afraid to keep on living without him."

She was more afraid of facing her failures head-on and existing in the Heavens as though nothing had happened. Carrying on as though her and Aric hadn't reunited for a fleeting moment, only to have it taken all away.

They couldn't guarantee Fate would even grant her entry, let alone give her Ariel wings and position back.

"The Willow I knew created life, not destroyed it."

She flinched. "I didn't ask Aric to do this. This was his idea. I'm not making him do anything he doesn't want. Anyway, I'm not the same Willow you once knew."

"Is that what you truly believe?" EJ raised an eyebrow. "You don't get it, do you? He's always chosen you. Every choice he's ever made has been to keep you safe. To return to you. And I know he'll do anything not to lose you again."

I'd Fall for you, Lo-Lo—the words Aric had said to her.

EJ stood. "Okay, I've said my peace. Our little chat is officially over." He descended the steps and gave her a brotherly peck on the cheek. "I truly hope I made it in time because it totally sucks when I don't."

She stared into the night as EJ flew away, his black wings like shadows passing over the thick clouds. Wispy fog rolled between the trees toward the cabin, like ghostly beings stalking her, closing in, choking her into deciding.

The pre-dawn glow peeked from behind the mountains, reminding her of the time. Aric had left a couple of hours ago to finalize things with Raven—do the honorable task and let him know his decision. He would return any minute.

Her time was running out.

Could she really let Aric Fall for her? Let him sever his connection with the Heavens just so she healed her soul and avoided returning there? Damn Fate and her twisted paths. Somehow, she still influenced her choices, and because Aric chose her, their paths were a package deal.

Facing the cabin, she peered through the open door to the wildflower standing tall in a shot glass. The cabin a replica of the one he'd conjured for them in the Heavens that had been their home.

She inhaled a deep, slow breath, exhaling even slower. If Aric held on for this long, could he hold on for a bit longer or would another separation break him and send his soul into darkness anyway? Could she draw on his strength to save him, even if it meant losing him at the same time?

In this moment, she had to make the right decision, because EJ had a point. Signing a soul to Zath and becoming a Fallen wouldn't only affect her and it wasn't easily undone.

She sagged against the railing. Her connection with Aric was so strong that he pulled her soul into Anahel when she Fell. He said he held her back but maybe what he'd done was save her. Maybe he'd prevented her from becoming a Fallen, from making the biggest mistake of her entire existence.

In the beginning, she'd wanted to bury the pain of him abandoning her, to sever their bond and get her powers back. But that was before she knew the truth, before she knew what Aric had suffered, too.

Healing her soul and having her wings back meant everything to her, but was it worth destroying her soulmate? It didn't matter whether she was broken or a failure, Aric loved her regardless.

She had to free her soul, but only one path also saved Aric.

Lifting her chin, she turned her back on the cabin. Now was her turn. Time to repay Aric for saving her, show him she wouldn't give up on them either. Show Aric that she loved him for eternity. Whether he wore the band or not, she'd honor their soulmate bond no matter how far apart they were. She'd prove that she'd wait for him, regardless of how long their mission took.

With her mind made up, she closed her eyes and imagined the pristine landscape of the Heavens. Imagined a connection to her soul in Anahel, and envisioned it filling with the bursts of light Aric gave her. Imagined the warmth of his love filling her heart.

"Gabe," she whispered. Hoping like hell she summoned him in time.

Chapter Thirty-Four

Aric trudged through the forest, head down, lost deep in thought. He'd landed away from the cabin intending to walk off the damn sinking feeling low in his gut. He needed that gone before he saw Willow. She always saw through his bullshit—now wouldn't be any different.

It didn't matter anyway. He'd decided, made a deal with Blaine, and squared things over with Raven. There was no point delaying it any further.

He stomped on a twig and the snap echoed in the still, pre-dawn darkness. Between the trees, the first tendrils of sunrise snuck through the branches, warning him to hurry his ass up.

He hadn't been able to face EJ and was too much of a coward to send a text. EJ would've hunted his ass down and talked him out of it quicker than it would've taken to text a reply. Raven would break the news, and EJ could kick his ass when—if—he ever made it back to the mortal realm. As a damn Fallen.

The root of his gut churning—if. Because, there were no guarantees he and Willow would make it back. No guarantees Blaine wouldn't double-cross them both, and no guarantees Zath wouldn't destroy their souls before they had enough Fallen power to fight back.

No one knew whether he and Willow would even give a shit about each other once their souls blackened.

Cutting their tie with the Heavens meant severing their soulmate connection for good. Another might form, but what if it didn't? He slammed his open palm into a nearby trunk, cracking the bark. So many fucking ifs.

"You gonna leave without saying goodbye?"

He stopped dead in his tracks. Glancing up, he found EJ standing at the perimeter of the forest, hands tucked in his ripped jeans, shoulder leaning against a tree.

A shuddered sigh left his lungs. So much for not wanting to face EJ.

He cleared his throat, trying to rid the damn knot forming. "I'm shit at goodbyes."

EJ tsked at him. "And here I thought we were brothers."

"I don't wanna make this harder than it already is."

EJ rubbed the back of his neck. His usually youthful face seemed older, harder. "I don't think it can get any harder than this, Ric."

A prickle danced along his nape. Peering past EJ, he spotted the cabin in the distance. Light spilled through the uncovered windows, yet, he couldn't see any movement inside. The porch swing hung still. The door closed.

Something was wrong. Why couldn't he see Willow inside? Why didn't he sense anyone in the cabin?

Without realizing, his feet took off toward the cabin. EJ snagged the shoulder of Aric's jacket.

He shot him a glare. "I'm sorry, man. I've gotta go. Something's wrong"

"She's not there, Ric," EJ muttered.

He frowned. "Whadda you mean, she's not there?"

EJ lowered his voice. "She's already gone."

Heat rose on his neck. Gone? Gone where? Surely, she didn't go to Hell without him?

He pulled out of EJ's grasp and raced to the cabin, slamming open the door. His heart hammered in his chest as he searched inside. Everything was how he'd left it a couple of hours ago; the sheets tangled on the bed, his clothes from earlier in the day lay on the wooden floor. But Willow wasn't there.

He bolted to the bathroom. She wasn't there either, yet, her scent still lingering in the air was a solid sign he hadn't dreamed the whole damn thing. Willow had been here.

He spun to EJ who hung back by the door. "Where the hell is she?"

EJ's lips thinned. "Gone, Ric. She's gone."

Pressure clamped around his throat. "I told her to wait for me. Why would she go without me?"

EJ's face softened as he entered the cabin. "Because you can't go where she's gone."

Out of the corner of his eye, the bright yellow wildflower caught his attention; standing tall in a crystal shot glass. The same wildflower he gave her, handpicked from his stash in the greenhouse back at the mansion. His stomach dropped when he noticed a handwritten note underneath the makeshift vase with his band beside it.

From behind him, EJ mumbled something about a vision, but his voice was distant. Everything around Aric drifted away as though the only thing that mattered were the words written on that damn note. He willed his shaky hand to still long enough to hold the paper and read:

My dearest Aric,

We are soulmates—though that word could never fully describe the bond between our two souls, a connection no mortal could comprehend. You are the soil that grounds my roots, the sunlight that greens my leaves, the air that breathes life into my limbs.

You are my everything.

I was so angry, for so long. Resentful that you chose your oath to the Guardians over us. I was bitter to the point I no longer saw through the darkness. But now, I understand. I see that if you didn't save Blaine, you wouldn't be the angel, the Guardian, that completes my soul. It is your loyalty, your courage, the love in your heart, that drew our souls together.

After you left, I lost sight of those qualities, and for that, I am truly sorry.

It is why I write this letter to you now. The reason I cannot ask you to choose again.

I will not make you go back on your word, on your oath, to the Guardians. Blaine deserves the chance for redemption, and only his brothers can return him to the Heavens. I also will not make you forsake your connection with the Heavens for me. Instead, I will make this choice for you and for us.

Over these past few weeks in the mortal realm, I have seen your true self through fresh eyes. Your willingness to do whatever it takes for those you love and your loyalty to me. For this reason, I summoned Gabe and will return to the Heavens alone.

I want you to keep the band. I made it for you, and I was wrong to ask for it back. The joining of our souls happened long before I tied my powers to you. Taking it off may have stopped the transfer of my powers, but it never broke our bond.

Stay strong, as you have this whole time and know that I will wait for you, for as long as it takes to complete your mission and return to me. Each day we are apart, know that my heart remains yours for eternity.

Until we are together again,

Your Lo-Lo xx

He scrunched the paper in his fist and hurled it at the wall. How could she do this? He was giving up his soul for her, and she fucking walked away. She left him here in the mortal realm without her.

"I'm sorry, Ric," EJ muttered behind him.

He spun; jaw clenched. "Why? Gabe did this. He convinced her to leave. He took away the only thing that mattered. My fucking soulmate. This was my choice, not his."

He'd lost her again. He balled his hands into tight fists.

As he stared at EJ standing in the doorway, the words he'd muttered earlier resurfaced. "What was the vision?"

"You, Ric. The vision was you as a Fallen."

"Fucking Fate," he shouted. "Why doesn't she leave me the hell alone? Why would she tell Gabe about—"

Time seemed to slow as clarity seeped into his brain. Gabe didn't convince Willow to leave...EJ did.

Rageland exploded through his body. Red dots clouded his vision.

He crossed the cabin in a second flat and shoved EJ's chest, slamming his back against the refrigerator. "You did this! You guilted her into leaving without me.

How could you do that?"

He swung his fist, but EJ slipped from his hold and ducked. Instead, his fist slammed through the wall. Blood burst from his knuckles but the pain didn't register. Nothing was worse than the agony clawing inside his chest.

"She made the right choice, Ric, for everyone."

"No, she didn't," he roared. "It's not the right choice for us."

He grabbed the first thing he could and threw the lamp at EJ. EJ side stepped, and it smashed into the wall, the shade rolling along the floor until it collided with the couch.

"It will be, Ric. You've gotta just get through this part."

No, it wouldn't be. He hurled a whiskey glass. With lightning speed, EJ snatched a nearby pillow to protect his face. The glass bounced off and shattered at EJ's feet.

"I thought you were my brother. I'll never forgive you for this."

EJ flung the pillow at him, smacking Aric in the face. No damage, but the childish action diverted his attention for a moment from the rage.

"Listen to me!" EJ yelled, shoving Aric in the chest.

What the hell had EJ said? He sucked in sharp breaths as his mind came back online and the whole damn situation became more screwed up. The red dots faded and disappeared. Willow had left without him. Left him a damn note that said she returned to the Heavens. But…did she lie?

It wouldn't be the first time she lied to him. She

lied about walking, about where she landed. She didn't tell him about her wings until it suited her. Maybe she started off small and worked her way up to pulling off this epic betrayal, so she freed herself and ran off into the fiery sunset with Blaine. Maybe this was their plan all along, so Willow could have her revenge.

"The note's a lie."

EJ drew back. "What?"

He stormed passed EJ, crunching his boots on the broken glass. "She made it crystal clear she wouldn't return to the Heavens. Her note's a goddamn lie."

"Ric, I'm positive she returned to the Heavens."

He spun lighting fast and got right up in EJ's face. "Were you here? Did you see Gabe mist her?"

EJ didn't say a goddamn thing, but he didn't need to, the look in his eyes said enough.

"She's lied before. She's lying now."

EJ squeezed his shoulder. "Ric, don't go down this path. She made the right choice, I know her."

He shrugged off the hand and kicked the first thing at his feet. That damn pillow flung across the room, collided with the window and fell limp on the floor. Just like his heart. "I thought I knew her, too. I offered her everything she ever wanted, and it still wasn't enough. I never thought she'd do this to me."

"Why would she lie in a note?"

"It's the only thing that makes sense. Unless you guilted her into going without me."

EJ sighed. "That's not fair, Ric. I did it to save you, to save both of you. This was the first frickin' vision Fate sent me where I had time to make a difference. Don't you think that means something?"

He faced EJ, who snagged another pillow and held

it in front of his chest like a goddamn squishy shield. Standing before him was a brother who always had his back, who he'd confided in since their creation, who he trusted with his life. Now, he was the brother who betrayed him and sent away his soulmate.

He turned away instead of hurling another innate object at EJ's face. "Get out."

"Ric—"

"I said get out," he growled.

EJ shoved the pillow against Aric's shoulder. "This was the only way, Ric. You'll see that."

"No, I fucking won't," he snapped, not bothering with eye contact.

The pillow fell to the floor before EJ trudged out of the cabin, leaving him alone, wallowing in the fact that one choice shattered his entire existence.

She must've lied. EJ wouldn't have done this to him, he knew how much it meant to have her back in his arms. Blaine must've convinced her to lie. He never should've trusted Blaine—he was the only one who could've misted her to Hell. Blaine double crossed him, just as he predicted.

Time to settle his score with Blaine once and for all.

****

He landed in front of Blaine's pretentious mansion. He stalked forward, murderous thoughts consuming his mind. Blaine was ready and waiting.

Blaine narrowed his eyes and exaggerated a lean to one side, peering around Aric. "You seem to be missing half your package, friend."

"I'm not your friend." Aric shoved Blaine's chest. "You agreed to take both of us. Instead, you broke your word and took her without me."

Blaine frowned, tilted his head slightly. "Say again."

"Willow, damn it. You took her without me," he shouted. "Stop the damn lies."

"How could I?" Blaine motioned to the ground by his feet. "I'm standing right here."

Muscles in his jaw popped. The fact Blaine stood in front of him now didn't mean he hadn't taken Willow. There was a two-hour window where she could have left. Was that enough time? He had no clue how quickly or slowly time moved in Hell. If the time situation was like the Heavens, then…he must've dropped her off and left her there. Blaine was a fucking dead man.

"We had a deal. Where she goes, I go."

Tiny flames lit inside Blaine's irises and Aric braced for an onslaught of power. "I can assure you, neither Slater nor I have taken Willow anywhere." Blaine inched closer. "Are you sure you haven't hidden her to stop her from Falling?"

"Why the hell would I do that? I told her I would Fall…"

The words caught in his throat. He'd told Willow he'd Fall for her. Then EJ had told her about the vision Fate sent. Shit. Clarity cleared the fog of rage in his mind as he pieced it all together.

His stomach sank. She didn't lie; she told the truth. She returned to the Heavens. Willow left on her own, so he didn't become a Fallen.

"Damn you, Fate," he muttered.

A vicious roar erupted beside him. Heat lanced his upper arm as a white-hot fireball whizzed past a second before a tree behind him exploded into flames. He gaped at the hole in the sleeve of his jacket.

That fireball missed his arm by less than an inch. By the sulfuric smell and the crimson undertones, Blaine had just thrown hellfire at him. Before he reacted, Blaine threw another.

Aric ducked and the fireball narrowly missed his head. "What the hell?"

"That bitch," Blaine seethed, not giving a shit where those bombs hit. "I'm done with her meddling. Fate's cold-blooded heart didn't skip a beat when I Fell. Why won't she bloody leave me be?"

Aric retreated a step, while formulating the quickest escape plan in history. No way he'd wait to see what happened if that fire exploded on him. "I'm done with the shit between the two of you. Why can't you and Fate fight it out in another realm and leave us the fuck out of it?"

Blaine flexed his fingers and fueled another flame inside his open palm.

Holy shit. When did he become so powerful? They were running out of time to save him.

"Don't blame me. She's the one that keeps changing the bloody rules," Blaine said in an icy tone matching the menacing look in his eyes. He wiggled his fingers, increasing the size of the flame.

Aric retreated another step. How far could Blaine throw? How quickly could he fly? "Better yet, why don't you go back to the Heavens and face Fate? That would solve all this in one move."

"Oh, I plan to, don't you worry."

"Hurry the fuck up then, so we can all move on from this stalemate of trying to save your ass."

Blaine threw his head back in a wicked cackle that sent chills dancing over Aric's nape. "Save me? You're released from the pointless exercise remember? You're on the fiery-winged team now. We had a deal."

Like hell they did. No way would he destroy his soul for the sake of it. He agreed only because it released Willow from Anahel, saved her soul and regenerated her wings. Him Falling with her would've kept them together, even though they'd be Fallen.

Instead, she rejected his willingness to sacrifice his soul for her and skipped off to the Heavens without him. She decided even without discussing it. By leaving, Willow threw away everything he'd worked for in one swift move. She also ended them.

He stepped back further from the hellfire flickering in the center of Blaine's palm. "Nope. We were a package deal, remember? I'm not going anywhere. If you've got an issue with her returning to the Heavens, then take it up with Fate." He held back a smirk. "Think of this as karma biting your ass for taking my Chosen's soul."

It happened all at once, so fast he barely tracked the movements. Blaine hurled several fireballs at him in quick succession. Aric unfurled his wings, but not quickly enough. The last fireball exploded at the bottom of his wing, scorching the flesh and incinerating a handful of feathers.

Raw, excruciating pain ripped through him.

Blaine didn't care, nor did he wait. He hurled another, aiming for Aric's other wing.

"You keep choosing her," Blaine roared. "I saved your soul. I saved Willow. Me. That should count for something. But still you chose Fate."

A new kind of pain tugged inside his chest at Blaine's words. Blaine had saved his soul, rescued Willow from Hell and saved her from Zath. But that couldn't murky his decision. Even though Willow left without him, he'd always choose her. Hanging around here would turn him into an incinerated pile of ash and he'd never find out why.

"I didn't choose Fate; I always chose Willow. I'm sorry, man," he muttered before he shot to the sky while he still had wings.

Another deafening roar sounded from below followed by a series of fireballs thrown in short succession. Two whizzed passed him. One got so close the heat billowed underneath his wings. He soared higher. As soon as he was out of range, Blaine directed the fireballs at the forest, incinerating every tree in sight.

Fate had better be ready, because Blaine's powers were a helluva lot more powerful than anyone anticipated.

Turning away from the nightmare below, he flapped his wings and soared high into the sky.

Payback was a goddamn bitch. His soulmate was back in the Heavens without him. Now, he was back to saving that bastard so he could return there. That was one vow he wouldn't break.

Here we go again…

Chapter Thirty-Five

Willow materialized in the Heavens near the narrow riverbank, in front of the cabin she and Aric once shared. Of all the realms in the Heavens Gabe could've misted her to, he brought her here.

Gabe materialized beside her and they stood side by side for several quiet moments, staring at the cabin. Water trickling over the rocks behind her was the only sound she registered. Her throat burned while her heart tore apart so painfully slow, she thought it would never stop.

"You made the right decision, Willow." Gabe spoke low and soft, breaking the silence.

She exhaled a heavy breath that ended in a sob. "I hope so, Gabe, I truly hope so."

He lay a comforting palm on her shoulder. "I will watch over Aric, as I have for centuries in the mortal realm."

"Tell him…" Her eyes stung. "Please tell him I'm all right."

He squeezed her shoulder. "I will. You have sacrificed a great deal for your soulmate, my dear. The act will continue to fuel light in his soul even though he doesn't wear the band."

She faced him. "And what do I do? Just sit here and…wait?"

His face tightened. "Fate will contact you when the

time is right. I will speak to her, but I cannot guarantee a positive outcome."

"Great. I can't wait for that conversation." She didn't bother holding back the sarcasm in her voice.

"Take this time to heal, my dear. You will need all your strength."

The pain inside her chest doubled as the gravity of her decision sank in. "And then what?" she said, her throat tightening. "Things go back to how they were before I…?" *Fell.* She couldn't even say the word aloud, just thinking it caused her throat to tighten. How could she have ever thought that would solve her situation?

Gabe glanced at the clear blue, cloudless sky. This time he spoke in her mind. *Fight for the path you wished for all along. Fate paves more than one. There is always another choice.*

He inclined his head. The surrounding air rippled, shimmering with golden light a split second before he misted away. Instead of taking her with him, he left her alone, facing the empty cabin.

She twisted the sash on her dress around her index finger, tighter and tighter until her fingertip throbbed and turned a nasty purple. Then she unwound the ribbon and tightened it again, all the while staring at that cabin, searching for life. Searching for a reason to carry on living.

The wooden swing hung at one end of the porch, gently rocking in the constant summer breeze. Though this one didn't squeak like its replica in the mortal realm. Because every damn thing in the Heavens was perfect, pristine and without imperfections. A thunderous storm, a snowy blizzard, a squeaky porch swing, those things didn't exist here. If an angel willed it to rain, the drops pattered down always a comfortable temperature, neither cold nor warm.

Bright rays of sunlight burst through the surrounding pine trees, tingling her exposed arms. But it did nothing to shift the cold and empty feeling inside.

Her existence here was so lifeless, in a realm so perfect it was almost…nauseating.

Returning to the Heavens was the right decision, the only choice that broke her soul out of Anahel, regenerated her wings and prevented Aric from becoming a Fallen. But that decision returned her to this stagnant, hollow existence where she resumed her never-ending Groundhog Day again.

Her chest tightened. *I can't do this.*

Her knees buckled, and she collapsed on the grass. So cushiony and warm, she tore at it with her bare hands. Aric said she was full of courage, stronger than anyone thought. But the strength needed to escape Hell was nothing compared to an eternity in this retched flawless realm without him.

In her note, she begged him to hold on, complete his mission and return to her. But who knew how much time passed in the mortal realm before Gabe delivered the message she'd arrived? Before he told Aric she was okay.

Being stuck here didn't lessen her worry for him. Would her leaving, coupled with him not knowing if she was all right, cause him to make hasty choices? How much could he endure before it broke him?

Physically as well as mentally exhausted, she flopped on her side and curled up in a ball. At this point, she had neither the strength nor the courage to enter that cabin, and being back in the Heavens, under Fate's command once again, she couldn't mist without an Ariel assignment. Like it or not, she was stuck here.

But that didn't mean she had to play along.

Underneath her, the earth hummed with power, a soft echo that thrummed through her veins. Familiar tingles danced along her fingertips as they weaved through the long thick blades of grass. At her touch, the grass lengthened and thickened, curving around her until it encased her entire body in a light blanket, as though it welcomed her home. Waves of light washed through her soul, bringing with it a sense of peace. Her eyes grew heavy.

She'd lay here on the grass for as long as it took until her soul fully healed. Out here was a hell of a lot easier than lying inside, alone in the bed.

Chapter Thirty-Six

An empty bottle of whiskey sailed through the air before it smashed against the wooden steps of his cabin. How many bottles would cure the crippling pain inside his chest?

The pungent stench of gasoline drowned all remnants of Willow's lingering scent, instead, filling the air with a filthy, thick smell resembling death. Fitting, given the cabin would soon burst into flames.

Willow had left without him. He'd given up everything for her and it still hadn't been enough.

Every choice he'd ever made had been aimed at returning to her and for a measly few weeks, he'd had her back in his arms. A blink of the eye in his long, dreary existence. Then she threw it all away as though it hadn't mattered.

The irony of the whole damn situation wasn't lost on him. Over three centuries ago, he'd done the same. He'd fought alongside his brothers and left her safely in the Heavens. Now, she flipped the damn cards on him. But when he left, he hadn't known his choice would be for an eternity.

Using his thumb, he flicked open the lighter in his hand, igniting a tiny flame for a few seconds before extinguishing it. What held him back? He had no use for the cabin anymore. He'd built it to feel closer to her, to feel connected to her even though she existed in another realm—one he would likely never re-enter. But over the years, he'd stopped coming here because the memories became too painful to bear.

"Goddamn it," he growled.

Broken glass crunched under his heavy boots as he stomped up the steps and inside the cabin. He snatched another bottle of whiskey from the kitchen cabinet. As he turned, he caught sight of the wildflower he'd picked for her, still alive, upright in that stupid shot glass. That crippling pain increased, burning his lungs. Why wasn't he enough for her? He thought she felt the same. That being together was more important than choosing sides in the war between Fate and Zath.

Turning away, he returned to his viewing point on the grass, screwed the top off the whiskey and chugged. Nothing would change how he felt about Willow nor permanently sever the connection between their souls. He sensed her even now, with her in the Heavens and him stuck on this damn earth.

Willow thought taking off the band destroyed their connection. She was wrong. Removing it only broke the link to her powers, preventing the light from transferring between their souls. Their bond was stronger than that. It had been there the entire time, simmering under the surface. He'd just forgotten what it felt like with all cylinders firing.

Through the open front door, he focused on the bright yellow flower on the nightstand. The flower had always reminded him of how her Ariel powers created life. But when he looked at the cabin everything felt…dead.

Again, the lighter flame ignited with the flick of his thumb. No more wasting time. He couldn't come here again. The cabin only served as another painful reminder of what they'd both lost.

He chugged from the bottle of whiskey and crouched. Holding the lighter against the grass, he ignited a gasoline trail. Flames roared to life and raced to the cabin. The steps lit a second before fire engulfed the porch.

He stood there, dead and numb on the inside, staring at the flames. Heat billowed as the fire entered the cabin, causing him to stagger back. Windows popped; glass sprayed onto the grass. The single wildflower drooped over the rim of the shot glass before alighting.

He grabbed the band from his jeans pocket and held it in his open palm. For more than a thousand years it stood the test of time, held together, held *him* together. Nurtured that tiny seed of hope inside his soul. But no longer. All his remaining hope died the moment Willow left. He was done with that useless feeling.

He hurled the band into the blaze. If Willow wanted a new start, then he'd give it to her.

As the flames reached the swing on the porch, the agony became too much. The bottle of whiskey fell from his hand. The black hole in his chest widened, sucking all remaining life from his heart. Fire engulfed the swing in a matter of seconds, rising to the beam hanging above. The wood cracked and split as the entire swing collapsed in the blaze.

"Goodbye, Lo-Lo." A sob caught in his throat as he turned and walked away.

****

Willow stood at the open doorway of the cabin. Since returning to the Heavens, she'd spent the entire time outside. Then, suddenly, something had compelled her up the steps.

Fate? But why? She hadn't spoken to Fate since she returned. The dread of that conversation increased each waking moment.

The entire cabin remained untouched, frozen in time, just like her. After so long, Aric's rich, masculine scent no longer lingered in the fresh, pure air. The last bunch of wildflowers he'd picked for her remained upright in a crystal vase by the couch, despite not being watered since Aric left. A crease remained in the linen on the edge of the bed, where she'd sat and sobbed, sensing even then, he wouldn't return.

Every piece of furniture and their belongings were exactly as she'd left it when she'd closed the door on that part of her existence. But standing here now, the whole space seemed empty, despite housing lifetimes of memories.

Stepping inside, she padded to the bed and sat on the edge of the mattress. The void inside her heart was once again front and center. Such a stupid move, thinking she could leave Aric. That she could return to the Heavens and wait until he completed his mission.

Through the uncovered windows, she caught the sun beaming on the grass outside, mixing with her Ariel powers, illuminating the lawn in an otherworldly glow. Everywhere she glanced, magic and life mingled together in a beauty that before, took her breath away. Only now, it left her hollow.

Aric had always chosen her, she knew that now. She just couldn't see it through her bitterness. This cabin no longer felt like home because her home was with him.

Without the concept of time, she had no clue how much time had passed in the mortal realm since she left. Each day, her Ariel powers intensified. With her first burst of power, she grew a field of wildflowers along the edge of the riverbank outside the cabin. Like the one Aric found her in when they first met.

She'd lay in the middle of the vibrant colors for hours, staring at the cloudless sky, imagining Aric lying beside her, his rough hand holding hers. But nostalgic memories overshadowed the thrill of using her powers and made her heart ache anew. Each time she turned her head to the side, hoping to catch his whiskey eyes staring back at her, he wasn't there.

Even though her powers had returned, her wings hadn't. Not a single feather. Nor her ability to mist. But still, she held on, because when they did, this horrific, tragic mistake would end.

On the wooden nightstand by the bed, a single yellow wildflower appeared, upright in a crystal shot glass. A replica of the glass Aric used as a makeshift vase in the mortal realm. The glass and flower materialized, as though her subconscious had conjured it so her heart could ache a little more. She reached to touch it but recoiled. Heat singed her fingertips. The flower shriveled and sagged. Black soot smudged the glass. As though in slow motion, single petals burned and floated onto the table before vanishing. The stem disappeared last. But the makeshift vase remained, melted in a mangled heap of blackened glass.

She shot to her feet with a sense of urgency that centered in her bones. Something was wrong with Aric.

Gabe's last words appeared in her mind. What the heck was she doing? She'd spent the entire time back in the Heavens wallowing in self-pity when she could've been fighting for a different path.

She paced in a tight circle as she decided on a plan. It wasn't in her nature to hurt others, cause them pain or suffering, nor was it in her nature to deceive. But every choice had a price.

Aric needed her. Now she would fight for him.

She was done with waiting. This time, she wouldn't make the same mistake. This time, when she jumped off that fence, she'd follow through the whole damn way.

Chapter Thirty-Seven

The bench creaked when Aric relaxed back, stretching his legs out in front, crossing at his boots. A dull ache burned in his lower back, a painful reminder of the hours he spent dozing on the hard slats, listening to the rain hammer down on the roof.

Morning light spilled through the glass panes covering the gable roof, the flowers beside him stretching for every ray of early sunshine. The greenhouse gifted year-round warmth to the plants, and gave him a tranquil space to relax, unwind, and soak up the sun's healing rays.

Today though, the wounds he healed weren't visible on the outside.

He'd built a greenhouse on the properties he and his brothers occupied during their time in the mortal realm, and this place was no exception. A brick base construction off the rear of the mansion, with the point of the pitched roof reaching just below the second-story windows. Oversized rectangular windows lined the walls and roof, letting light stream in from every direction. Inside, wicker baskets hung from the ceiling with dark green foliage spilling over the sides, while raised garden beds lined the perimeter, filled with an array of fruits and vegetables. Ellen enjoyed tending the space as much as he did.

But the narrow garden bed positioned down the

center was the reason for the greenhouse: Growing those goddamn wildflowers. The thing he did to feel closer to Willow.

Over the years, he'd perfected the right seed combination, ensuring a year-round bloom of color, regardless of season. So, when he was without her, he wasn't without the memories.

Twisting around, he reached behind him, plucked a dainty yellow daisy from the sea of color and twirled it between his thumb and forefinger. The same daisies that had hugged the edge of the river near their cabin in the Heavens. God, the memory of that cabin felt like a lifetime ago. How the hell would he make it through the next year or decade, a century even, until he saw her again?

Five weeks and six days had passed since Willow left, and it seemed like the entire mortal realm had ground to a halt. Time passed at a crawl, each day dragging longer than the last. At this rate, he wouldn't make it another week.

A soft rap sounded at the door, and he peered up to find EJ standing in the doorway.

"You up for company, Ric?"

At his nod, EJ strolled in and plonked his ass on the edge of a garden bed, leaning forward with his forearms on his thighs.

Goddamn it, EJ looked as shitty as Aric felt. Wrinkles covered his white T-shirt, short stubble covered his usually clean-shaven jaw, and he looked like he hadn't slept in weeks.

Welcome to the club.

He'd barely spoken to EJ since Willow left. The tension wedged between them had placed a big-ass strain on the household. Sure, he was pissed at EJ for telling Willow about the vision, but now that his brother sat in front of him, he couldn't help but let all that anger float away.

Though EJ never said, he sensed he carried a heavy burden because of those fucked up visions. Ever since Fate sent him the vision of that ornamental cherry planted in front of the mansion; he'd trusted Fate to guide their way. But the visions tortured EJ with failure after failure. How the hell did he cope with that every day?

He had to trust Fate. If she sent EJ the vision of Aric Falling, then he trusted she had a damn good reason for doing so. He hadn't looked forward to the adventure in Hell, but for Willow, he would've done it.

In the end, Fate had saved Willow's soul and his own. He owed EJ one helluva apology.

He glanced at EJ. "Listen, man, I—"

"No, me first." EJ took off his beanie and ruffled his hair. "I don't want this to be weird between us anymore. I miss my brother. I miss my best mate." He paused. "I'm sorry I told her, Ric. I truly am."

He cursed under his breath. "I'm the one who's sorry. I've been an ass. I know your heart was in the right place. I also know because you gave a shit Willow is back in the Heavens where she's safe. It's just…" His damn throat closed, stopping the words.

EJ didn't move, just sat there, letting him process the stupid-ass feelings overtaking him.

He leaned forward, elbows on his knees. "It's like Fate's exiled us all over again. Only it hurts so much more." He twirled the daisy between his fingertips. "I was so goddamn wrong. I thought it wasn't enough for her. I wasn't enough. Then I realized, she didn't choose the Heavens over me. She chose an eternity alone there to save me. And because I was a fucking idiot and threw the band in the fire, these flowers are all I have left."

"You may wanna lock Raine outta here then, she has an unnatural ability to kill things. Plants included."

A chuckle rose in his chest, but it fizzled out before fully developing.

Absently, he touched his wrist hoping the band was there, but once again his fingers came up empty. Why the hell did he throw it in the flames? In the mortal realm, that band meant more to him than air. It had gotten him through the darkest of times, kept the light in his soul burning bright. It had kept that useless feeling of hope alive and kicking.

Now the band was toast, just like the cabin.

When he'd woken from his whiskey coma in the middle of the nearby forest, the weight of his actions sank in. For hours, he'd rummaged through the ash searching for the band. He didn't give a shit about the cabin or its contents. Nothing mattered except that band.

But he never found it. The second biggest screw up of his entire existence.

"She held onto the hope that one day we'd reunite and in return I burned down the damn cabin." He peered around the greenhouse. "I miss her so fucking bad, man," he mumbled.

"I know, Ric."

Last night, he'd slept in here. He'd wandered down during the night, drawn to the space like a magnet, just like the first time he'd searched for her in the Heavens.

Some unknown force compelled him to lay beside the daisies and breathe in their sweet fragrance, while an angry thunderstorm raged in the darkness.

Returning to the greenhouse gave his broken heart a single seed of hope.

He scrubbed his hands over his face and glanced back at EJ.

EJ stood, dug a hand in his pocket, pulled out a leather band and dangled it in front of him.

Wait a minute. That wasn't leather. "Is that…?"

EJ nodded. "I've kept it safe, waiting for the right time to give it back."

He shot to his feet, his heart flipping upside down. "You had it all along?"

"Yep. I had to be sure you weren't gonna torch it again. 'Cause let me tell you, Ric, there's no way I'm diving through flames and saving it a second time." EJ exhaled a long, exaggerated sigh. "A pair of my favorite shoes were sacrificed that day."

The moment his shaky fingers touched the band, a single burst of light shot into his veins, white and hot, centering in his soul. He held the band in his palm, tightening his grip. God, he hadn't realized how lost he'd been without it. He wouldn't wear it again though; he wouldn't make Willow's powers suffer. Having it close was enough.

He blinked hard. Damn dirt in his eye again. "Why give it back today?"

EJ half shrugged. "I had a vision last night of you and Red lying in a field filled with those frickin' flowers." He motioned to the garden bed behind Aric. "You looked so goddamn happy, I thought you might spring up and dance around like a little girl."

A smile warmed his cheeks. "That wasn't a vision. Fate sent you a memory."

It had to be Willow. No one else knew of that moment they shared in the field of daisies. Fate must've sent the vision to let him know Willow was okay, that she held on. Back came that single seed of hope, sprouting inside his beating heart.

"I'm sorry about your shoes." He held back a grin as best he could.

"It's cool. I have a few spares. I also put the fire out before the mortals reported it, but I couldn't save the cabin."

Opening his palm, he glanced at the band. "This is the only thing that mattered."

EJ shifted the weight between his feet. "So...we good, Ric?"

He squeezed EJ's shoulder. "Of course we are, man. We always were." He slipped the band in his pocket. "You don't know how much this means to me."

"I can imagine. And just so you know, if anyone throws my car in a fire, I want you to haul your ass in there and save it. Understood?"

Aric barked out a laugh. "Copy that."

EJ plucked a white daisy and tucked it behind his ear. "C'mon Ric, I could use a drinking partner. While we're catching up, let's sort out a plan to rebuild the cabin when you're ready. Somehow, I don't think Red would be too happy if she found out you torched it."

Just like that, his world semi-righted itself again. He didn't have Willow in his arms, but EJ's vision confirmed she was okay, and at that moment, that's all he needed.

EJ waited by the door while he took a moment. His

heart swelled as he smoothed his fingertips along the petals.

"Thank you, baby," he murmured, before striding back into the main house.

Chapter Thirty-Eight

Willow rapped her knuckles on white paneled double doors. Given she still couldn't mist to a destination of her choice, she trekked all the way across the Heavens to Fate's sanctuary. Now, she stood outside. Totally freaking out.

The oversized doors opened and after a few heartbeats, she stepped inside.

Each time she entered Fate's sanctuary, the sheer size and elegance took her breath away. Perfectly cut pink diamonds were embedded in the white marble floor, sparkling under the filtered sunlight, making a kaleidoscope of colors dance across the pristine white walls. Towering arched stained-glass windows filled one side of the sanctuary, while on the opposite side, a gigantic window faced a massive waterfall plunging into a blue lake.

The view from that oversized window constantly changed, and she suspected Fate used it as a gateway to showcase the breathtaking scenery in the mortal realm. But the gesture was wasted on Willow. She hadn't come to sightsee, she came to bargain.

From a concealed door at the far end, Fate glided into the room dressed in a lacy, pale pink summer dress, a tall crown of cherry blossoms and delicate vines positioned on her head. Fate halted in front of the crystal fountain, its jeweled tiers stretching to the glass

315

dome ceiling.

Had Fate stood in that exact spot when she'd made a deal with the Guardians all those centuries ago? The thought made her stomach flip.

She approached Fate with light, careful steps. When standing before Fate, she extended the sides of her dress in a curtesy. "Your Grace."

Fate inclined her head. "Willow. I see your faith is finally strong enough to return to my sanctuary. I've been expecting you."

That didn't sound good.

Straightening, Willow swallowed the lump forming in her throat. Hopefully, having her faith back meant Fate wouldn't punish her. "I wish to discuss the situation involving the Guardians."

"Go on."

"I'd like to request you lift their exile so they can return to the Heavens."

Fate lifted her chin slightly. "My Guardians knelt in this very spot and swore an oath to me. One I will not revoke. Nor will I explain my reasons."

Right, that plan went up in smoke. Luckily, Aric taught her to always have more than one.

"Would you consider an amendment, one that permits me to reside in the mortal realm for as long as Aric does?"

Fate narrowed her sapphire blue eyes. "In case you've forgotten, let me remind you. The last time you departed the Heavens, your soul was destined for darkness. Nothing you could offer me in exchange would be worth the risk."

Her heart thumped inside her chest. Damn it. She knew this wouldn't be easy; Fate wasn't stupid. A tight knot coiled in the pit of her stomach. She had no choice. To reunite with Aric, she had to offer her the one thing she knew Fate wanted. She had to make the sacrifice.

I'm sorry, Blaine.

She squared her shoulders. "I have information on Blaine. I know what he's planning, and I also know why you can't see his actions in the mortal realm."

If the news shocked Fate, she didn't show it. Not a surprise. The Queen of Destiny had perfected masking her emotions.

Fate brushed her thumb over a circular burn on the inside of her palm, about the same size as one of the blossoms in her crown. Willow held her breath, waiting for a reply. Would Fate risk an angel's soul for information on Blaine's plan? If Willow held the power, she'd risk anything for information on Aric.

After agonizing minutes, Fate's gaze met Willow's. "Tell me his plans and I shall consider your request."

Not "yes" but not flat out "no." She had no other option but to take it.

She wound the sash on her dress tightly around her finger while divulging Blaine's plans. Everything from his Raziel ability to cloak his presence, to his army hidden in Hell. She left out the part about Blaine's festering resentment because that wouldn't aid her cause.

She'd aligned herself on Fate's side, the side of the Heavens, and she'd respect that alliance. Because there was no way she'd switch sides again.

"So, while you're up here plotting everyone's future, Blaine's down there with a plan of his own.

317

Plotting his revenge against you." She tightened the sash. "How could you let him Fall in the first place?"

Aric hadn't known about Willow's Fall, but for Fate, Blaine had severed his connection to the Heavens right in front of her. And Fate did absolutely nothing to stop him.

Fate peered at that waterfall for a moment, then back at Willow. "Blaine's Fall was a necessary step."

What? No angel's Fall to Hell was necessary. How could Fate stand back and let that happen? Had she done the same when she Fell?

"Are you for real?" she snapped. "Are you sure you didn't let him Fall just so you'd never have to admit—"

"Watch your tone, Ariel." Fate's voice boomed off the walls, brimming with power. "Just because we are two females engaged in a conversation, does not mean you should forget who I am."

Big mistake. Forgetting Fate was the most powerful angel in the entire universe would undo her plan. Fate would probably lock her out of the mortal realm for the rest of eternity.

She wound the sash tighter around her palm and lowered her voice. "My apologies."

The second the words spilled from her mouth, her stomached lurched. The surrounding air swirled and glimmered, spinning so fast her eyes couldn't focus. Her body swayed. She squeezed her eyes shut, covering them with her palms so she didn't throw up on the marble floor.

As quickly as the sensation began, it disappeared. The dizziness eased, and the urge to bring up her last meal faded away. She lowered her palms and opened her eyes, blinking hard to adjust for the glare.

They weren't in the sanctuary any longer. Instead, Fate had misted them to one end of an expansive estate.

Ancient cherry blossom trees lined the lush, green manicured lawn far into the distance. The delicate pale pink and white flowers covered the weeping branches like a cascading waterfall. Or tired, hanging limbs.

She'd heard of this place. Dread filled her stomach. Fate had misted her to Tartirim.

Before she spoke, Fate strolled down the center of the lawn. She raced to catch up with her.

"In the mortal realm," Fate said as Willow fell in step beside her. "The cherry blossom flowers are a symbol of new life. Rebirth. In some cultures, mortals worship the trees, planting them in the center of their towns as a symbol of hope." Fate paused under an extended branch. She brushed her fingers over the petals making the sweet scent drift through the air. "But they are also a symbol of death."

When a light breeze ruffled the trees, one delicate flower fell from its anchor on the branch. She stood silently, mesmerized by the pale pink blossom as it tumbled through the air, caught in the breeze, before, as though in slow motion, it vanished. The flower disappeared into the ether as though it never existed.

Fate continued, "Each soul I create is linked to the magic of a single petal. While connected to the tree, the flower flourishes, strengthened by my power in the soil, rising through the trunk. But when that soul brushes with darkness, it marks the petal, like a tarnish if you will. Over time, that petal wilts until it withers away and falls from the branch."

She surveyed the estate. Thousands of ancient trees

dotted the lawn, overflowing with millions of pale pink and white blossoms. Her breath caught as her gaze narrowed on the handful of trees in the far distance, where blackened, burned bark covered ghostly bare branches and a misty fog crept over the ground. Only one petal remained intact on the furthest tree, but not the same shade as the others. That petal was dark crimson.

"All those souls…" she whispered.

Fate maintained her stony expression. "The game of war is brutal," Fate said in an equally flat tone.

Before she said any more, Fate led her along the manicured grass until they came to a white wrought-iron table with two matching chairs.

"Why did you bring me here?"

Fate folded her dress behind her legs before sitting. "Your brush with darkness left its mark, Willow. I cannot permit you to depart the Heavens until your soul is healed. The risk is too great."

"Are you serious?"

At Fate's glare, she bit her tongue, so she didn't shout what she really thought. Instead, she lowered her butt onto the seat.

"What do I do, just sit at the cabin and wait until I heal?"

Fate peered at the never-ending lawn. "The healing powers here among the blossoms are the most powerful in all the realms in the Heavens. This is the only place a stain on an angel's soul can be removed."

Lightness filled her chest. Maybe Tartirim wasn't as bad as she thought.

"If I stay here my soul will heal?"

Fade nodded. "But the powers only heal your

soul."

The lightness disappeared, replaced by a sinking feeling. *And there's the catch.* "Staying here won't heal my wings," she murmured.

"Each path comes with its own sacrifice."

She stood, took a few steps then faced Fate. "Let me get this straight. Because I have a stain on my soul, you won't let me return to the mortal realm. I'm too much of a risk. The only way to heal that stain is to sit here…" She waved her arm, motioning to the thousands of trees. "In this prison of cherry blossoms. If I return to the cabin, or another realm in the Heavens, my wings will regenerate but the stain will remain on my soul? I could never again mist to the mortal realm."

Fate inclined her head. "The choice is yours."

Bet Fate had fun creating those two paths. What a bitch.

She placed her hands on her hips as she paced in a tight circle. She wanted so bad to stomp all over the cushiony grass like a cranky mortal toddler.

To reunite with Aric, she needed to sacrifice her wings. They were a part of her and without them she didn't feel whole. She'd spent her entire time in the mortal realm wanting them back. She'd even severed her bond with Aric just so she could return to Hell before Aric struck a deal with Blaine to help her.

Then EJ had spoken with her and she sat alone in the Heavens, replaying her decision over in her mind. Aric nearly became a Fallen for her. His soul would have joined those countless of withered and infected cherry blossoms, eventually falling from the tree and disappearing into God knows where.

Aric told her over and over he didn't care about the

color of her wings. He said he loved her because of her soul. He made her feel whole. Not her wings, not her Ariel powers. Aric. She wouldn't be at peace until she was back in his arms.

She pivoted and faced Fate. "I won't stand by and let you separate Aric and I any longer."

Fate's eyes flashed with silver. "Yet, you were so willing to sever your connection with him."

She flinched. Yes. But that was before she had all the facts, before she knew the truth. She'd regret that choice for eternity if she didn't return to Aric.

"I was wrong. I thought my power and wings were more important. But they aren't. They don't define me." She raised her chin. "I chose Aric because that's what soulmates do."

Fate stood, straightening her dress. "Voice your decision, Ariel."

"I'll stay here in Tartirim and heal my soul."

"Very well."

"I have one more question, if I may."

Fate waved a hand through the air for her to continue.

"If you can't influence the path of a Fallen, how did Aric and I cross paths? How did our bond hold my soul in Anahel?"

Fate's shoulders tensed, though her expression remained neutral. "The tether between two soulmates is a powerful bond. Yet, freewill must decide each path. Your Guardian's devotion to you prevented your soul from transitioning to a Fallen, and his loyalty to his duty, to his assigned Chosen, led his path to cross with yours."

She frowned. "Hang on. How would Aric's duty to

his Chosen bring us together?"

"I couldn't see your choices, Willow. I needed to draw you out."

She gaped. "You created a Chosen to use as bait?" Her voice rose. "You willingly sacrificed a mortal?"

Fate remained unfazed. "Aric's decision to save that mortal's soul put this entire path in motion. The path that resulted in you standing in this exact spot, at this exact moment, making this exact choice."

She retreated a step. Fate was in control the entire time. She should've known.

If Aric wasn't in that parking lot at the back of the nightclub, she may never have crossed paths with him. Their connection would've held her soul in Anahel until she died. Or if she returned to Hell with Blaine, she would've become a Fallen and severed her bond to Aric. She never would've known his side of the story, his version of events. She never would've known how sorry he was.

"You knew Aric would Fall for me. You knew I wouldn't let him," she whispered.

"I am the Queen of Destiny," she said, like it was the most obvious thing in the universe.

The entire time she'd tortured herself with decisions—regenerating her wings, reuniting with Aric, trusting Blaine, returning to the Heavens, and Fate had known the path she'd choose. The whole freaking time.

Her heart sank a little. If Fate knew, then why didn't she prevent this massive mess?

"Why didn't you stop me from Falling?"

Fate glided to the nearest tree, reached high into the branches, and plucked a blossom. "It seems I underestimated Blaine's powers. A mistake I won't repeat."

As Fate turned around, she tossed the pale pink flower in the air toward Willow. It hovered just out of reach, shimmering with power, twisting and turning, as a silver glow brimmed around the edges.

The instant she held out her hand, the blossom floated onto the inside of her palm. She sucked in a breath, noticing the faint, thin black veins swirling underneath the surface of the petal, as though infected by a disease.

Which, it was, just like her soul.

By the time she glanced up, Fate was already halfway down the lawn.

"Wait!" Willow shouted. "How will I know when my soul is healed?"

Without breaking her graceful stride, Fate replied in her mind before she misted away. *When the petal heals, so will your soul. Then you may return to your Guardian.*

She cradled the blossom in her palm, protecting it as though it were her most treasured possession. Because it was. The blossom was her soul.

Chapter Thirty-Nine

Three months had passed, and EJ still hadn't received another vision slash memory from Fate regarding Willow. Three goddamn months. And Aric had asked every fucking day.

In that time, he'd exhausted all avenues of message-travel. Gabe hadn't seen Willow since he misted her to the Heavens, Cole couldn't find her...that was all he had.

The only logical explanation was Fate had imprisoned Willow in Tartirim. If so, that was royally fucked up. He'd heard of the place Fate sent angels for rehabilitation—death by fucking cherry blossoms. Regardless, exile anywhere was a goddamn bitch. No matter the outcome.

He couldn't think like that. He had to remain positive and hold on for her. Sooner or later, Fate would send another message. He just had to keep moving forward. He hadn't rebuilt the cabin yet, but he would when the time was right.

As a dusting of snow melted into the earth, he took his frustration out on a helpless piece of wood. Snatching a split log from the ground, he tossed it into the nearby wheelbarrow then reached for another.

Using his shirt, he wiped the sweat from his brow before tucking it back into the waistband of his sweatpants. He cranked up the volume on his music, blasting his ear drums so loud it drowned out all remnants of life. Exactly the point.

Today's song of choice on repeat: "Rain." But outside, the weather was the complete opposite. The first sign of spring hinted in the chilly air. The sun shone bright in the cloudless sky, bathing his bare torso in warmth; the familiar tingle of healing power tickled across his skin. Healing not only his physical wounds but right into his soul.

Swing axe. Split wood. Repeat.

As he swung the axe over his shoulder for the umpteenth time, the surrounding air shifted. He froze. The breeze stilled, birds silenced, as though the entire realm halted. Time stilled.

He lowered the axe to his side but kept it in his grasp. What the fuck was going on?

Pivoting, he scanned the nearby pine trees. The late afternoon sun beamed through the branches, creating shadows along the dirt, stretching beyond the forest perimeter. No movement.

A prickle danced across the back of his neck. He spun, facing the mansion. He surveyed for threats, peering through the uncovered lower-level windows. A few scattered lights were on inside, but nothing out of the ordinary.

The ornamental cherry, planted in the feature garden, caught his attention. He inched closer, narrowing his eyes. As though in fast-forward, pale pink buds formed on the tip of each individual branch before they burst open. Like one of those nature shows where they capture an entire life cycle in a one-hour episode. Only in this case, the blossoms were the only thing moving on the whole estate.

A gust of wind came out of nowhere, swirling up the gravel drive and around the base of the tree. He crept closer. A blossom, caught in the gust, blew his way and he plucked it from the air. As soon as he closed his palm around the flower, another drifted toward him. Then another. In a split second, a whole damn tree full of blossoms swirled around him as though he were stuck in the center of a cherry blossom tornado.

"What the fuck?"

He dropped the axe, flicking the blossoms away from his face, waving his hands in the air like River on the dance floor. A moment later, as though nothing had ever happened, the gust of wind vanished. Each blossom stilled in the air before floating to the grass like snowflakes.

Kneeling on the lawn, he picked up a flower and turned it this way and that, inspecting the petals. It warmed in his fingers as though made from angelic powers. As though created using…

He sucked in a sharp breath.

A blast of heat raced through his blood at the exact moment the air thickened with the heavy anticipation of a brewing thunderstorm. The scent consumed his nose, even though his eyes confirmed the absence of clouds in the sky. His goddamn hope sprung to life as a familiar connection, deep inside, sparked and fused together.

In the center of the scattered, fallen blossoms, the space glimmered with power and buzzed with energy. Holding his breath, he stared at the angelic form materializing. When he noticed the fiery red locks, his brain misfired but his heart pieced everything together.

It took a second for the mist to clear.

"Aric!" Willow cried, leaping into his arms.

He caught her, wrapping his arms around her waist, holding her so goddamn tight. "Lo-Lo, is it really you?"

"Yes!" She giggled, curling her arms around his neck. "Who else were you expecting?"

Drawing his head back slightly, he admired her gorgeous face, the glint in her hazel eyes, the brown freckles scattered over the bridge of her nose.

"You're really here? How the hell are you here?"

She smirked. "I found my inner badass."

"That's my girl." A deep laugh rose in his chest and it felt so damn good to let it out. While he sat in the mortal realm feeling sorry for himself, his soulmate was in the Heavens kicking ass.

He smoothed his knuckles along her jaw. "How the hell did you convince Fate to let you leave?" His hand froze. "Please tell me she knows you're here."

She bit the corner of her bottom lip. "She knows."

If Fate knew, then that meant Willow must've… "Tell me you didn't make a deal with Fate."

She exhaled a long breath. "Not quite. I had information she wanted, so I used it as a bargaining chip. I had to heal first though, before she'd let me leave, which is why it took so long."

He leaned closer and grazed his chin along the sensitive part of her neck. "I bet your new wings are even sexier."

At her silence, he drew back. She lowered her head.

"Lo-Lo, what's wrong?"

She pursed her lips. "They didn't…I chose not to…"

Her chest rose with a deep inhale.

"I chose healing my soul instead of my wings." She met his gaze, her eyes glassy. "You said it didn't matter…"

"It doesn't." He brushed his thumb over her bottom lip. God, it felt so good to touch her skin again. "I love you, Willow. Nothing's ever gonna change that. You hear me?"

Her eyes shined with relief.

"Are you sure it's what you want?"

"Yes. I'm at peace with it, I really am. And trust me, I've had a lot of solitude to think about it. I'd rather be here with you."

Pink dusted her cheeks as she blinked up at him through her long lashes. Her skin was warm under his touch, no gray circles under her bright eyes.

"I'll just have to wrap my legs around your waist while you fly both of us."

His hands slid down to firmly squeeze her ass. "Damn right you will."

She cupped his face between her palms, rubbing her thumbs along the stubble on his jaw. "I've missed you so much."

He leaned into her touch. She was here, in his arms. Somehow, she'd made it back to him. "Me too, baby. Me too."

"Yeah? Show me how much."

He'd missed her more than life itself, more than the air he breathed, more than he ever could've imagined. Lifting her off the ground, he locked her legs around his waist.

"Copy that," he whispered hotly against her ear.

A blast of heat scorched through their shared

connection the moment she peered up at him, her eyes sexy as hell.

"Good. I need to reacquaint myself with those arms."

With all control lost, he took her mouth with his in a hungry, hot kiss. Poured out all the love in his heart, all the need in his soul, all the hope for their future.

His feet moved on their own, long strides toward the mansion, his bedroom the intended destination...or whatever room they came across first that granted them some privacy. Midway to the front door, he unfurled his black wings and flew to his balcony because walking took too fucking long.

Epilogue

Aric stood mesmerized as a single sprout pushed through a patch of dirt, weaving upward, reaching for the sunlight between the pine trees. Willow crouched beside it, nurturing the seedling to life, Ariel power pouring from her palms in a deep orange glow as beautiful as a summer sunset. The seedling grew in height and width, maturing into a tiny gum tree right before his eyes.

Raine screwed up her face. "I don't know how you do it, Willow. I can't even keep mint alive and that shit grows anywhere."

EJ threw his head back and laughed. "This realm should leave you in charge of cilantro, Rae. Wipe it out. You'd be doing the mortals a favor."

Raine frowned. "What exactly is your issue with cilantro?"

EJ's eyes widened. "What isn't? That shit is nasty."

Beside him, Willow chuckled as she stood. "We all have our strengths, Raine." Something she'd once said to him. "I, for one, have no idea how you forge Purah into a weapon."

Raine lifted a shoulder like creating a weapon out of heavenly water was no big fucking deal. Like hell it wasn't. He'd seen her in action.

He wrapped his arms around Willow's middle,

pressing her back against his front. "I'll never get bored watching you do that. It's sexy as hell."

EJ snorted. "Ric, if your idea of sexy-time is watching a plant grow, then you seriously need to get out more."

"When it comes to your soulmate, nothing is sexier than watching them do something they love."

"Good thing I have no intention of signing up for a soulmate." EJ scoffed.

Warmth expanded through his chest as a chuckle rose. "If Fate's twisted paths over the past two years are anything to go by, Chosen visions lead to soulmates."

"Well, thank-frickin'-Christ I haven't had a Chosen vision." EJ tucked a strand of blond hair under his beanie. "I reckon something's blocking my visions anyway. I haven't had Fate's standard the-world-is-ending vision for over a fortnight."

Given how regularly EJ had that vision, a fortnight without was a huge abnormality.

Raine crouched and dusted dirt off her shiny death-defying heels. "Have you seen anything else?"

"I keep seeing this flash of a frickin' beach over and over," EJ squawked. "Fate must be taking a vacay or something. The image is all sand and ocean—it never ends quick enough."

Willow's chuckle rumbled against his chest. He squeezed her tighter. "Not a fan of the beach, EJ?"

EJ screwed up his face. "I'd take the Infernal Pits in Hell over a pile of gritty, hot sand any day."

He barked out a laugh. "Get ready, man. I bet you're next."

"No frickin' way. I like my existence just the way it is."

Aric squeezed his arms around Willow a little tighter, leaning down to nuzzle her neck. "There's nothing better, trust me."

"Annnnd, that's our cue to take off, Rae, before those two get freaky up against a tree."

He ignored them as EJ and Raine sauntered off toward the mansion. His hands roamed around Willow's hips. "It's still surreal having you back."

Remaining in his embrace, Willow pivoted to face him, brushing her fingers along his stubble. "You know, for all her faults, I think Fate's heart is in the right place."

"I'm not sure her head was in the right place when she let Blaine Fall."

Her expression softened. "No, maybe not. But we both know how spur-of-the-moment choices can end. Sometimes, they're worth the risk, sometimes they turn out to be our greatest regrets."

He crooked a finger under her chin. Man, what did he do to deserve a soulmate as smart and beautiful as her?

"Taking that deal and walking away from you will always be my biggest regret."

"But that choice led us to this moment."

He kissed her forehead. "You're beginning to sound like Gabe."

She smiled, causing his heart to melt into a gooey mess. He drew her in tighter, so her cheek rested against his chest. This was it. This was what he longed for over the past three and a half centuries. Having her back in his arms, waking beside her each morning, sharing a connection so strong it felt like their souls were one.

Right here, right now, he was finally home.

"I want to show you something," he murmured against her hair. "Take a flight with me?"

Through their connection, he felt her heartrate spike. He drew back and took her hands in his.

Deep down, he suspected she hoped that one day her wings would regrow. That the stronger her Ariel powers became, the more chance she had of regenerating them. But he knew better. Fate's deals had no loopholes.

Willow resumed her Ariel duties last week when her power to mist returned, minus all the restrictions Fate had previously placed on her. The two times she'd misted to regenerate a nearby burned forest, she took him with her. She never returned to the Heavens, though. He sensed she feared that once she arrived, Fate might not let her leave. He feared the same.

Over the past month, since her return to the mortal realm, the closest she came to flying was on the back of his bike. Now that was an activity he encouraged daily. Having her legs wrapped around his waist as he drove them over the mountains was a pleasure he never thought he'd experience with her. Most of the time, he stuck to the narrow, windy roads, because it gave the illusion of flying between the trees without leaving the ground.

But each time he suggested flying with him, in the air, she found an excuse and said no. Someone needed her help, something important needed tending in the mansion. Each time she said no, his heart ached. She'd given up so much so they could be together.

Worries plagued his mind. Was she happy here without her wings? Did she regret her deal with Fate?

He didn't want to pressure her, but he wanted her to know she could have the pleasure and freedom of flying without her wings. He could give her that.

Her lips parted, about to speak but he held a finger against them. "Please, I've got a surprise for you."

That piqued her interest. "Tell me."

He grinned. *Gotcha.* "I'd rather show you."

Her eyes narrowed. "Aric, I…"

"Please." He gave her hands a gentle squeeze.

She sighed. "You won't give up, will you?"

"Nope." He unfurled his wings and lifted her in his arms. "Is that a yes?"

A sexy grin hinted at her lips. "Will you stop whining?"

He snorted. If she thought this was whining, she hadn't seen nothing yet. He could be rather convincing when he wanted. "Yep."

"Okay then, show me."

"Hold on tight, baby."

A thrill traveled through his veins when he took to the sky with Willow in his arms. They weren't going far, so he risked a quick daylight flight. As he leveled out in the clouds, she brushed her lips over his before resting her head in the crook of his neck. It gave him the much needed concentration to fly without colliding with a damn bird. Though her warm breaths skating across his flesh stoked the raging fire inside him, muddling his brain anyway.

"I'd forgotten how beautiful flying is," she murmured.

Nothing compared to the beauty he had cradled in his arms. He kissed the top of her head before banking to the right. The cool wind caught her hair, blowing it across his face.

"Luckily, I know where we're going," he sputtered. "'Cause I can't see a damn thing."

She chuckled, trying to tame her wild locks without success.

A few minutes later, he landed at the edge of a flowing stream. Her legs slid from his waist. Cupping her face, he brushed his lips against her forehead, a gesture that made him feel so whole he thought he might burst.

"I was so lost when you left. I knew you made the right choice, but I couldn't see it." He curled a crazy strand of hair around his finger. "You said you don't mind living at the mansion, but I think now and then, it would be good for us to have some privacy, you know?"

There was that sexy grin again. "And why would we need that?"

"Lo-Lo, you're…ah…pretty vocal in the bedroom."

She slapped his chest. "I am not."

"Oh, don't worry, I'm not complaining."

"Well, it's your fault anyway. You're the one who makes me loud."

He pulled her closer. "Damn right I am. Which is why I brought you here."

With his hands on the tops of her shoulders, he pivoted her. Her breath hitched.

"But you burned it down…"

"I did. I couldn't stand knowing the cabin was here without you. Another stupid decision on my behalf."

She glanced back at him. "So, you rebuilt it?"

"An improved version." He wrapped his arms

around her middle, leaning forward to rest his chin on her shoulder. "One we can make new memories in, rather than reliving old ones."

"It's...beautiful." She rested her head against his. "Did you do this all by yourself?"

"I had a little help."

She smirked. "No wonder you disappeared all the time. I suppose everyone knew?"

He nodded but couldn't hold back his grin. "It's been quite the project. Everyone's had a hand in rebuilding it. Turns out Tayla has an eye for interior design. I think she's found her calling there. The Guardians helped build it, so I could get it finished before you questioned where I kept running off to. Even Ellen pitched in."

"And Raine?"

He smirked, recalling Raine's housewarming gift to them. "Just wait till you see the headboard. Gabe's gonna have a fit at the amount of Purah she used."

She shook her head. "I can't believe you did all this without me knowing."

"I felt shitty for burning down the other one."

She cupped his jaw between her soft palms. "Maybe that choice forced us to have a fresh start?"

"I like that idea. When we both make it back to the Heavens, let's conjure a replica of this cabin and get rid of the old one."

Coaxing him down, she kissed him, full of love and adoration. A kiss that marked the beginning of their fresh start.

He took her hand and led her to the cabin, up the timber steps, onto the wide porch. Heat seeped through their shared connection as she eyed the new swing hanging at one end. Double the size of the previous one, so many colorful pillows covered the seat, he didn't know where the bloody hell they'd sit.

He swung open the door, but Willow pulled him back.

"Wait."

"What's wrong?"

"I also have a gift for you." She retrieved something from her pocket and held it out to him.

He eyed the band in her hand. His band. The same one she gave him when they first met. She must've grabbed it from where he kept it on the nightstand. "I won't wear it. It drains your powers."

"No. I had it all wrong. When I was in Tartirim, I had a lot of time to think. A lot of time. There wasn't anything else to do. Anyway, I realized it wasn't because you wore the band that my powers faded. It was because I lost faith in us. I stopped the band from working both ways. The more bitter I became, the more I resented you for leaving, the more I sealed off the flow of power. But you held on. You continued believing in us even when I didn't. That's why the power still flowed to you. I'm sorry, Aric. I'll never make that mistake again."

His eyes stung. "Don't apologize. We've both made dumbass choices."

She laughed. "True." She pressed the band into his palm.

"Are you sure?"

"Yes. I want you to wear it."

He took it from her and slipped the band back on his wrist. A burst of light entered his soul, reviving the connection, strengthening it, fusing it back together as though the fracture had never happened. Everything fell back into place.

"You wanna hang on the porch or check out the inside?" his said, his voice thick and raw.

She peeked through the door. "Is there anything inside better than that swing?"

He half shrugged. "I can think of a few things. The leather couch...the bed...the kitchen counter." He lowered his voice. "The shower."

Her thrill of desire coursed through his veins.

"With all those choices, where should we start?"

He hooked an arm around her legs and lifted her into his arms. "At the beginning, Lo-Lo. We're gonna start at the beginning."

With Willow cradled in his arms, he stepped over the threshold into their new cabin. The cabin he built to symbolize their new life together.

Their new beginning.

Glossary of Terms

Anahel—A realm between the Heavens and Hell, where a soul is trapped when it's conflicted or with an equal balance of light and dark.

Ariel—Angels of Nature who regenerate flora using angelic magic, often in the aftermath of a natural catastrophe such as a wildfire. Ariel have bronze wings.

Azrael—Angels of Death who transport souls from the mortal realm to their final resting place in either the Heavens or Hell. Azrael have silvery gray wings.

Chosen—A mortal created by Fate; whose destiny restores the balance in Fate's favor. Chosen souls are the brightest among all mortals, and because of this, they're hunted by the Fallen.

Fallen—Once angels of the Heavens, Fallen now reside in the many realms in Hell and give their allegiance to Zath, the current ruler of Hell. Fallen have crimson wings, with poisonous talons.

Guardians—Fate's warriors, tasked with protecting Chosen mortals, so they can fulfill their fated destiny. The Guardians were exiled to the mortal world over three hundred years ago. They have midnight black wings.

Purah—Crystalline water from the Eternal Fountain, found in the Heavens. Purah is toxic to Fallen.

Raziel—Angels who cast magic, commonly used to disguise the immortal world from mortal eyes.

Tartirim—A realm in the Heavens where Fate imprisons angelic souls that require intense rehabilitation.

A word about the author…

Growing up in a military family, Cassie had a childhood filled with countless crazy adventures. Eventually, sunny Queensland stole her heart, and she now calls it home with her husband and their two BMX-crazy boys.

Borderline obsessed with the paranormal world, Cassie loves nothing more than crafting stories involving strong, otherworldly characters in need of redemption. She's a self-confessed book-a-holic and a sucker for a gut-wrenching happily ever after.

When she isn't narrating imaginary characters, Cassie loves binging on TV shows, spending time at the beach, and curling up listening to the rain.

For exclusive bonus scenes of The Fallen Guardians, visit:

http://cassielaelyn.com

Thank you for purchasing
this publication of The Wild Rose Press, Inc.

For questions or more information
contact us at
info@thewildrosepress.com.

The Wild Rose Press, Inc.
www.thewildrosepress.com